T0128557

Also By Antonio F. Vianna

Non-Fiction

Career Management and Employee Portfolio Tool Kit Workbook, **3rd edition (2010)**
(ISBN: 978-1-4107-1100-7)

Leader Champions: Secrets of Success **(2004).** (ISBN: 1-4184-3684-4)

Fiction

A Tale from a Ghost Dance **(2003).** (ISBN: 1-4107-1384-9)
The In-ter-view **(2003).** (ISBN: 1-4107-0876-4)
Talking Rain **(2004).** (ISBN: 1-4140-6648-1)
Uncovered Secrets **(2005)**. (ISBN: 1-4208-1795-7)
Midnight Blue **(2005)**. (ISBN: 1-4208-6397-5)
Veil of Ignorance **(2006)**. (ISBN: 1-4259-1695-3)
Yellow Moon **(2006)**. (ISBN: 1-4259-5112-0)
Hidden Dangers **(2007)**. (ISBN: 978-1-4259-9710-6)
Haunted Memories **(2007)**. (ISBN: 978-1-4343-2852-6)
Bound and Determined **(2008)**. (ISBN: 978-1-4343-7450-9)
Stranger On A Train **(2009)**. Book 1 of a vampire trilogy. (ISBN: 978-1-4389-1490-9)
The Hiding **(2009)**. Book 2 of a vampire trilogy. (ISBN: 978-1-4389-6206-1)
The Vampire Who Loved **(2009)**. Book 3 of a vampire trilogy. (ISBN: 978-1-4490-2488-8)
Second Son **(2010)**. (ISBN: 978-1-4490-7473-9)
Unintentional Consequences **(2010)**. (ISBN: 978-1-4520-6901-2)
Time and Money **(2011)**. (ISBN: 978-1-4634-3945-3)
Unordinary Love. **(2012)**. (ISBN: 978-1-4685-4677-4)
Scarlet Rose **(2013)**. (ISBN: 978-1-4817-0577-6)
Chase **(2014)**. (ISBN: 978-1-4918-3575-3)
Secrets Kept Hidden **(2016).** (ISBN: 978-1-5049-8075-3)
Betrayal **(2017).** (ISBN: 978-1-5462-0834-1)
Historical Fiction
Far From Ordinary **(2015).** (ISBN: 978-1-5049-0522-0)

CHOICES WE MAKE

A NOVEL

ANTONIO F. VIANNA

authorHOUSE

AuthorHouse™
1663 Liberty Drive
Bloomington, IN 47403
www.authorhouse.com
Phone: 1 (800) 839-8640

Published by AuthorHouse 01/23/2020

ISBN: 978-1-7283-4431-7 (sc)
ISBN: 978-1-7283-4437-9 (e)

Library of Congress Control Number: 2020901164

Print information available on the last page.

Prologue

This has been on my mind since it happened. Nothing like what I'm about to tell you has ever happened to me before. I must be changing somehow as I get older or maybe it's something else. I don't know but I've got to tell you this or else I think I'll go crazy. It's about choices.

I was driving alone in my own car, returning from pitching my screenplays at a weekend pitch event, going south on the *Interstate* when my mind drifted off to something or the other. I don't know what I was thinking of at the time but evidently something distracted me because at the Y-intersection where I should have taken a left I veered right. All of a sudden I was in a bad part of town. I don't think I've ever been to that place before at any time. The Mayor's got to do something about it because it's definitely not a place to raise a family. Anyway I checked my gas gauge and it was about half empty so I figured I'd fill it up and then find my way back to the *Interstate*. There was a gas station that had fast food … you know the kind I'm referring to.

I pulled alongside a pump, got out of the car and started to go inside to give the attendant cash for the gas I was going to pump when out of the blue came a young woman … I'd say 25 or 26 years old but I'm not good at judging someone's age. Anyway, she was dressed in shabby clothes, hair twisted in all sorts of ways, but with a beautiful smile that you'd want to look at all the time. She didn't know me, we had never met before, I'm sure. She asked me for a few dollars for food. Said she hadn't eaten in two days. My immediate reaction was to ignore her, so I turned my back to continue walking into the building. But she was persistent … I gotta say that about her. She asked a second time. So I turned and stared at her. I got a better look at her face and honest to God she looked like an Angel from the Heavens. Her voice was soft and sweet sounding with a slight accent from someplace I couldn't figure out nor did I care or ask her about. Her skin was light brown and looked smooth as silk, and her hair was dark. She looked fit … in good shape. For a split second I lost focus. I was really disorganized, but then I quickly pulled myself back together. I then said that she shouldn't be doing this, you know, begging for money. I told her to get a job. She didn't seem to listen to me … she begged me for a few dollars, only a few bucks, but I refused her again. I wasn't about to give her a hand out … I've fallen for the act before only to see the guy who I gave money to drive off in a BMW.

I turned to step inside the building, but I hadn't forgotten about her. It was her voice and face that confused me as contrasted to her otherwise grimy appearance. I started to think that maybe she was an actress doing a documentary about the homeless. How crazy is that? Anyway, I paid the attendant inside and headed back outside to pump the gas.

As I stepped outside the station there she was again. But this time she was sitting on the steps, head between her legs with her hands on top of her head. She was crying, and

I do mean crying. I stopped to look at her. I wanted her to stop crying … I really did. So I said to her to stop crying. Then she looked up at me, face to face with those beautiful brown eyes neatly placed on her smooth looking face. Again I thought I was looking at an Angel … honest to God … a real Angel. She asked again for a few dollars for food. Then, I started to cry like a baby. It just happened. It was uncontrollable. I couldn't stop. She didn't say a thing. She just looked at me as if she could see my soul. So I told her I was going to fill the gas tank and then move my car off to the side but I'd come back to her. I don't think she believed me, but I did. I returned to where I left her. She hadn't moved but I saw a bit of a surprise on her face. I grabbed her by the hand and said that I was going to buy her anything she wanted from a nearby diner across the street.

We walked hand and hand to the restaurant across the street that, quite honestly, had the best spiced chicken I've ever tasted. She told me a little about her awful life. She said she was born to poor parents and grew up that way, never living in anything more than two-bedroom run-down apartments on the poverty-stricken side of towns. Her toys were fantasized within her own creative mind and her travels were between school and apartment, and then when she was old enough to work, part-time jobs filled in her day … her life. Without keeping up with the changing times her skill-set quickly became outdated, whatever those skills were. Not even she knows. Now she finds herself just trying to survive, one day at a time. I began to feel somehow connected to her in some strange way although, like then, I still can't think of anything about her that relates to me.

After we finished our meals we walked back to my parked car. I gave her some money … I don't remember how much … and then began to drive off to leave her alone where we found each other. But before I was too far away she yelled out to me in a sweet and pleasurable sound a marriage proposal! Can you believe that … a marriage proposal! I stopped the car to look at her. Her face hadn't changed one ounce. We just looked into each other's eyes for a short time. Then I said to her she deserved someone better than me. As I drove off she said something else, but I really didn't hear what it was.

As I drove off, I thought I was going to feel like a sucker with this woman, but I didn't. I guess it's too easy to not notice the lonely and desperate people in the world because they seem to stay hidden. Yet, doesn't everybody need somebody? But I think the truth is I don't think I really know why I felt the way I did. I just drove away. Yet I'll always remember her and even think about what our lives would be like if I took her up on the marriage proposal, but it was the choice that I made. We didn't even exchange first and last names with each other.

CHAPTER 1

It's muggy, one of those nights when she's not sure if it's going to rain. Regardless, Lilli Jackson is dressed in the approved uniform … dark blue long sleeve shirt and pants, same color jacket, black high-top laced boots, with a .38 caliber Smith and Wesson holstered gun, reserve bullets, a high powered flashlight and a can of mace snugly wrapped around her waist. She wears a Company issued dark blue ski cap with the Company logo. Inside the pocket of her jacket is a Company provided cell phone to use in emergency. *Public Safety Officer Jackson* is imprinted on her shirt and jacket along with the name of the property security firm she is employed with, *Verity Security*.

She checks her watch … it is 11:30 pm … just another 30 minutes before her shift is up at midnight. She looks around … sees and hears only the quietness of the night. Then she smiles, thinking of Natalie, her three year old daughter that ushers in a tear to form at the corner of her eye. She'd do almost anything to be with her pride and joy. But it is what it is. Bills have to get paid. Fortunately, she has the high school daughter of a friend who stays with her daughter when she's at work. This is the last night of her five-day shift. She has two days to be with Natalie until it starts all over again.

Lilli was born in a hurry, screaming into life and having a problem catching her breath. Her heart was either not beating at all or so fast that the doctors couldn't figure it out at first. Nobody thought she would live, not even for a second, yet she did. Her parents divorced when she was just short of her fifth birthday, and for the next several years she lived with her maternal grandmother and mother, both of whom had severe drinking problems. When her maternal grandmother died, her mother couldn't care for her so she lived with various relatives until she graduated from high school. It was then that she started to date her soon-to-be-divorced husband of the same age. She was pregnant at eighteen, gave birth at nineteen, and then reluctantly married the paternal father of the same age. It's not been a marriage made in heaven since then.

Lilli and her husband eventually finalized no-fault divorce papers that gave her complete custody of Natalie without any alimony from him. She's committed to finding a higher paying and more satisfying career where she can go to an office wearing a skirt and blouse with nice shoes and begin to work her way up the career ladder, but with only a high school education, her options seem minimal. She figures life would be fine if only she knew what she wanted to be. And that is the problem ... she has no idea, and no one to turn to. What got her to where she is now won't get her to where she wants to be in the future ... whatever that is.

She can't wait for her turn to be at the top of the Wheel, the roster that gives all full-time Public Safety Officers with *Verity Security* a day off the street and inside a warm building. When you're at the top of the Wheel, you're answering phone calls and performing other administrative duties until the next Public Safety Officer's name on the roster takes over. The current thinking is that more than two consecutive days out of the field reduces one's readiness to perform in the field although there is no scientific research to support the argument. Regardless, that system does not spare anyone.

She continues walking on the Centro Rail Service platform, a high speed rail service, taking a glimpse now and then at the rail tracks to make sure no one has fallen.

Rail service is provided between the hours of 6:00 am and midnight, and *Verity Security* provides security service during those hours each and every day of the year. Homeless people, those who smuggle into the country drugs and people, and others without a legal green light to be in the country seem to find a way to use the area as a place of safety. Rail service passengers have repeatedly complained about their fear of being an innocent victim.

She slowly continues her inspection. This time she is headed for a ticket machine that often times is the target of those needing cash. Some machines provide change while others do not. No machine gives more than $3.50 in change. Nickels, dimes, quarters, $1, $5, $10, and $20 bills are accepted. Machines sell tickets from $1.50 to $40. She closely examines one ticket machine to find it in order, and then moves toward the remaining ones. Everything seems to be OK.

Her next stop is the parking lot, free to all passengers but often times the place where some people sleep. Signs are everywhere that indicates the restrictions, but often times they are ignored. She automatically touches her holstered gun as she proceeds towards the parking lot. She remembers part of a prior experience that reminds her to be alert.

It was about a year ago when she came
upon one person sleeping,
and she wasn't 100% prepared. As
she approached the person
whom she later discovered was male,
she removed her gun from
the holster, stood about five yards away,
and yelled out something.
The male slowly rolled over and then
raised his torso to give her
a look. What she didn't see or suspect
was another male behind
her who might have been peeing,
but that's not certain. She
heard a gunshot so loud that it nearly
deafened her. But the
smell of the bullet's gun powder from
the shooter mixed with
her own blood from the shot was
more than she could take.
Confusion infused her head more
than she could handle. She
wanted to cry but the sounds ran
into each other negating one
another. Her mind at that point was
a mere spectator. An image

of Natalie flashed through her mind.
She awoke an hour or so later
in the hospital. She felt blessed to be
alive to see Natalie once again.

There are overhead solar powered lights that provide sufficient illumination during the nighttime. Except for her parked vehicle that is badly in need of engine repair under one of the lights, the rest of the parking spaces are empty. She feels safe, although in her job, one should always be on the alert. Yet, while her internal radar tells her there is no imminent danger, she keeps her hand tightly around her gun in spite of everything being very quiet. She starts circling the parking lot looking repeatedly to her left and then right. Occasionally she stops to hear the dead silence. Then she starts up again. Satisfied that there's nothing out of the ordinary, she heads to the main building that opens at 8:00 am and shuts down at 5:00 pm each weekday. Sunday and Saturday schedules are shortened to 9:00 am to 3:00 pm, while the building is completely shut down on all Federal and State holidays.

She stops at the rear entrance door that is usually used for deliveries. She jiggles the door handle that tells her it is still locked and secure. As she makes her way totally around the building, she peeks into each window as she flips on her flashlight to check inside. Everything seems to be in order. Once at the two main front doors she repeats the process until she returns to the rear entrance door. Finally, she stops to take a look up into the sky. The moon is bright, and she no longer feels that rain is in the air. She smiles, yet life has a way of changing rapidly.

Lilli turns to her left at a noise sounding like the groaning of a man. She quickly removes her gun from the holster, takes the flashlight out of its pouch to turn on, and points it in the direction of the sound. She feels her heart pick up its beat. "Who's there?" She stands motionless but her voice wavers.

"Uh."

She moves the flashlight in the direction of the sound. She spots a man lying on the ground with a frail snarling German-Shepherd alongside seemingly protecting him. The man grabs an armful of air but there is nothing to hold onto. He lifts his head, and then recoils at seeing her handgun.

"The last thing I want to do is hurt you. But don't move or it'll be on my list." She waits for him to respond, but all she hears is her own deep breathing. As she steps closer to the man and his dog, the German-Shepherd takes another try at protecting the man with another drained snarling growl.

The man closes his eyes, his breathing is steadied. "I need help." There is no fire in his voice wilding out of control rage, interested in doing harm to her. His nose seems to be twisted, most likely broken more than once, possibly from an overuse of his mouth to the wrong people. Maybe he just didn't know when to shut up and listen or how to pick the right audience. But then again, some people can't handle the truth, and so they take it out on the one telling it.

"Can you keep your dog from coming at me?" She moves another step closer.

"Lady's just trying to protect me. We've been through a lot." He coughs a few times as saliva drips out of his mouth.

Lilli thinks to herself that her problems don't come close to what he's probably going through. "I'm gonna call in an ambulance for you." She reaches for her cell to make the emergency call.

The man coughs again. His face looks like he hasn't bathed in weeks, if not months, and he probably hasn't eaten a meal for as long. The German-Shepherd crawls closer to him ... the same appearance could be said for the dog as well, yet neither seem to be complaining.

Holding onto something of value is not uncommon for many people. It's a way to keep sane in an insane world that is full of unpredictable uncertainties. In a way it all goes back to looking for and keeping love.

Lilli awkwardly smiles at the man and his dog, Lady. She thinks what a name for a dog, but that's what dog owners do. She feels a rush of emotion blast through her body as she thinks of her love ... Natalie ... and what she would do to protect the love of her life. She feels her mouth go dry as her body goes still.

The sound of a speeding vehicle interrupts her thoughts. She turns towards the noise to see a late model black Jeep Wrangler entering the parking lot about thirty yards away. The vehicle abruptly stops. Then two people jump out and run away, both in the same direction. She thinks one is chunky and the other is thin but it happens so fast she can't be sure. They both seem, however, to be about the same average height. They wear loose fitting untucked striped shirts, dark colored cargo pants, and sandals.

Without warning a late model white colored Chevy panel van arrives in the parking lot a few seconds later and stops behind the Wrangler. Two wiry young people leap out of the Chevy van. Again, Lilli can't make out much of their appearance. Both of them wear cotton caps, black T-shirts and faded blue jeans. The taller of the two holds a gun, aims, and shoots three times as the shorter one stands alongside.

You can't run faster than 1,200 feet per second, the average speed of a bullet fired from a gun. The chunky one running away doesn't have a chance before it happens. It doesn't hurt because there isn't anything to feel. The victim falls forward on the parking lot pavement, presumably dead before the body hits the asphalt. The thin one disappears.

The two wiry people hop back into their van and drive off.

Lilli stands motionless for a short time. The image of Natalie flashes through her mind. She's confused.

It all happens so fast, Lilli doesn't have time to get involved. The next thing she does is call for law enforcement.

The ambulance arrives first, consisting of a paramedic and a driver who also acts in the same capacity as her partner. Lilli meets them. "There's someone who's been shot." She points in the direction of the chunky one who had fallen. "And also there's what appears to be a homeless man with his dog. They're in that direction." She points towards the man and the dog. "I've also called law enforcement."

The female paramedic shouts to her partner. "Let's get first to the one who's been shot."

They take their equipment from the ambulance to the fallen victim. Her first action is to feel for a carotid pulse on the side of the victim's neck. The carotid arteries carry blood from the heart to the brain, thus a key factor for sustaining life. While she performs that, her partner rips off the victim's shirt to give him access to the victim's chest, thus allowing him to apply electrocardiogram patches to determine if there is any electric activity from the heart. He quickly discovers the victim is dead … there is no electrical activity.

The next sound is the siren of a police car, who when they arrive, secure the scene and get debriefed by the paramedics and Lilli.

"Stay with the dead victim while I attend to the homeless man," the female paramedic says to her partner. She rushes away.

During her drive home Lilli thinks of what's coming next … dreading having to spend an hour or so filling out paperwork and talking to more law enforcement about it all. All she wants are a few days off to be with Natalie, but the overtime money she'll receive could be put to good use.

She steps into her one bedroom apartment that is not as tidy and orderly as she would like, some boxes still unpacked that are stuffed into every possible corner of the place. She spots Ginger, the babysitter, sprawled out on the small worn out couch. She is face up with a copy of a novel, "Betrayal," from her favorite author novelist, lying alongside her. It is quiet. Lilli smiles thinking that her daughter is sound asleep.

She tiptoes past Ginger to take a peek at Natalie in her bedroom. She stands nearby the crib-bed where her daughter peacefully sleeps, and then she returns to wake up Ginger.

"Hey," she softly says as she gently nudges Ginger.

Slowly Ginger responds. Her eyes open first, then puckering of her lips and finally a gentle nod. "Ah, I must have fallen asleep." She straightens her body, stretches her arms, and breathes out. "Time to go." She stands, and then bends over to pick up the novel by her feet. "This guy sure knows how to write. I'll loan it to you if you want."

"Oh, thanks. That would be nice." Lilli dips into her pocket to pull out cash to pay Ginger. "Sorry I'm a little late. Some unexpected stuff happened. And tomorrow I'll probably have to complete more paperwork and talk with real law enforcement. But what the heck, its overtime pay." She smiles as she hands over cash. "I really appreciate you being flexible with me."

"No worry. Natalie is a sweetheart. Never a problem." She takes the cash from Lilli's hands. "So you're saying you'll need me tomorrow? My schedule this year is all online, which I hate, so I'm flexible."

"Yeah, I really do." Lilli's face only emphasizes the necessity.

"No problem." She gives one of her comforting smiles. "What time?"

"Is nine OK?"

"Nine it is." Ginger gives another one of her comforting smiles, turns, and leaves the apartment.

CHAPTER 2

The next morning Lilli wakes up to the sound of her alarm clock. It is 8:00 am. She turns to switch off the sound and then returns to lay flat on her back. She remains flat on her back for a few more minutes, enjoying the peacefulness for another few moments. It feels so good.

She thinks that life is strange and love is even stranger. People often times never say what they mean, making a response even more troublesome. But, she guesses, that might be the defining human characteristic that you don't find in dogs, cats, and other like animals. Sometimes, when she has trouble falling to sleep she imagines all the words, actions, and feelings that are never said between people … the honest stuff. She admits that she's part of it as well. Her love life with a man is currently non-existent.

Then she gets out of the internal conversation to whisper something aloud to herself, "I've slept close to eight straight hours. No wonder I feel so good. Now for some strong coffee." She yawns again, stretches her arms over her head, sits up in bed and looks towards Natalie's crib-bed.

She switches her body to let her feet touch the wooden floor, and then stands. With a broad smile on her face, she walks towards her daughter who is playing with a doll. "Good morning."

Natalie looks innocently at her mother, smiles, and says, "Mommy." She lets go of the doll.

Lilli picks up her daughter, holds her tightly in her arms, and together they head for the tiny kitchen. "Mommy's got to go to work today … not long. I'll be back soon. Ginger will be here shortly."

Natalie looks at her mother, "Mommy."

"I'll take that as an OK." She gently squeezes her daughter in her arms. "I love you." Then she kisses Natalie.

Now in the kitchen Lilli checks her cell that lies on the kitchen counter. The screen lists a text message from *Verity Security*.

> *NEED TO FINISH PAPERWORK FROM RECENT SITUATION.*
> *OT! HOMELESS GUY DIDN'T MAKE IT, BUT THE DOG DID.*
> *NO ID OF WHO THE DECEASED YOUTH IS. PROBABLY BE*
> *JOINED BY LOCAL DETECTIVE …*
> *DON'T KNOW WHO EXACTLY …*
> *SHOULDN'T TAKE LONG.*

She knows better. There's no such animal as a brief interview. They'll be repeated questions again and again, some with identical wording while others modified for one reason or another. And then there's the paperwork that will pile on the time.

Lilli places Natalie in a safeguarded chair and then turns around to get some food out of the refrigerator for her daughter and grab a bag of expresso grounded dark-roasted coffee. First she takes care of the making the coffee and then sits alongside her daughter to feed her.

A short time slips by when she hears a knock on the apartment front door. "It's me, Ginger. I've got my key, so I'm coming in."

"Got coffee for you."

Ginger enters the apartment, holding her laptop, and heads for the coffee machine to pour a cup for her, and a refill to Lilli's cup who stays seated alongside Natalie. "Good morning to the both of you."

"Thanks again for helping me out on such a short notice." Lilli stays focused on feeding Natalie. "You're the best."

"Hey, let me finish up with Natalie. You've still got to get dressed."

Ginger and Lilli exchange places as she places her laptop on the table.

Ginger repeats, "Go ... get dressed. I've got this covered."

A few minutes later Lilli reappears. She is dressed in casual plain clothes ... jeans, untucked long sleeve shirt, and Dexter's without socks. Her short hair is as it always is ... hanging straight down. She leans over to kiss Natalie. "See you soon."

There is something about a woman with her child daughter that can't be explained, but it's magic, maybe the glow from both of them that is captivating to any and all observers of human nature.

On her way out, she says to Ginger, "I owe you."

"Forget about owing me anything. Go, get out of here."

Now outside the apartment building, Lilli walks to her parked car in her assigned space, suddenly stops and stretches her neck. She notices the trunk is partly open. She hurries towards the vehicle to fully open the trunk. "Jeez!" She shuffles through the items inside the trunk, yet missing is her Smith and Wesson 9mm/.38 caliber gun, holster and 15 round ammunition bandolier belt. She feels her body heat up with anger. "Jeez," she repeats with the same intensity as before.

Still shaken up and pissed over the missing items, she gets into the car to drive to work, thinking all along who did it, why, and how will she pay for the stolen items. Fortunately, the drive is short.

She enters the building, nods without words as she passes by the front desk where Fred sits. He peeks just a bit without looking up, "Morning." He's not excited in working on a Saturday.

She continues towards the boss's office, knocks her knuckles on the door.

"It's open."

John Walker went into the U. S. Army right out of high school … not interested in upping further academic challenges. He is from Scottish heritage and often was teased about his name. At first he had no idea what was so funny, but that didn't last long once he turned the legal age for drinking alcohol.

He had come from living in a neighborhood composed mainly of Scottish, Polish, and Slovakian families … each so different from one another, yet many similarities. The most important similarities among them were: family comes first and everyone works hard.

Their homes were constructed in a modular fashion and close together with little space between them. When windows were open during the hot summer days everybody heard each other's conversations … air conditioning was financially out of the question.

Fathers worked in low paying jobs in local factories while the mothers took clerical jobs anyplace they could get once their children were able to take minimal care of themselves while still living at home. Most of the children's ages were about the same.

John never experienced combat during his Army service … stationed at U. S. domestic bases during the four years. He was bored and didn't reenlist.

Once he left the Army he returned to his home town and worked his way into local law enforcement that he immediately loved … much to his surprise as well as to his family, school teachers, and friends … life has a way of carving its own path.

Eventually he developed a reputation in law enforcement with a good deal of admiration from within the force and community at large. He was conscientious, hardworking, and fair.

Encouraged to take the Sergeant's Exam, he easily passed, and soon he was the topic of choice from the local media ... print and television ... as well as speaking engagements at schools.

He eventually married a widow who lost her husband through a freak hunting trip. The daughter, from his wife's first marriage and John bonded immediately. Life was very good, but only for a short time until one summer day his wife drowned while swimming in a local lake.

John became the only family member in his daughter's life. And, with John's encouragement, his daughter worked hard and went to college. Months before graduation she was pursued with multiple job offers from high-end advertising firms. She eventually accepted one in Paris, France ... moved, married a Frenchman, and had a girl and boy.

As far as John knows everyone is fine, although he'd like to spend time with all of them if he had both the time and money.

It was just about that time that he felt the urge to be his own boss. That's when he founded *Verity Security*.

She enters the small office, cluttered with boxes and paper almost everywhere. John sits behind a worn out metal desk. Another man, about her age she figures, maybe slightly older, sits to the side.

She nods, "John."

"Lilli, this is Detective Abrams. He's local. He's got some questions ... shouldn't take long."

Abrams stays seated, nods his head once, "Hi. Call me Jeff."

She ignores Jeff for the moment to turn toward John. "Stuff got stolen from my car … the trunk was jimmied … sometime between this morning when I got off and now. Revolver, holster, and ammo belt were taken … left the utility chest vest, gloves, interview book, can of mace, and handcuffs. Jeez."

"Your boots and cell?"

"I kept the boots on, and the cell is in my jacket pocket. They're still in my apartment."

John lets out a puff of air. Frustration fills his face. "Not good. Anything else taken … any damage to the vehicle other than the trunk's lock?"

"Not that I could tell."

"And you keep your equipment in the trunk of your car for what reason?" John's stare is intense.

"I've got a baby girl. Don't think it's smart to have my weapon and equipment inside the apartment."

Jeff inserts a comment. "That makes sense." He pauses and then continues. "This might be none of my business, but then again it could … the shooting during your shift and your stolen items could be connected."

John asks, "How so?"

"Well, I don't know everything that happened during her shift … that's why she's here to tell me … but she might have been followed by the two guys responsible for the shooting death. Don't know, but it's possible." He shrugs his shoulders.

John turns to Lilli, "It's your turn. Tell us what happened during your last shift."

Thirty minutes later, Lilli says, "That's it."

John turns to Jeff, raises his eyebrows and lifts his chin.

Jeff answers, "I think there's a strong possibility that the two who are responsible for the murder of the dead victim might have waited around for a while, and then followed Lilli to her place. No evidence, just my gut … my sense … that's all." Then he turns to look at Lilli, "Do you live in a safe neighborhood?"

Her eyes widen. "I've never thought of it as either safe or not. It's just an apartment building. I parked the car in my assigned parking space. But, come to think of it, I doubt if there is any security … like someone patrolling the place or cameras. You know."

Jeff asks another question. "Did you drive the same vehicle you used in your last shift to get here?"

"Yeah, it's the only one I have."

"Is it your personal vehicle or does it belong to *Verity Security?*"

John chuckles. "A company car … please." He rolls his eyes.

Jeff tilts his head to the side. "I'm just asking." He pauses. "Maybe I should take a look at it. There might be something left inside that is some sort of evidence from whoever stole your equipment." He pauses and then continues. "I can take a look now if that's OK."

"OK with me, if it's OK with Lilli."

She nods, "Definitely."

John and Lilli watch Jeff search Lilli's vehicle. He wears gloves.

The first spot Jeff checks is the trunk. "Yeah, the lock has been jimmied … not real professional but enough to get the trunk opened." He then rummages around inside the trunk. "Did you check to make sure nothing else was taken?"

Lilli answers, "Yeah, just the gun, holster and ammo belt."

Jeff continues examining the trunk. "Don't see anything the thief might have accidently left behind." He moves to the passenger's side. "Hmm, looks as if this door lock was pried open. Did you know that?"

Lilli puts her hands to her mouth. "No."

Jeff opens the passenger door, gazes at the inside, spots something, and leans over. "There's a cigarette butt on the floor. Do you smoke, or does anyone who's sat here smoke?"

"No." She swallows deeply.

"Could have been left by whoever took your equipment. I'm gonna consider this possible evidence and get it tested for prints but we won't be able to match it to the guy who shot the victim last night unless we have his prints on file and who seemed to be sitting in your vehicle for some reason. The same goes for the saliva on the butt." He keeps looking around. "Nothing else stands out." He stands looking at the vehicle, and then turns to Lilli. "Are there any distinguishing marks on the revolver, holster, and ammo belt that could be used to identify the items as belonging to you?"

John says, "The S and W, holster and belt are all marked. I've got them listed for each of my employees."

"What about the other gear?"

John switches looking at Jeff and Lilli. "Each employee creates their own four-letter, four-digit or four-letter-digit combination ID that is placed on those pieces of equipment used. I've got them listed as well."

Jeff asks Lilli, "What's yours?"

Lilli grins, "1 B A S."

Jeff chuckles as John remains silent having already experienced her sense of humor many times before. John thinks to himself that's just how the younger generation get their kicks … doing something they want to do because for some strange reason is funny or rebellious contrasted with what you are told or expected to do … whatever.

Jeff settles down to become serious again. "The forensic side of the murder during your shift is almost done … nothing unusual so far. Shot with a .38 caliber revolver, probably a Colt or Smith and Wesson, 4 inch barrel length, cylinder-loaded, exposed hammer selective double action. That's my best guess." He pauses to look at John and Lilli for any comments. When there is only silence attached to their attentive behavior he continues. "The revolver can be fired at the full-cock position or double action by a longer, heavier squeeze of the trigger. I suspect the shooter fired double action."

Here is where John adds his insights, "So in case the killer missed with the first shot, he would keep firing until he hit the mark."

"Yeah, that's right," nods Jeff.

With a sigh John asks, "Anything else to sink our teeth into?"

Jeff shrugs his shoulders, glances at Lilli and then back at John, "No, not yet."

Lilli asks, "What about the ID of the shooter, the accomplice, and the other one who ran away?"

Jeff says, "Nothing more than what I've just said. We're still working on it … missing person's reports don't usually show up for a few days, if at all. We only know the victim is a male, a kid, probably 15 or 16 at most, but that'll be up to the coroner to state more specifically. Nothing else about the others." He pauses as something pops into his head. He turns to John and then asks Lilli, "We know the victim is a young male … that's a definite, but did you clearly see well enough the gender and anything else specifically about the other three?"

Lilli hesitates, feeling the pressure of four eyes staring at her, waiting for a definitive answer. "Well … uh … it all happened so fast and I was twenty, maybe thirty yards away when it happened. I … I must have seen their faces and … you know … the way they ran … to … uh … conclude they were male."

Jeff raises an important point, "But you can't describe what their faces looked like so that one of our forensic artists might prepare a sketch of their faces. Is that what you're saying?"

Lilli clears her throat, feeling it quickly get dry. "Yeah, I can't."

Jeff adds, "Even if I gave you a book of photographs to look at so the artist might be able to hand draw a facial image?"

Lilli's voice is soft and low, "Even with that I wouldn't be of help. I'm sorry."

John adds, "The longer it takes the less likely they'll be an ID."

"I'm fully aware of that," Jeff agrees.

Lilli gets back to ask a question, "And the vehicles … who they're registered to?"

Jeff responds to her question in a similar tone of frustration as before, "Don't know that yet as well … both or one could be stolen. There's a lot we don't yet know."

Lilli thinks the meeting is over but Jeff adds something. He turns to look at Lilli, "I still want to investigate the break-in and robbery of your vehicle, especially if there turns out to be a connection between the two events. I'll keep both of you informed as I find out more. OK?"

John nods his head followed by the same response from Lilli.

Lilli's feeling of inadequacy comes almost immediately and is greater than she could have ever imagined. Why hadn't she been more observant of what these 4 people looked like? That's part of her job … to be diligent, observant, and vigilant while on duty. And come to think of it … as well in her personal life as a mother of a young child. Will the two responsible for the male's murder ever be found? What if it was Natalie, her daughter, who was murdered in front of her, and she couldn't identify the killer? Just thinking about it makes her skin feel creepy and her muscles tighten everywhere. She suddenly has a hard time breathing as her eyes begin to shut, and her head bobbles uncontrollably.

Jeff notices the sudden change in Lilli. "Lilli, are you OK?"

Lilli's eyes, now completely shut, slumps over in her chair as she makes out the image of her daughter. She manages to say, "Yeah," but she isn't convincing to anyone including herself.

CHAPTER 3

Eric Jackson keeps his head down so others can't look him in the eyes. It's much easier that way to avoid seeing them read him like a book, and not enjoying his pathetic story. He got Lilli pregnant at eighteen, freaked out at what it would be like to be a father and a husband at such a young age and without first reading the *HOW TO* manual. After he reluctantly married her he knew this too was a big mistake. So, he told her he'd accept a no-fault divorce and sign the papers immediately. Then he took off. It wasn't that long ago, but he's not counting. He roams around a lot calling no place his home. He tries to forget his past, but that's easier said than done.

He grew up in a small town near nowhere and there wasn't even a town drunk, so everyone had to take a turn.

When his old brother died from a gunshot while robbing a convenience store to help feed his parents and him, his father told him, "too bad it wasn't you." You've got to give his father credit for being blunt. The truth can hurt.

Right now, Eric cleans up all sorts of messes in the rooms of a seedy motel, from toilets to vomit from the guests. It's not ideal, obviously, but he gets a free room with a television set, three meals, and a minimum payment each week. He hoards as much money as he can. He feels doomed.

He'd like to have a girlfriend with no attachments, and he'd promise her he'd always have ample supplies of condoms, just to be safe. But that's not working out. Maybe he needs a real plan … maybe not.

The truth of the matter is he's scared to venture out. Look what happened when he and Lilli met! But he wants to believe in himself that he's a changed man.

There's a local community college within walking distance of the motel that sponsors all sorts of social events for their students. He could roam around to check it out. But he's lying to himself … he'd be invisible to the students. And then there's the clothes thing, respectable ones that he'd have to buy, and probably a cell phone whether it's one of those prepaid ones or not. He can't afford any of it, so for the time being he'll spend his free time watching television reruns alone.

As Eric counts his saved money of two hundred thirty-one dollars and seventy-five cents, his mind shifts to a sobering thought … he's stuck with nowhere to go. His life hasn't amounted to anything. He needs a plan, but he's said that before without taking any action. He's got to get a real job with a future, go to college even if it's with a crappy online school, and start living. But again, the problem is he has no plan to make that happen. He's got to get out of the hole he's put himself in and not go back.

The next day Eric gets paid, and wastes no time to tell his boss, Miss Palcovic, that he's quitting. He lies to her, "I've got a family emergency."

She doesn't buy it or care one way or another as she shrugs her shoulders *so what*.

He continues. "It's serious. I've got to go." Why doesn't he give it up and stop expanding on the lie?

Miss Palcovic says, "Can't it wait until next week's pay cycle? I've got to hire a replacement."

He continues with the lie. "No, this is very serious. I feel bad in walking out with no notice … I really do."

"Yeah, right." She doesn't believe him at all.

"No, really." He pushes the lie to a point of it being ridiculous.

"And nobody else in the family?" She figures two can play the same game.

"No there isn't." He reaches down towards his feet to grab a duffle bag that is full of his clothes and incidentals. "Thanks for everything." He walks away towards a nearby bus stop just as the sun goes down.

He waits fifteen minutes before noticing the nearby sign that indicates the bus's schedule. Nothing until tomorrow morning.

He looks back at the motel, but decides against asking Miss Palcovic to stay overnight. He decides it's better to hitchhike to wherever the driver is headed. He lucks out within ten minutes.

Eric sits in the backseat of a late model Chevy. His duffle bag is where his feet should be which means his feet are atop of the bag, uncomfortably crunched. He's not complaining … it's a free ride to someplace.

"Where are you going?" he asks the driver.

The driver is an older man whose age could be that as his parents. There's a woman sitting in the front passenger seat who keeps quiet. She could be the driver's wife, but no one's talking and he's not asking.

"We're headed East," the driver says.

Eric wants to ask the driver a follow up question that would lead to a more specific destination, such as a city name, but that's not how it's working in this situation, so he keeps his mouth shut.

The driver asks, "Ever been on a road trip?"

"Each one is different." It's the first thought that comes to Eric's consciousness.

The driver laughs as he looks to his right at the woman who remains silent. "You got that right. That's what I've been tellin' her."

Eric isn't interested. He doesn't care one way or another. He just wants to get *there*, wherever *there* is.

The rest of the drive is in silence, which for Eric is better than carrying on a conversation with the driver and the silent woman passenger.

Soon it's dark and the car's headlights are shining. Eric is asleep, but is awakened when he hears the driver's voice again.

"I'm hungry!"

The unexpected sound causes Eric's body to jump a bit. "Huh?" He blinks his eyes a few times to refocus into the night.

Up ahead is a seedy looking restaurant whose name is unfamiliar to Eric, regardless if only half the neon sign above the building is lit.

"Burger, fries, and a beer or two … that's what I want." The driver doesn't ask anyone else their preferences because he doesn't care.

Eric remains crunched up in the back seat. He has no idea where he is, other than crunched up in the back seat of a late model Chevy with a male driver and a silent female passenger in the front passenger seat. He begins to feel unhappy about the situation but he figures there's not much he can do about it. He decides to stick it out to the final destination, wherever that is. He can bail anytime he wants. He now feels hungry himself, and also needs to take a pee.

The driver is the first to get out of the car, stretches both arms over his head and walks towards the front doors of the seedy looking place whose neon sign is only half lit without offering to open the front passenger door where the woman sits, or even waits for anyone to join him. He doesn't even lock the car. He acts as if he is by himself without anyone else … solo.

Eric steps outside of the car and then opens the front passenger door. He then steps aside as he extends his hand to help her get out. There is a slight smile on her face of appreciation, a *thank-you*.

As the silent woman and Eric walk side by side behind the driver, it is obvious to Eric that the man is big … really big … not necessarily tall but heavy in weight, and not in tip-top physical condition. He wonders what the connection between the couple is, but he isn't about to get into that conversation, at least not now.

As they enter the place, they notice it isn't crowded. Eric figures the crowd was earlier or it will happen later or it will never happen. Doesn't matter. He spots the big man already seated in a booth holding a menu.

Eric says to the woman. "There he is." He points in the direction where the big man is seated. "I've got to go to the restroom." He walks away to take care of business as she heads towards the big man.

A few minutes later, Eric exits the restroom to head towards the booth where the big man and silent woman are seated. There's something different … very, very different.

A small crowd of people are standing near the couple. The big man is slumped over the table, not moving. The silent woman is no longer silent … she's screaming something.

A woman within the small crowd yells, "Call 911!" But that callout is too late for medical help. The big man is dead from a sudden heart attack.

An ambulance arrives within ten minutes to confirm the death and then takes him away, but not before two local police officers question those nearby. No one has any useful information to share, including the previously silent woman, whose silence is soon discovered to be based on her not speaking English.

As weird and wonderful as it may seem, there is a family of a husband, wife, and two pre-teen children on vacation from Slovakia who speak the previously silent woman's language. She is Viktoria Loscius, an undocumented worker in the United States performing servant and companion duties for the dead man, Stephen Starnyski.

Viktoria is detained for further questioning while Eric remains motionless several feet away. He isn't sure what all has happened since he was taking care of business in the restroom when it happened. This also means he's not questioned by law enforcement, something he's very happy about.

As Viktoria is escorted out of the place, passing by Eric, she motions with her eyes towards him and then towards the booth. She doesn't say a word but offers a slight grin.

He keeps quiet, and once the small crowd settles down, he casually walks towards the now empty booth that has been setup for the next customer. He quickly takes a seat, still wondering what her eye signal and grin meant to say. His feet nervously shuffle under the table, and then he hears something move along the floor. He bends over to check out the sound. What he finds is a wallet and car keys. Slowly, without trying to be noticed, he reaches for both items. He opens the wallet to find a driver's license, a vehicle registration card, one credit card, and several bills in various dollar denominations. He figures the wallet belonged to the driver and the keys are to the Chevy. His mind temporarily goes blank for a second, and then reboots back into working order. "What the hell," he softly says and then asks, "Why did she do this?"

He then is suddenly interrupted when he is asked by a waitress, "What'll you have honey?"

He does everything he can to hold back a cry.

Eric finishes his meal, pays cash with a decent tip, and heads for the spot where the Chevy was parked. He's not sure the car will still be there thinking the police probably already towed it away. He's happily surprised. The car is still there and it's still unlocked. He spots his duffle bag on the backseat floor. He's relieved, but it dawns on him that the big man and the previously silent woman must have had some luggage if they were really on a road trip. He takes a look in the trunk to find two suitcases, opens each to check out their contents hoping he'll find something useful to take. It's not easy breaking habits. He doesn't find anything of importance to him, so he places both suitcases on the pavement, still with a smile on his face. Maybe the tide has changed to favor him.

He re-enters the car, this time in the driver's seat, starts the Chevy and drives away to someplace he's not sure of. He figures he might have to stay invisible for a while. The further away from this place is the safest. He can't risk being tracked down. It is what it is.

His jaw moves around like he's trying to decide something. Then he retakes control of himself. You can see it in his face, the way he nods his head up and own, and the determination in his eyes. "It's going to be fine," he counsels himself, but he has no idea what that means and how he'll do it.

His past will never be officially behind him and forgotten. But he's determined to have a place of his own even if it's a dump. He'll soon know that for a fact.

CHAPTER 4

A few days after the debriefing with John and Jeff, Lilli meets with John in his office.

"You look a little better from a few days ago, but, well, not completely back to yourself, if you ask me."

"I – I don't know what came over me," she unconvincingly lies, too embarrassed to tell him the truth. "I'm good though; ready to come back to work."

"I'd like to agree with you but I'm not so sure."

She knows she's not good at lying … best at telling the truth. Yet, she persists. "I'm good … really I am."

"I don't want to put you at risk." He sounds fatherly. "You need to take some time off … to recover."

She persists despite agreeing with him. "Come on. I'm good to go."

"If I were you I'd reconsider very carefully whether or not you really want to continue working here. Maybe a career change is what you need." He pushes his glasses down to the tip of his nose, now looking fatherly to buoy the sound of his voice. "A few days off from this place would help."

Her eyes are now wide open, more than usual. "But I need the money. I've got a daughter, and well … so many other financial obligations. I can't afford to be off from work."

"Consider a week or two paid sabbatical. How does that sound? Would that work for you?"

"Really ... you'd do that?" She's confused at the unexpected compassion. Is she refusing to let someone show her unconditional affection? Is she that hardened at such a young age?

"I can manage it."

"Are you sure?"

"Like I just said, I can manage it." There is a slight pause in their conversation before he adds, "Oh, by the way, Jeff's been asking about you. He seems concerned about you, like, how you're doing. I think he's really worried about you more than he is of the case. But that's just my two cents."

Against her hardened cynical instincts, she relents. "Come on ... really?" She squints with a grin.

"He asked if it was OK to stop by your place or give you a call. Imagine that ... asking me for permission." John chuckles.

Her thoughts are flipping upside down and all over the place. "What did you say?"

"I told him you were both adults ... that he'll never know until he tries. It would be something he might regret if he didn't at least give it a try."

She thinks how unlikely whatever that might be ... friends, associates, supporters ... whatever. Her eyes dance with joy.

Her thoughts are interrupted when he says, "You're immediately on a two-week paid sabbatical. End of discussion."

A week later, Lilli is barely out of bed when her phone rings. There is a sign of nervousness from her voice. "Hello."

"It's me, John. Want an update on the case?"

She smacks her lips, swallows before she replies, wishing the caller was someone else asking about something else. "Sure," although further, she's not fully awake to carry on an adult conversation.

"We still haven't found them … the shooter and the accomplice, but the buddy of the kid who was killed came forward … actually his parents. It seems their son and the victim have been in trouble before for using drugs. An autopsy of the victim showed contaminated opioids in his system. The victim's buddy said that they were running away from the sellers … also kids, males, a little older than them, 'cause they didn't pay … just took the drugs and took off. From what Jeff told me, the kid was scared as hell. I mean, why wouldn't he? But his parents were forgiving … some special parents if you ask me … promised Jeff they'd have close reigns on the kid … very tight on him. According to Jeff, the victim's parents haven't come forward, and the victim's buddy claims he doesn't even know the victim's last name, if you can believe that, so there's no way to find the parents." He pauses again. "Speaking of Jeff, has he called you or stopped by? None of my business, I know, but, well, I just had to ask."

Lilli blinks her eyes a few times to take it all in. "Uh, no."

"Well, that doesn't surprise me. He's been busy as hell … they're short staffed, not able to hire any more due to budget restrictions. But anyway, I've got to believe he'll call you … you know … just to check up with you … I mean if it's still OK with you. Cops are unique … not easy to figure out."

"Uh, sure."

"You're doing OK yourself? You seem quiet."

"Uh, yeah, I guess the week off is something I really needed. Thanks for everything."

"Yeah, sure." John pauses. "Don't want to seem pushy or anything like that but I'm just wondering if you're coming back to work here. I mean, no rush, you've got another paid week I promised, maybe more after that if you need it … I mean really need it."

"I'm still not sure, but I promise you I won't take advantage of your generosity. Really."

"No problem." Another pause from John. "Anyway, I gotta go. Talk with you soon. Give Natalie a big hug and kiss from me. OK?"

Lilli sniffles, "Sure."

The phones disconnect as she thinks to herself … "Cops are basically good people, but probably horrible husbands." She doesn't know this for sure, but it's her best guess. "They probably chicken out when they're needed the most. It must be in their cop-DNA she concludes. Where else could it come from?" Yet she wants someone special in her life. And to eliminate all cops just decreases the odds she'll meet the right guy.

She believes she is not meant to be a single mom … to be alone without a husband. She's met only a few guys who could be considered possibilities since the no-fault divorce, but none really knocked her socks off. They all seemed to blend into the same profile … looking for someone who is funny, yet serious; athletic, yet enjoys just watching television; takes chances but is really conservative; and so on to the point of nausea.

"Sometimes" … she thinks … "men are just trying too hard to be Mr. Right and come off like a phony-baloney, in other words, insincere and desperate, maybe just trying to get into the sack for a one-timer." She wonders to herself … "Could she be the one who is insincere and desperate, hoping that there really is a Mr. Right someplace in the galaxy? Is she missing the obvious … whatever that might be?"

Her eyes begin to tear of the mere possibility that there isn't the perfect guy for her … ever. "Damn," she says aloud. "I wonder if Jeff will call. But I shouldn't count on him. I can't put all my eggs into one basket. If it's meant to be, it's meant to be."

Suddenly, as if on cue, her phone rings again. "Hello?"

"Hi, it's Jeff, thought I'd call you before I leave my place for the office to update you on the case and see how you're doing."

She shakes off her inner desires. "Just finished talking with John who gave me an update on the case."

"Oh." He pauses and then continues, "They usually take longer than you want and don't always have happy endings, but it's the career I chose, so I'm not complaining." Jeff pauses, waiting for a response, but when there is only silence he changes the topic. "So, how are you doing?"

Her voice lifts slightly, feeling a little nervous about sharing too much with a man she really doesn't know but imagines she'd like to. "The good news is I'm spending time with my daughter. I wouldn't know what I'd do without her." She feels awkward for a brief moment for some reason, not sure why. Then she continues. "John has been so nice to me, giving me time to think about returning to work, no pressure from him, just from me. I feel I've got to make a decision sooner and not later."

"Don't rush it. You'll know it's right when it is." He temporarily halts talking before picking up again. "You sound good." He feels foolish with the superficial comment.

"And so do you." She almost laughs out loud with the ridiculous reply, like a teenage girl about to giggle on her first date.

It's been quite a while since he's talked with a woman about non-work things. He doesn't want to blow this opportunity. "Do you like animals?" The question rushes out of his mouth before he can stop it.

"Ah, yeah, I guess, but I don't have any ... you know with a child who takes up a lot of time." She isn't sure why they're talking about this, but she's not about to put a kibosh on the conversation. "And you?"

"I adopted the German-Shepherd who was with the homeless guy. I still don't know why I did ... I mean I've never had a pet, even as a kid. But she was going to be put down, and I couldn't let that happen. I hope I know what I've done ... time will tell."

"Really?" There's nothing else that comes to mind to say.

"Her name is Lady, but you already know that ... you told John and me. Now I'm living with a woman again. It's been a while." He almost laughs wondering why he added the last part.

"That's real sweet of you. I kind-of felt sorry for her but I just couldn't see me supporting both Natalie and Lady at the same time." Her mind goes blank, empty of thoughts for a split second, and then she lets slip something. "So, I take it you were married before?" Lilli scolds herself for the question, totally out of line, yet it seems to be the right opening for Jeff to give some details.

"We divorced after 3 years of marriage. It was not a good marriage and my feelings about her are ... shall I say ... at best ... neutral. No children ... thank God. She was attractive and I was dumb." There is a cup of coffee in front of him on his kitchen table. He reaches for it to take a needed gulp as he questions the motivation for sharing such personal information.

Lilli mentally observes him from their prior meeting ... about 30 she guesses, in good shape, handsome, but holding back some anger. His finger nails neatly cut, clear almost to a polish. "What does she look like?"

"Huh?"

"Can you describe what she looks like?"

"Please."

"No, really."

"Why are you interested?"

"Well for one thing, you brought it up."

"I'd only have bad things to say."

"I understand, but, uh, I thought you said your feelings about her are neutral. Maybe, I misunderstood."

"Really?" He doesn't intend to sound sarcastic.

Lilli wonders ... "Why does he seem to have become so defensive all of a sudden, or is it something else."

Jeff wonders why she's interested. Is she just a nosey person, or is there something more?

Lilli thinks for a moment, wondering what he's doing right now and how he looks, searching for the right way to turn the conversation around into something positive. "Did others feel the same way about her as you?" Oops, the question is out ... too late to retrieve it.

He's tried to put aside his thoughts about his wife sleeping around, although that's easier said than done. Further, he's never had any proof, just a gut feeling. Anyway, he thinks back to an incident when he was married, in bed with her. He tried snuggling up to her, to her naked back and kiss the nape of her neck and then let his hand slide down to reach between her legs to get some sort of reaction. But nothing ... there was no response from her ... too drunk, dead to the world. But what about that scratch on her back ... how the hell did that happen? It seemed fresh. Maybe he had his proof, but then again, he never confronted her.

His face, broken eyes, eyebrows appear darkened contrasted to how he imagines Lilli right now ... her eyes, short hair and her posture as straight as an arrow. Then he blurts out, "You don't lie to people you love." He loved his ex-wife ... doubts that will ever go away, yet that is exactly a big part of the pain he is feeling.

His head tilts forward showing a longer and downturned nose.

His voice is now softer, eyes appear smaller and squinty. "I trusted her but she betrayed me." His posture doesn't change.

Lilli remains a bit confused, but she keeps quiet to let him go on.

"I don't know. I'm not thinking straight right now. It was, well, all so confusing to me. I'm sorry to have brought you into my past."

His eyes soften yet his lips are pursed just enough to be noticeable. "I want you to believe, I mean really believe what I'm about to say about her. OK?"

Lilli's eyes widen, teary, her stare focused on the wall imagining him and what he's about to say. She, for the time being, is speechless.

He continues. "I loved her. I always have and always will."

She keeps starring at him still looking at the wall but it's unclear if it is based on confusion, shock, or something else. Nothing comes to mind to say, so she remains silent.

"You think I shouldn't have done it." He stares off into space ... motionless. "To have divorced her."

She doesn't answer.

"I know what I'd do, I'd do it again."

Again, she doesn't say a thing.

"And that's not a lie." His lips twist. "And <u>that</u> is not a lie!"

She blinks and her mouth opens ever so slightly. "So ...."

He doesn't hesitate to interrupt her. "Yes, I'd probably do it again under those circumstances. I'd leave her, but I'd still love her. Is that crazy or what?"

She slowly lets out a long and audible breath of air and closes her eyes, feeling the pain he's feeling as if it was her own, which it is. "OK." She pauses and then adds, "You're not a bastard."

"I know that," he quickly responds.

He grins ever so slightly. "And there's a *but*, isn't there."

She senses wanting to run away, but doesn't. Instead she says, "No *buts*."

He continues, "It's still not easy for me to talk about this anymore."

He feels hollow and lonely as he visualizes Lilli turning away. He finds enough oomph to ask, "We can still talk? I can call you again?" He hopes he knows her answer before she says it.

"Of course. I'd like that."

Jeff doesn't want the conversation to end. "What about you … how did you become a single mother?"

"How do you know that?"

"John told me, and you told me enough about caring for your daughter and not being able to take in Lady."

"Maybe at another time … I hope you don't mind me saying that."

"No, not at all … perhaps later on."

"Do you smoke or drink?"

Jeff frowns, taken aback by the sudden change in topic. He tells a partial truth. "Never smoked, but I do enjoy a glass of wine now and then. And you?"

"Same here. Chardonnay is my favorite. The reds give me a headache. Don't want Natalie to pick up any bad habits from her mom."

"Are you saying you don't have any bad habits?"

"Oh no, that's not what I mean. We can talk about that at a later time." He doesn't see her grin and wiggle her eyebrows.

"How about dinner some time?"

"I'd like that very much."

Jeff's face glimmers with joy ... a big and wide smile. "Anyway, I gotta go."

"OK, thanks for calling," she answers.

After the phones disconnect Lilli remains motionless ... she doesn't know why. Then it creeps up on her, flashes ever so slow briefly, and then vanishes, but she knows it was there if just for a split second ... she's convinced without a doubt. It dawns on her that maybe, just maybe, it could grow into something special. But she knows she's got to be cautious. She's been careless in the past ... something she has no intention of repeating, especially now with Natalie to take care of.

She hears her daughter's sweet voice that dislodges her from the thoughts. She smiles and takes Natalie into her arms. Her eyes are now a bit moist from pleasure. "I love you."

Jeff, on the other hand isn't sure what to make of their talk. He initiated it for sure, but he's now somewhat mixed up about it all. He tries to assess what just happened. It shouldn't be difficult for him ... he's an experienced law enforcement professional ... he's been trained in sound, objective profiling and investigative techniques. His intuitions are usually spot-on. But this is different, very different ... it's personal.

It wasn't supposed to be like this. It was supposed to be clear. The waters weren't to be muddied. It seemed to go just fine … the talk that is … he thinks, but he wonders what she thinks about it. Maybe he should have asked her right then and there, maybe not. Was he too blatant about his thoughts of his divorced wife … too soon? He has no idea except for one thing … she agreed to have dinner with him. "That's positive," he says aloud grinning from ear to ear.

He hears Lady bark, not as strong of a woof as she's capable of right now given her circumstances. But give it time. He's committed to follow the Vet's specific instructions, and in no time she'll be in good physical shape … strong and vigorous. He turns towards her, kneels down to gesture for her to come closer. The German-Shepherd slowly agrees. "This could be the start of something good." He pets her on her head. Lady barks as if she knows exactly what he's going through.

CHAPTER 5

Two days later in the afternoon Jeff and John meet in John's office. There are half cups of coffee in each of their hands, the third for each of them since meeting only a half hour ago.

Jeff says, "I've tried looking for them."

"And?" John takes a slow sip from his cup.

"They don't seem to exist."

"Don't exist?" John's eyebrows rise.

"Impossible so far to find out anything about them."

"You've tried everything?" Now it's John's lips that pucker.

"Maybe not a psychic."

"Not funny." John's brow furrows.

"I know." Jeff's inner corner eyebrows rise. He too is disappointed of essentially no progress in finding those responsible for killing the kid.

"So what are you going to do?" John's gaze is more intense than before.

"I've been thinking about that."

"And?"

"Don't know." Jeff shrugs his shoulders and then takes a sip of coffee that has lost most of its flavor.

"Put somebody undercover." John's face is deadpan in spite of the suggestion.

"Undercover?" Jeff pauses. "You're not serious."

"Oh yes I am. You've got the resources."

Jeff's eyes widen and his voice is bleak sounding. "Only in my dreams. We're short staffed."

"Be creative."

"Easier said than done."

John takes another sip of now tepid coffee. "I have an idea." He looks at the cup with annoyance.

"Don't keep me in suspense." Jeff matches John's sip with the same reaction. "Too cold." He moves the cup away from him.

John's face is deadpan. "How about Lilli?"

Confused, Jeff answers, "Huh?"

"You know who I'm talking about."

"Oh, I do." Jeff frowns.

"And what's the problem?"

"What's in your coffee ... a little brandy or something?"

"No, I'm serious."

Jeff straightens his body, picks up the coffee cup again and then moves it from one hand to the other. "For starters, she's not trained in this. Come on ...."

Without much emotion John explains in simple terms, "So train her."

"It's not that easy." Jeff shakes his head. "You sure there's nothing in your coffee?"

"Important things are never easy."

Jeff twists his nose. "Why her ... isn't she coming back to work here?"

"She's undecided."

"Why would undercover work make her decision easier to make?"

"Hell, I don't know. Maybe because it'd be a change, and that's something she needs right now … a change."

"And we both know more dangerous. Hell, she's got a daughter to take care of." Jeff pauses, looks at the half cup of coffee, and then shakes his head. "I don't think she's cut out for something like that. Hell, she's got a young daughter."

"Why not just ask her? Let her decide."

Jeff shakes his head sideways as his head remains tilted downward. "That's too much paperwork, the approval process is complicated and lengthy … it's complicated. No, I'm not in favor of it."

"It sounds as if your only alternative is to let the case go cold. Let the killer of the kid stay free. Let their parents never get closure. Make it …."

Jeff interrupts, "OK, I hear you. Don't lay it on me." He lifts his head to squarely look at John.

"It's about solving a murder, keeping punks from pushing drugs, and preventing others from getting killed."

Jeff shakes his head a few times and then shifts it back to looking at the coffee cup in his hand. "First, I'd have to create a past for her that is simple but close to the truth. Her daughter would have to be protected at all times. She'd never be able to keep notes or anything else personal that would expose her identity. She'd have to play one hundred percent of the time by the rules of the street, yet at the same time be her own person. In other words blend in to be somebody else but not become one of them, not to mention make some pretty difficult decisions on the spot." He looks up at John. "Is that what you want Lilli to do … to become … really?"

John stares unblinkingly at Jeff, "What's the alternative?"

Jeff says, "I guess there are some good sides for her going undercover." His eyebrows rise.

John agrees, "Sure. Talk to me."

Jeff takes in a shallow breath of air and explains. "She can mostly keep her own hours, roam the streets to nose around at her own pace for the most part, and carry a gun."

John asks, "And the flip side ... what?"

Jeff cocks his head to the side. "Of course there are some bad sides like being away from her daughter, although she'd have to deal with that with any job. The conditions could be dangerous on the street. And, uh, sleep patterns get messed up with probable irregular hours."

Now it's John's turn. "Listen, Jeff. We've known each other for a while. You know things about me that very few others do. We've teamed up before to put enough of the punk-heads away for a while, although it seems they have a way of reproducing. Anyway, this is the career each of us chose. And, I know a few things about you as well that, in order to save time right now I won't bring up. What I'm leading to is we can both, at the same time, convince Lilli to go undercover. What do you say?"

Jeff clenches his mouth. "I called her recently to see how she was doing."

John nods. "That was nice."

Jeff tilts his head slightly to the left and then straightens it. "For some dumb-ass reason on my part I started talking about my ex." He notices John's eyes bulge. "Yeah, what the hell was I thinking?" He pauses and continues. "I guess I wasn't thinking. Anyway, I felt something between us ...

something good … I mean as if I was beginning to care about her."

John shakes his head in major disappointment. "What the hell were you thinking?"

Jeff holds up his right hand. "Yeah, what was I thinking?" He looks away for a split second and then back to John. "It just happened and I wouldn't want to place her in any extreme dangerous position. Know what I mean?"

John lets out an exasperated breath of air. "Let her decide. She's an adult. I too admire her as a single mom. She's strong. I know that's not what you're referring to, but she's smart enough to make her own decisions, not us."

Jeff clears his throat. "OK, I'm in."

John nods his head. "I'll set up a meeting to meet with her. I'd keep your personal feelings private for the time being. Can you do that?"

Jeff nods his head, "If I agree, will you?"

John nods, "You've got my word on it." He extends his hand to shake on it.

The next day, Lilli meets with John and Jeff in John's office. John is the first to speak. "Thanks for coming down to talk with us."

Lilli worries she's acting as nervous as she feels. With a slight nod to Jeff, she replies to John. "Sure. Let me say first, though, that I appreciate everything that each of you have done to help me get through this. I'm really forever thankful."

John continues. "Our word is our word." He shifts in his chair, a sign that he too feels a bit uncomfortable for some reason. "Jeff would normally take the lead on this, but since you're still an employee of *Verity Security* we agreed that I'd take the lead. So, I'll cut to the chase. The case is at a standstill. Jeff and I think we need someone to go undercover. We think, make that believe, you are the right person for this. We'll make sure there's ample security for you and Natalie as you blend into the environment. You're smart and conscientious with high integrity. You'll be trained properly. And you'll report to Jeff and me. That's what we're offering you. Oh, yeah, one more thing, your pay will increase by twenty-five percent."

There is silence until Jeff speaks. "While we want you to say yes, this is entirely your decision. We'll both respect your answer, whatever it is."

John adds, "Your position with *Verity Security* as a Public Safety Officer is still yours in case you decline."

"I – I don't know what to say. This is … well … so sudden … something I wasn't expecting."

Jeff asks, "Do you want some time to think this through?"

"I need more information." She pauses and then asks, "What's my undercover … who do I become?"

Jeff suggests, "How about a newspaper reporter or maybe a novelist … whatever you're comfortable with."

Lilli's normal looking confident face is overshadowed by creases in her face indicating worry, surprise and maybe even more. Then she shakes her head a few times. "I don't think so. My daughter could be caught in the middle. I'd be thinking about her all the time. No thanks. This isn't for me under my present situation. Maybe I need to entirely switch to another career field."

John and Jeff were not expecting a turn-down. They quickly glance at each other, and then John offers an alternative. "Jeff and I hadn't discussed a back-up plan in the event you said no, but I have an idea." He looks at Jeff to see him nod his head to hear further.

John directly faces Lilli. "How about still working for *Verity Security* in a promotional role? I'm thinking as a Supervisor and Lead Public Safety Officer. You'll wear your uniform with full equipment when on duty patrolling our clients' grounds, but you'll wear whatever you want when you're the Supervisor working on this case. You'll still get a twenty-five percent pay bump. You'll still report to me while I keep Jeff up-to-date." He waits for a response, but then quickly adds, "It's not a career change to another field, but it'll take advantage of your strengths."

Lilli frowns not from confusion but from the revised offer.

Jeff chimes in, "I'll agree to that. Yeah, that makes sense. I guess they'll be times when we'll work together on this case, and then you'll work with John on *Verity Security* issues."

Both John and Jeff focus on Lilli wondering what she's thinking.

She pauses and then says, "You've both got to promise me that Natalie will never be in harms-way."

John and Jeff look at each other. They nod in agreement.

John adds, "We'll do everything possible to keep Natalie safe and protected. You've got our word on it."

Jeff suggests, "We could relocate you to another apartment in another city."

She swallows, still processing the information. "OK, I trust both of you. I'll stay in my current place. I'm in."

CHAPTER 6

It is the least favorite responsibility of Chief Cooke ... a press conference ... but he's obligated to the public. There is something about the atmosphere that is created when a group of overachieving and often incompetent journalists, reporters, and photographers come together, trying to outdo one another even if it means asking biased and insinuating questions in an attempt to boost their own frail egos. And, it's anyone's guess what they'll actually report as the truth, although in the atmosphere of today's fake news it isn't surprising what it will be. It isn't only the media but the politicians and government officials to mention two other groups who share the blame. And the public is the ultimate victim.

Chief Cooke, dressed in his standard blue uniform, quasi-military in appearance, enters the room, walks towards a podium to stand behind it where there is a microphone and an opened bottle of water. The room goes silent. He taps the microphone twice to get everyone's attention, introduces himself although not necessary since they all know who he is but it is customary just the same, and explains the situation with partial truths ... somethings must be withheld from the public during an investigation.

"The murdered victim's name is being withheld in respect to his parent's request. He was shot in the parking lot of Centro Rail Service Station at around midnight ten days ago. The victim and what appears to be a friend, not known if the alleged friend was male or female, the age or anything else descriptive, were allegedly running away from two others, not yet identified. The victim was struck once by a bullet. The weapon was a .38 caliber revolver, most likely a Colt or Smith and Wesson, 4 inch-barrel length, cylinder-loaded exposed hammer selective double action, or something close to that. There was another person with the killer. Presently, we don't know either of their identities." He pauses to take a gulp of water and then continues, with a few untruths. "Further we do not know the motive or motives for the shooting. Our efforts are concentrated on finding the two responsible for this situation, and anything else that may lead to solving the case. That's about it. Any questions?" He looks around the room.

A woman reporter raises her hand.

"Yes, Ms. Malone."

With a bit of sarcasm in her voice, she says, "It seems you don't know much."

He ignores her attitude. "At the present time we are early in the investigation. Who's next?" He looks around to point to a man from a local television station in the back of the room. "Mr. Renovo. You're up."

"Chief, so you're saying you have no suspects?"

He nods his head. "That's exactly what I've said." He looks to the edge of those seated. "Ms. Price."

"Is the public at risk?"

"We believe this is an isolated incident." The Chief scans the room again. "Ms. Pruett, your turn."

"Are drugs involved?"

"Not that we know of at the present time." He quickly glances at the audience. "Mr. Chen."

"Do you have someone devoted to solving this shooting?"

"We have highly qualified and dedicated law enforcement personnel presently working on many cases to ensure the safety of our public." Another quick once-over of the room leads him to call out, "Ms. Schell."

"What theory or theories do you have? Surely, you must have multiple ones."

"We're gathering facts at the present time."

A man in the middle of the room stands to scream out, "So you don't have a theory!"

The Chief ignores the outburst, realizing the guy wants to create a spectacle. "I'm old fashion, I guess, in that I stick to the facts." He stares down the man and then closes the press conference. "Thank you all for coming. Have a good day." He quickly leaves the room while many in the audience incoherently yell out.

CHAPTER 7

Dressed in casual clothes, Lilli stands against a boarded-down building that might once have been a profitable business … difficult to tell since there is so much graffiti on the outside she has no idea. There're signs of homeless sleeping arrangements up and down the block … not a place to bring-up a child. It is close to 10:00 pm as she waits to see what'll happen across the street at a bar. Thirty minutes pass and still there is no activity across the street. She wonders if she is chasing something she can't catch, but she's agreed to work with Jeff undercover so she's not complaining. At least Natalie is safe. Suddenly her cell phone pings.

She reads the message … ANYTHING TO REPORT?

Lilli frowns and texts back … QUIET AS CAN BE. HOW MUCH LONGER DO YOU WANT ME TO WAIT?

The reply is … GIVE IT ANOTHER 30 MINUTES. THEN LEAVE. MAYBE A BOGUS TIP.

She replies … OK, ANOTHER 30 MINUTES. She sneezes once. It's gotten cold outside.

Lilli waits.

Five minutes later a male wearing dark colored loafers and socks, dressed in a black shirt, jeans, and a brown leather jacket casually walks down the sidewalk across from Lilli, and then enters the bar. Lilli texts … ESTABLISHED VISUAL CONTACT WITH A MALE PERSON OF INTEREST. Now she waits to see what happens. She sneezes again.

Twenty minutes later the male who walked into the bar re-emerges with another person who appears to Lilli to be female. She texts … FOLLOWING THE MALE WHO NOW IS WITH A FEMALE.

The reply is quick … BE SAFE. DON'T TAKE UNNECESSARY CHANCES.

Lilli tightly holds the cell in her hand and as covertly as possible follows the couple staying at least a half-block behind them until they turn down an alleyway. She texts … ENTERING AN ALLEY.

Still far enough back to stay unseen by the couple Lilli looks around to make sure she's not the one being followed. She's doing her best to apply the techniques taught by Jeff. A raggedy dressed male sleeps just a few feet from her as someone next to him is playing a flute-like instrument … not very well. She keeps visible contact with the couple and a safe distance behind as the darkness of the alleyway gets darker with every step. She squints as her eyes struggle to adjust but keeps walking until she spots the couple walk below an overhead sign … **EXIT**. Then they disappear. The filthy smell of the alleyway gradually changes to something more pleasant yet difficult to describe, something she's never smelled before.

She picks up her pace in a jog-like action so she doesn't lose them. All of a sudden she hears music … pleasant sounding music to her ears as the man and woman meet up with another couple and then suddenly many more people. It seems almost like being at a party of some sort. They all stand outside a warehouse that appears to have experienced the last of its regular and planned usefulness.

Lilli stops walking to figure out what's going on. She stares straight ahead. The people are dressed in sensible casual clothing smoking and drinking as if she's just crashed a party, uninvited. She's not sure what's happening. The people seem to be celebrating something, but what is it? Then the crowd enters the warehouse through a front door. She rushes closer to the warehouse's entrance.

Close enough to the warehouse to touch it, she swivels her body to make sure no one is behind her. Then she slowly opens the door to take a peek in. She sees several people looking at a specific spot on the wall, so she stretches her neck to take a look-see. She puts the cell in her jacket pocket.

There is an assortment of paintings on the walls of the warehouse, some brushed directly on the wall while others shown on canvas hangings. The chatter of the crowd has grown. She wonders if this is the city's underground art scene.

"Excuse me." The voice comes from behind her.

Lilli turns to see a man, tall and lean with wavy black hair stand behind her. She remains composed and in her undercover role. "Yes?" Her face is stoic looking.

"What are you waiting for? There's no charge to check it out." He smiles.

Lilli feels her muscles tighten. The sudden appearance of the man gives her some alarm. She can't be exposed. She must play the role.

He waits conveniently long enough for Lilli to respond, but when she doesn't he adds, "Do you like something you see?" He raises his eyebrows.

She feels a sigh of relief. "I – I'm not sure I know what I'm seeing."

"We're celebrating. One of us just sold a work of art for twenty thousand dollars." He smiles. "Not me unfortunately, but I'll never give up on my dreams."

Her previously tightened muscles relax a bit. "This is sort of like an art gallery, except it's …."

"Unconventional." His smile is sincere and comforting. "So, do I assume you're not an artist?"

Lilli gets her voice back, "Excellent assumption." She grins in relief.

"How did you find this?"

"I'm nosey."

"Nosey can be sexy," he says as his eyes stay glued on Lilli.

She's prepared to take on his comment with one of her own. "Curiosity is sexy and both are rare."

"Touché … I stand corrected."

Suddenly the buildup of tension between them is obvious.

"You don't take many people seriously, do you?" he asks, but it's really a statement of opinion.

"Why do you say that?" Lilli frowns. She thinks he's so far off the mark, but she's got to play the role.

"Because you don't, I can tell." He shrugs his shoulders, pauses as he looks away briefly and then looks back at her. "Too many people are not serious about what matters." He looks away again and returns to her. "They judge others by their superficial appearances, splash on the fringes of politics without even knowing their own, and are so much in love with themselves that it disgusts me."

"So, I take that as your opinion, I guess." She figures she's got to be careful. This guy may be playing a role as well.

"Bingo," he answers.

A chill runs through her body. For some reason she reminds herself that it is better to see the devil that you know than the demon you've never met … but which one is he … or is he something else?

He nods for some reason without much emotion as he continues, "And what are you curious about?"

"I'm a reporter for *Universal Gazette News*." Inwardly she applauds at how easy she responded. She's in control.

"Do you report on the art scene?"

"No."

"I've never heard of *Universal Gazette News*."

"Most haven't. We're a relatively new startup."

"I hope you don't report on what's going on inside."

"Why's that? Is it illegal?" She definitely feels like she's in a groove.

"Not really. The building is vacant."

"But aren't you trespassing?"

"There aren't any signs telling us that." He waves his hand in the air.

"I see." Lilli is not sure what to say next. The situation isn't what she originally thought it would be, yet she's proud of how well she played her role. She's about to leave, but the man continues.

"Reporting what's going on inside will throw us out of the building, as well as the hopes and dreams of us as artists to have our work noticed. I hope you don't. We're all struggling to make a few dollars off of what we all passionately love doing."

"And be famous."

"Not necessarily. Our body of work … yes for sure, but not necessarily who we are."

"Maybe I should go."

"You're more than welcome to stay, to enjoy the art, to talk with the artists."

"Maybe I should leave now. And I promise not to write about it."

"I thought you were curious?"

Lilli turns without saying anything else, finished with what she came to do and walks away to be home with her daughter. Now far enough from the warehouse she grabs her cell from her jacket pocket and texts … TIP LED NOWHERE OF IMPORTANCE. CALLING IT A NIGHT.

The next day, Saturday, a little after 10:00 am, John unexpectedly shows up at Lilli's apartment.

"What are you doing here?"

"We've got to talk." His voice is serious sounding as is his unsmiling face.

"About what?" Lilli mimics his dour appearance and sound.

"Can I come in … it's important."

She hesitates, but then steps aside to let him enter her apartment. "I hope this is important. I've got a ton of things to do today that includes spending quality time with Natalie."

He stands outside the apartment. "Anyone else here besides you, Natalie, and me?"

"No." She frowns.

"Good." He steps inside, takes a quick look around to verify no one else is present, and spots Natalie playing on the floor. He gives the girl a sincere grin.

Lilli can tell from John's eyes that something important is up, but exactly what is still unclear.

"This can only be between us … no one else … OK?"

"OK." She feels her muscles tighten up. "What's up?"

John repeats, "Only between us."

"I heard you. Did you hear me?"

John nods his head affirmatively.

"Cross my heart." She keeps her eyes focused on him.

"Now that you're undercover … I should never have pushed the idea to Jeff … it's all my fault."

Lilli's brow knits. "What are you saying?"

John shakes his head sideways, tilts his eyes downward to avoid direct contact with her, and then squarely faces her. "There's a huge difference between your real life and your undercover life when you work with Jeff. Your real life is the only thing that matters. Don't ever forget that."

Her brow remains puckered. "I don't understand."

Slowly and calmly John says, "I'm gonna sound like your father, but, uh, well, I don't want you to put your life in jeopardy."

"What?"

"Jeff told me of yesterday's situation … how well you handled it … maybe too well."

"What does that mean?"

"You could easily find yourself in a dangerous situation the next time out."

"And?"

"Between you and me … right."

"We've already agreed on that."

The sound of his voice is alarming. "I've seen this happen before. It can be addictive."

She somehow retains her composure. "What?"

"Danger can easily be addictive … a rush. It can catch up to you very quickly. And then …." He doesn't finish the thought.

She takes a strong look towards him. "Finish your thought."

"You'll purposely put yourself in increasingly more dangerous situations thinking you can handle them all. You'll forget about Natalie. You could get killed. So I've said it."

Lilli shakes her head, confused about what he said. She keeps quiet but tells herself it would never happen to her.

"It's not too late. Fortunately, you're not in deep enough."

"That's not going to happen." She crosses her arms.

"Denial does not solve anything. In fact, it may make it worse for you and Natalie."

"It's not too much pressure. I can take care of my daughter."

"Don't believe that."

"Then what am I supposed to do?"

"I'm here to warn you to be careful. You can always count on me. I'll stop by occasionally as if just to check up on you and Natalie. Don't get reckless, be resourceful."

"This is crazy. I think this is more about you than me."

"I don't see it that way."

"Jeff has asked me to have dinner with him some time. What am I supposed to do ... say no?"

"What's wrong with that?"

"Because I've already told him it would be nice."

"So, you've had a personal conversation already with him?"

"Sort of ... I guess so."

"I don't know how to advise you on that ... only, just be careful about what I've said ... the addiction to danger. Would you promise me at least that?"

Lilli nods. "Sure."

John isn't convinced. She's shown to him an alarming increase in hardness in such a short time since going undercover. He wonders what else he can do, if anything, to intervene, beyond what he's just done, and beyond the choice she has made.

CHAPTER 8

Prairie isn't his birth name, which is Roger George Poe, Jr., named after his father. But even as a baby he was mischievous, tending to cause annoyance, trouble and even minor injury to others that included him. What he thought was playfulness was interpreted as irresponsible and he continually was punished and scolded by his parents, then his teachers, and others. He had no real friends. He was nicknamed Prairie to reflect a prairie dog, in other words a rodent like creature. There were even others who thought of him as a prairie wolf, in other words, a coyote ... a small but dangerous wolf. He soon began to believe that he didn't belong to a normal human society. He turned out to be a very angry male human being. Not surprisingly to anyone, he ran away, essentially disappeared, and no one cared to try to find him. He wasn't surprised. The streets became his home.

It takes everything he's got to stay calm and relaxed in spite of him stealing for so many years. He should be settled, but he isn't. He dumps the box of bullets that are carelessly left on top of a counter waiting to be secured into his pants pocket, looks around to notice that no other customers or store employees or security guards are watching him steal the merchandise. He slowly walks towards the men's rest room next to the self-service checkout lane. Calmly, he enters the rest room where he is alone. He takes a pee, washes his hands and exits. Then he stops, looks around and makes a successful dash to leave the store. He's already preplanned his exit strategy well enough to get safely away.

The stolen bicycle is parked far enough away from the store and among the motorized vehicles in the parking lot that he has no problem in reaching it to ride off. Prairie's become a successful thief.

If you asked him how he became who he's become he'd tell you he has no idea. It just happened ... it was meant to be ... the stars were aligned ... and other such crap. He's not making any alibis ... it just is ... and he just as well be the best he can be. At least he doesn't have to be responsible for anyone other than himself, no errands to run for anyone other than himself, and no rules to follow except those for survival. He can still hear the way his parents, teachers and others sounded.

He leans against the bicycle before he hops-on and smiles. He's not a screw-up. He's no longer a kid. If you say the same thing to yourself enough times you begin to believe it. His motto is *tell the truth even when it's a big fat lie.*

He stares out at the parking lot of vehicles wondering what he might find if he was able to unlock a door. It doesn't bother him that he takes from others what doesn't belong to him, but he's convinced that's what coyotes do.

He looks away, deciding not to push his success. There will always be another opportunity. Right now he feels hungry, so he jumps on the bicycle headed to a convenience store to steal some food. Coyotes would approve.

CHAPTER 9

Striking doesn't do justice to describing her appearance, but at least it's a start. In some ways Lili looks like an innocent adult child, but in other ways it is clear she is now dressed just the right way for tonight. She feels a little naughty. Her tight fitting skirt, an inch well above her knees, accentuate her slender legs and show just enough of her thigh to make one's imagination run wild. The two top opened buttons of her white silk blouse add to her unmistakable message. And her spiked black shoes with stockings that have a black seam down the back add to the final touch. It's impossible not to be mesmerized by just looking at her whether you're a woman or a man. She just looks luscious and exotic. She's forgotten about John's recent caution to her regarding addiction and danger.

Lilli steps into the bar. This is her personal time. Instantly she feels out of place but comfortable enough even though it's been quite a while she's even thought about joining in. Hell, she's the single mom of a girl she desperately loves, Natalie. She's been working her ass off between John and Jeff, and there simply hasn't been any time to think of going out, looking at another guy, or anything else other than working and raising her daughter the best she knows how.

Fortunate that she's met some incredible people who sit with Natalie while she's working. And Vincent, an older man, has become sort of a grandfather to Natalie. And fortunate that he lives in another apartment in the same building and doesn't charge her anything for his domestic services, which, by the way, are considerable to her but seemingly small to him. No one's complaining. Everyone seems to be getting what they want, or so it seems. According to Vincent, his wife unexpectedly passed on a few years ago and his kids don't seem to take any interest in him at all. At least she and Natalie do the best they can. It seems too perfect to be true.

Lilli glances around the place, checks her watch, and then spots an open spot at the bar. She's got about 15 minutes to wait for Sandy, a girlfriend from high school. They've recently kept in touch on social media as friends, and when Sandy mentioned to her that she'd be in town on business, they agreed to meet up. Evidently Sandy is a published author meeting with her literary agent on a project she's working on. It seems the timing is just right.

On her way to the open seat at the bar Lilli notices him … a very handsome man about her age, she guesses. It seems he's by himself just enjoying the live music and having a drink by himself. She pretends she hadn't noticed him as she takes the open seat, but the truth is she noticed him a lot. Wavy brown hair with deep blue eyes, and looks way too cool to be her type. The bartender politely places a small bowl of cashews in front of her, smiles, and asks, "Good evening. Welcome to *The Broadway*. What would you like?"

Out of the corner of her eye she spots the cool looking guy looking her way. Well, maybe not directly at her and more like he shifted his body to catch a glimpse of the singer to her left. "I'll take a Chardonnay, buttery, not smoky."

"We're pouring a new wine, right from Italy … ViAntonini. It's a Pinot Grigio, not Chardonnay. We've got a special tonight … half off. I think you'll like it" His pause confuses Lilli for a split second, and then he says, "OK?"

She clears her throat, "Yes, that's fine." She thinks to herself … "What the hell … take a risk … what will it cost?"

"I'm not much for whites, I prefer the reds." The body of the cool looking guy is now more directly facing Lilli. He holds up the glass of Cabernet. "It's also a ViAntonini … very good body and smooth."

She figures he's not too forward, just enough to show interest in her. She's flattered, but honestly, not sure how to reply. He helps her out.

"How are you tonight?" His smile is warm and inviting.

She collects her thoughts, immediately trying to throw out that it's been a while since she's been at a bar, at night, by herself, and talking to a very good looking man. She quickly says, "Waiting for someone," and then as quickly suspects she sounds rude to him.

"Oh, sorry if I was coming on too strong. It's just that …." He purposely lets the thought drift away and starts to shift his body away from her.

Right now it's the last thing she wants to happen. "Oh, I'm sorry. I didn't mean to imply …."

"No worry." He turns away to face the large mirror behind the bar.

Lilli doesn't give up. "Hey listen. My high school friend is in town on business, so we decided to meet up for a drink and dinner." She figures she's got a little time to further check him out before Sandy shows. Then her cell buzzes. She reads the message from Sandy … RUNNING LATE. GIVE ME A HALF HOUR.

Lilli replies … BETTER HURRY. HOT GUY AT THE BAR MIGHT REPLACE YOU.

Sandy answers … I'LL DO MY BEST.

Lilli looks up at him. His deep blue eyes are magical to her. Her heart picks up the beat. "Oh, I'm so sorry. Sandy is running a little late. What did you say?"

"Here's your Pinot Grigio. Enjoy." The bartender sets the drink on the bar and then moves onto another customer.

He smiles at her. "Sorry … it's all about the right time and place."

She smiles back. She wonders if he is really interested in her. She blurts out, thinking she might have been too harsh on him. "Who runs late at this time of the night?"

"Well, traffic's not predictable around here. Is he flying in from out of town?"

"Well, SHE's in town but tied up in a meeting." Lilli hopes she's emphasized the gender clearly enough.

"Sort of girls' night out."

He lifts his drink to Lilli, and he smiles gently, "Here's to a traffic jam."

They each take a sip of wine before he continues.

"What do you do?"

Lilli knows to keep her law enforcement work to herself … too many creepy people wandering around, and definitely doesn't want to turn off this incredible looking guy. She decides to fabricate something out of the blue. "School teacher."

"What grade?"

She wonders if he is truly interested in that particular fact or interested for some other reason. "Third grade."

"Married?"

She now wonders where this conversation is headed. She's not an accomplished liar but she might have to pick it up real fast. "No … just haven't found the right guy." She nervously takes another sip of wine.

"By the way, I'm Sean."

Without thinking she replies, "Lilli." Once she reaches out to shake his hand, she wonders if the move is out of place … juvenile or even stupid.

He takes her sweaty and cold hand in his warm and comforting hand. They stare at each for less than a few seconds but to her it seems much longer.

Suddenly, Lilli's phone buzzes again, and she suspects it's Sandy. "Excuse me," she reluctantly says to Sean. She reads the message … LILLI, I'M SO SORRY. JUST CAN'T MAKE IT TONIGHT. CALL YOU TOMORROW. SORRY. LOVE YA.

Maybe Lilli is feeling alone and vulnerable or maybe it is something else. Whatever it is, she has to make a decision on whether to stay or go. She figures she can leave any time she wants for any reason. Her eyes inevitably fall on Sean's. "Well, there goes girls' night out."

They continue to talk for a while about their interests, not to mention two more drinks each … more than she can ever remember consuming with someone she barely knows in a place she's never been to before. Yet during the entire time, their eyes come together and their smiles communicate. There is a twinkle from each of them as if to say, "I'm happy you're still here."

"So, Sean, what do you do?"

He tells her the truth. "I'm an HR guy. There's a professional HR meeting in town that I'm attending and I'm staying at this hotel." He wiggles his eyebrows as if to say, 'convenient.'

After they separately pay for their drinks, he and Lilli wind up in his hotel room. They stand, both still fully dressed, very close to each other, she feeling a bit disoriented as she wonders to herself … "What the hell am I doing here? This isn't right." And then suddenly she finds her arms tightly wrapped around him, smelling his body, feeling his reaction to her closeness. She feels electricity running through her entire body as his hands begin to explore her in ways she never thought was possible.

Their mouths are on each other, eagerly kissing like never before. His tongue dances against hers and his hands find their way beneath her clothing without any resistance from her. She feels a welcomed shiver, putting aside whether this was ever the right thing to do with a man she just met an hour or so ago.

He lifts her up and onto the bed. They each remove their shoes, and without a signal from her, he sheds his clothes as she excitedly watches, and then she copies what he did. They kiss. Now both naked on top of the blanketed bed, the critical incident is about to happen … serious and under the current conditions unavoidable. There is only a slight wiggle from both of them to make sure they are properly aligned. Then the unexpected happens.

Lilli feels a trepidation overtake her body, hesitating from going through with the final deed, something just a few minutes ago would have been farthest from her conscious mind. She pushes him away. "Stop!"

His tongue stops lacing her mouth.

Now, louder, she says, "Stop, please. I can't do this."

His body relaxes enough for her to push further away from him. "Sean, I just can't. I'm sorry."

"You're kidding, huh?" His face is completely confused.

"No, I'm not. It's just … well … not right for me. Please understand."

The passion in his eyes has completely drifted off to some other place. He blinks without saying a word but he's thinking … "What the hell just happened?"

"I'm really sorry. I am, really, really sorry." She sounds as if she is apologizing to him for something she's done.

His face is now looking confused. Then he blows out a breath of air and shakes his head. He manages to say in a humorous way, "So, this isn't your version of foreplay?"

Now a bit more relaxed, Lilli takes a deep sigh realizing she isn't in any danger of being with a wacko of sorts. "I wish it was." She takes in a deep swallow of air and slowly lets it back into space. "I really can't believe any of this happened."

"What's next?"

"I've got to straighten up, get dressed and leave. I'm so sorry."

"The bathroom is over there." He nods towards a closed bathroom door. He's convinced of the reality that sex is not going to happen.

She ignores him as she gets off the bed, picks up her clothes, and dresses in front of him. Then without saying a goodbye or see-you-around, she leaves him alone, naked on top of the bed.

CHAPTER 10

The man who holds onto the take-out double-cheese-pepperoni medium pizza with one hand as he unlocks the apartment door with the other hand is much younger than he looks. His hair has thinned and the bald spot at the back of his head grows by the day. There are random hairs on his face, ears, and nose that make him look even worse off than he is, although his life has not amounted to much since he and Lilli split. He wears a faded green T-shirt and his undershorts need a good washing … only if he was able to recognize it. His dirty feet are hidden by the worn out sneakers he wears and his arms have become thinner over a short time, obvious that he hasn't been exercising much. He needs glasses but he's short on cash at the moment. He opens the door with the same hand that still clings to the key.

He steps inside the apartment and kicks the door shut with his foot.

The studio apartment is a mess … looks as if it hasn't ever been cleaned or even tidied up a wee-bit for a long time, if ever. Food scraps seem to be everywhere but the beer cans are seemingly neatly stacked in a corner of the room for some reason. Eric walks near a sagging fake-suede couch whose color is a mystery to put the pizza on a nearby table.

He looks at the empty Styrofoam containers on the floor from a few meals ago, along with a lump of dirty clothes that need to be washed, but it seems that's not a priority for him at the moment.

He sniffles and then wipes his nose with the back of his hand.

He heads to a small kitchen area to get a cold beer from the refrigerator and then back to where the pizza rests. He flops on the couch, opens the can of beer, takes a deep swallow, and then reaches for a slice of pizza. His mouth opens wide enough to shove a good deal of the slice into this mouth. Then he chews just enough times before he takes a long swallow of cold beer. A fart finds its way into the air.

Chapter 11

A window of opportunity is not very large, considering the size of the window. Most are on the small size and therefore, logically so are the opportunities. And that's OK since opportunities are only looking for, at minimal, a small opening in order to take advantage of the chance to advance the progress. Most times, that's all you need is a small favorable circumstance as well as patience, even though it might feel like your teeth are being pulled out without the benefit of a sedative.

Vincent, the older man living in the same apartment building who has been helping Lilli care for Natalie when she's away at work, knocks on her apartment door. "Lilli, it's me, Vincent."

She casually opens the door, greets him with a warm smile as usual, and steps aside. "Come on in. What's up?"

He's hesitant at first, in fact quite odd behavior. His face is also tight looking and he remains silent.

She looks at him, wondering why he appears tentative. "Is there something you want to say to me?" She's confused.

He takes in a deep breath of air before saying what's on his mind. "There's been something I've wanted to say for a while, but I've been putting it off … kind of worried about your response."

She notices his usual calm appearance has quickly changed. His hand shakes. "You're not sick … are you?" she asks.

"Sick … hell no … just worried."

"About what … you can tell me."

"I'm worried you'll say no … you see the fact of the matter is I'm in love with you."

If fear doesn't move you, then love will compel you, because it all goes back to love … it's all that matters. You spend your life looking for the truth because truth is supposed to free you, but sometimes truth sucks. He believes if her answer is *no*, he'll not only look different but feel different without her. Maybe he should ditch the notion … it's too much of an impulse or urge … but maybe, no matter he's still going to chase the feeling until the day he dies. He's been in love before, once, the first girl he fell in love with and that's supposed to be it because, allegedly, it only gets worse after that because you'll never have the same feeling again.

She stares at him with total and naked astonishment.

"I'd like you to consider being my wife." His message is in his eyes.

It seems like forever there is total silence between them. Not even their breathing and pounding of their heart beats are noticeable. Then she's able to say, "I … wow."

"I know I'm older, too old for you … probably." His voice is now calm as he continues. "But we do get along real well, and I love Natalie like she's my daughter."

"I know you do, and she loves you too, as do I."

His heart soars, but only for a short time as Lilli continues.

"But I can't be your wife." If she could help him, she would, but it would only be out of pity … and that's not gonna happen … no way.

He takes in a deep breath of air. "Somebody else … is that it? There's someone else."

"Not in the way you mean."

His lips clamp together and his eyes are broken.

He continues. "Your ex … you're still in love with him … that must be it."

She starts to cry. Tears roll down her cheeks. "No, no, that's not it."

"Sure it is. Marry me. Chose me … your future … not him … your past. Please, don't say no."

"I know I'm happy right now, and Natalie is too."

"Yes, that's right. Just think about it, huh? Don't say no. Think about you, Natalie and me." His eyes sparkle with hope, as unrealistic as that may be.

"It's not that simple. Don't be angry with me. Please … but …." Her voice trails off.

He's got to find a way to gain her confidence … some way … any way. And that's the easy part. The tricky part is to convince her to marry him. He takes in a long breath of air and holds it for a second or two … but who's counting … before he lets it escape. He feels a little, but not much, less stressed.

Then he flashes back to his military days … not a real happy time in his life … a few specific days in particular when he was dropped off someplace in the middle of nowhere. He didn't know what or who he'd encounter once he reached the target location but he knew the mission … to gather as much intelligence information in the shortest amount of time about the enemy's strengths, weaknesses, opportunities and threats. And then, get the hell out of there as fast as possible … easier said than done. He made it through during his capture and detainment by the enemy alive somehow. Maybe he was praying to God, maybe not … it was a while ago and with time memory tends to fade. They were barely teenagers or so they looked, those who grabbed him. Why they didn't torture and kill him is still a mystery to him but he's not complaining. He was not classified as a prisoner of war because the mission was classified and even today there are no records of it ever happening, although he still is under a gag order. Those teenagers seemed only to want his clothes, at least mostly, before they tied him up standing until he passed out. He touches his left hand to feel the permanent injury. He shakes himself out of thinking about it anymore … the past is the past so just forget about it and move on. Yeah, right. What the hell was he thinking of when he volunteered for the mission … danger and excitement? Well, that's what he got 100 times over! He was young. Signing a final will to his parents should have signaled to him the mission was more than just danger and excitement. But if he wanted to be safe and secure, he would not have volunteered in the first place. There was no one pressuring him to do it, except of course, himself. It's that simple … or is it. Yet, it was the choice he made.

He blinks, sees Lilli still standing in front of him and then he mumbles something to himself that not even he understands. His shoulder muscles loosen and his pulse slows down. He takes in another deep breath of air and, as before, lets it escape to the area around him. Then he feels a sharp pain in his chest that lasts only momentarily. He ignores it as if it is unimportant, but he'll soon regret that choice.

Her phone rings. Lilli checks the caller-ID, smiles and answers to hear his voice, seemingly forgetting that Vincent is still standing in the doorway.

"It's me, none other," Jeff says.

"Where are you?" she asks.

"About an hour away."

"What's up?"

"I've got some news for you."

"OK, I'm listening." She frowns, thinking it's all about work stuff.

"I'm inviting myself over for dinner tonight at your place. I'll cook for the three of us."

"Huh?" She's obviously surprised.

"You, Natalie, and me … I'll bring the food and wine."

"Are you serious?"

"Very."

Her smile widens. "OK, tonight in an hour." Then she hears the phones disconnect. Slowly she brings her head straight ahead towards Vincent, but all she sees is him walking away. Her throat tightens so that she doesn't reach out to him … it's probably best to let it alone. She slowly closes the door, turns and heads back towards Natalie.

Within a few minutes from the call she gets a text message from Jeff … HEY, SOMETHING JUST CAME UP. I CAN'T MAKE IT. CALL YOU LATER.

She loves kids. Hell, she's a mother to a beautiful daughter, Natalie. But being without a husband isn't easy. Sure, she was married but the jerk bolted, that no-good-for nothing-twerp, and now they've finalized their no-fault divorce papers that gave her full custody. She had always imagined herself as a wife and mother, and as Natalie grew she would make it a point to glare at the boys who wanted to date her, cry when her daughter's heart got broken, and comfort her along the way. And that still might happen as the mother, but the odds are against her in the role of a wife. She reminds herself that she really does love kids. So, in a way, she's got a lock on one of the two.

Chapter 12

Lilli tosses and turns in her bed … something is bothering her … but what? Then it comes to her … she's trying to cope with the murder at the Centro Rail Service, her new job, Jeff, and Vincent. Then, strangely to her surprise she thinks of Natalie's father … the jerk! She says aloud, "I wonder where he is, who he's with, and what is he doing? Is he married, in jail, or even alive? Is he rich and famous?" Then she rubs her eyes. "I must be a perfect mother. My number one priority is to protect Natalie."

Unsuccessfully she tries to go back to sleep, but predictability that fails. Now wide eyes wide open, starring at the ceiling, her cell buzzes.

"What the hell? Who's calling at this crazy time?" She figures to let the call move to voice mail, but something causes her to change, not sure what, so she reaches over to pick up the cell. "Yeah?" She hears a familiar voice, not sure who it is, but before she can ask, she hears the caller say, "This is Patti Iverson. Camille Conroy is dead."

Lillis sits up in bed. "Who's this?"

"Patti Iverson, you remember, I'm sure."

"Patti Iverson? Is this you?"

"The one and only. I'm sorry to call you at this time and I know we haven't hung-out, well since high school. But that's life for ya. Anyway, I thought you'd want to know since you and Camille were the best of friends, and her parents asked me to tell you. I think they want to talk with you about something."

Lilli hesitates … times have changed, hell everything changes with time. "How did you get my number?"

"You've updated your records with your prominent high school class correspondent, which is me." She chuckles at what she thinks is funny. Then, without a rejoinder from Lilli, Patti continues. "Why on earth I ever accepted the role I'll never know. I get too much information from grads who I really had no special connection with during school. Guess I thought I didn't have much better stuff to do with my spare time. Anyway, that's neither here nor there. I've made the call. Hope you can make the funeral."

"What happened? How did Camille die?"

"Seems to have committed suicide, but her parents … they're still alive and living in the same place … don't believe it. Her mother asked me to contact you."

"What for?"

"Like I said before, you and Camille were the best of friends, and I guess her mom and dad think you could investigate."

"Investigate?"

"Yeah, that's what Mrs. Conroy said, and my answer was quite like yours. However, it seems they must think you're qualified, you know, equipped to deal with this sort of thing. I have no idea why. Maybe it was something that I said. Anyway, that's all I know."

A silence stretches out. Lilli hears her own breathing. Then she breaks the silent quietness. "The local police are really in charge, and I'm sure they will conduct a thorough investigation."

"Listen, Lilli, don't try to convince me of any of this. I'm just the messenger. Her parents, both of them, have it in their heads that something isn't right, that Camille would never take her life. Even if things were real bad, got mixed up in something unusual and couldn't get out. I don't know … I'm just the messenger."

"What do you think?"

"I think … I think Camille never really grew up. She trusted a lot of people. And it hurts me to say this but it wouldn't surprise me if something else happened. Maybe got mixed up with the wrong crowd. Hell, I don't know to be honest."

"How long have you felt this? Did you regularly socialize with Camille? Did she say or do anything that you thought might put her into some unexpected risk?"

"I agree with her parents, it doesn't sound like her. But again, I don't know anything specific. What should I tell her parents?"

"Hell, I don't know. I've got to think about this."

"OK, I'll tell her parents that you're thinking about it." Patti pauses and then says, "The funeral is tomorrow."

"Oh, that's out of the question. I can't make that, and I can't promise investigating the situation. I've got to think about that."

"Got it … that's what I'll say."

"Oh, what's her parents address?"

"They haven't moved. It's still 2763 Edge Avenue."

"OK."

Later in the day Lilli is still at her apartment playing with Natalie when her cell buzzes. She doesn't bother to check caller-ID. "Hello."

"It's me, John. Enjoying a day with your daughter?"

Her eyes light up. "Oh yeah, she's so adorable and curious ... the love of my life. What's up?"

"I've got an autopsy update on the victim if you're interested."

She twists her nose left and then right wondering if this is a good time to listen. She doesn't have many days when she can forget her work to be with Natalie. She exhales, noticeably to John and herself.

He senses her reluctance. "Maybe another time."

"No, no, tell me." Once the words are out, she regrets having agreed to listen, in spite of John giving her a way out. "I'm listening."

"OK. I don't know how much you know about examining a body by a forensic team."

"Not much ... I've never been in a situation like this before."

"OK, I'll give you a quick overview as well." He clears his throat. "The goal of an external examination is to create a descriptive record of the body at the time of an autopsy. They photograph the body and document all clothing. Then there is a head-to-toe physical examination. They cover areas like the physical development of the body, state of body preservation, body temperature, and level of body nutrition. They get very detailed in how they describe the body. Essentially the victim in this case was only a kid they believe to have been 14 or 15 years old, Caucasian male. Other than the gun shot there were no other external signs of trauma or fractures. I won't get into eye color, hair color and length, but those all have been documented. There were indications of needle punctures indicating use of drugs by injection but nothing else. Because this was a gun-related death from a distance there was no gunshot residue such as skin burning, soot, or tattooing. The size of the fatal wound was small and circular. The bullet was still lodged in his body … from a .38 caliber revolver. The victim had opioids stuffed in his system that probably came from both the injections and swallowing." He pauses, wondering how Lilli is taking it all in. Then he asks, "Still there?"

She sniffles. Natalie is now tightly cradled in her arms with tears formed at the corner of her eyes. "Yeah, it's just all so sad."

"I agree." He pauses and without a response from Lilli he ends the mostly one way conversation. "That's it."

"Thanks." She pauses and arrives at a conclusion. "I've got to take off on a personal matter for a few days about a recent death … her parents contacted me … Henry and Barbara Conroy. I hope that's OK."

"Ah, whatever you need. I'll let Jeff know. What about Natalie?"

"She'll be coming with me."

"OK, be safe. Talk again soon." John waits for a response that does not come, just the click of the phones disconnecting.

CHAPTER 13

Prairie pulls out the fake I. D. that he's had for a few years. It's up for renewal, a joke to him, so he's got to scout out another weak victim to start anew. He's not worried, but it might take some time since he looks a little older than what the picture shows on his fake I. D., which means he's got to find someone who more clearly fits his current appearance. It's just another job. He's not stupid.

His eyes get squinty, like when you spot an animal at night you don't want to play with. He levels his gaze at nothing in particular. He's thinking of his next move. The sun is just about to set. He stands on the sidewalk of a cul-de-sac where there are average looking homes and parked cars in the driveways and on the street. Then he smells smoke. He looks around to spot a house on fire. There's a rain of ashes headed his way. Next he hears a fire truck from behind along with an ambulance right behind it. Adults and their children have stepped outside their places, faces in shock. They're most likely in total disbelief.

Prairie leaves his bicycle to the side of the street behind a parked car and runs to get closer to the catastrophe. The colors of the flames are mesmerizing to him.

An elderly woman stands in front of her house that's on fire appearing to be surprisingly calm, or maybe she's traumatized.

Two firefighters have commenced their work to save the house and to keep nearby houses from catching on fire.

A paramedic from the ambulance runs to the elderly woman, and slowly walks her away to a place that is safer.

More firefighters wearing protective gear join in.

Prairie isn't able to hear the conversation between the paramedic and elderly woman. In fact, he could care less about what is said. He's more interested in returning to this place, as well as other houses here, sometime tomorrow to scrounge through whatever he might find inside them that is valuable to him and to the street for sale. Maybe he'll find the renewal for his fake I. D. inside one of the houses.

He doesn't care how the fire happened, who may have done it, or anything else. That's not his problem, and even if he knew what on earth could he do? It's not his end of the world.

CHAPTER 14

Lilli rings the doorbell. It sounds like chimes of some sort, like from a church or something similar. Then there is a bark ... a dog barking in a loud and frantic sounding way. She is not afraid ... she's heard the sound of protection before. She looks down at Natalie standing alongside her, who seems to be just fine with the barking for some reason.

From inside the house Lilli hears a woman's voice. "Henry, would you get that?"

Then there is the sound of a male voice. "Be quiet. Please, just calm down. What's got into you?" There is a pause, and then the sound of the male voice again. "Who's there ... what do you want?"

Calmly Lilli says, "I'd like to talk with you and your wife about Camille. I'm Lilli Jackson, a friend from high school."

She is interrupted by the re-emergence of the barking dog.

Then it's Henry who speaks. "Just shut the hell up! I can't hear what she's saying!"

The door cracks open very slightly, prevented further from opening wider by a chain linking the door to its panel on the side. Henry's head peaks out on the side. "What's this about?"

Lilli steps back a few paces to signal to the man and the dog that she means no harm to either one.

The dog barks louder than before.

Henry unhinges the chain to open the door more as he stretches his head through the wider crack.

Lilli sees his light brown eyes and the dog's dark brown eyes. They both stare at her, now quiet.

Henry says, "I couldn't hear you. She's very protective and well, since Camille has left us, she seems to be unhinged. I'm Henry, Camille's … father." He doesn't appear to recognize Lilli. Then he begins to cry.

Lilli studies the dog's eyes and says, "Your dog is scared and lonely, but that's just my guess. I think once the door is opened a little wider your dog will settle down more."

"I'm not sure about that. She's got strong jaws and sharp teeth." Henry wipes his eyes with the back of his hand. He still seems not to recognize who Lilli is.

"So, your dog is a she." Lilli kneels on one knee, still looking at the female dog. "What's her name?"

"Lucky."

Lilli reaches out to Lucky, "Good dog."

Lucky lowers both ears and stays quiet.

Lilli extends her right hand, fist tight, towards Lucky's nose. "Lucky, say hello to my daughter Natalie."

The golden fur dog with dark brown eyes named Lucky sniffs her hand and then lets out a soft whine.

Henry puts his hand to his mouth, surprised yet pleased. "I've never seen this before."

"She's a good dog. Take care of her." Lilly scratches Lucky's ears.

Lucky moves closer to Lilli, ears pulled back and tail wagging as she licks Lilli's hand and nuzzles closer to her.

Lilli runs her fingers through Lucky's thick fur and then scratches the sides of her head. "Good Lucky."

Lucky whines with pleasure.

Henry is astonished. "How do you know this?"

Still attending to Lucky, Lilli says, "Dogs protect their owners' lives." She doesn't answer his question.

Henry yells to his wife, "Barbara, come here."

Barbara, Henry, and Lucky stand alongside each other ... all six eyes towards Lilli.

Lilli says, "I'm Lilli Jackson. I'm sorry I couldn't make the funeral ... my condolences ... but I might be able to help out a little. I'm not sure ... I'm relatively new at investigative work. And, I had to bring my daughter with me since I'm a single mom. Patti Iverson called me on your behalf."

Barbara replies, "Please come in so we can at least talk. Thank you for coming to see us. It's been quite some time since we saw you last ... in high school with ... uh ... Camille."

Barbara steps aside, followed by Henry and Lucky. Lilli walks into the small entrance way with Natalie hand-in-hand, and instinctively looks around. The first room she spots is the living room ... small and cozy with aged brown carpeting that is reflective of the type of modular homes that were built 25 years ago. Light brown wall paper covers the walls with a good sized window facing the street and a smaller one in the adjoining wall. There is a well-worn couch and two soft chairs along with a small coffee table that, at the moment is bare. The room feels welcoming and if it could talk would have many stories to tell. There's a picture on the wall above the couch that is probably a cheap knock-off from a known artist at one time … a large family sits around a large rectangular table celebrating something. There are no other pictures that Lilli can spot at the moment … of Henry, Barbara, Camille, or Lucky. There is a 32-inch television resting on its own table with the remote control device on top of the television.

Barbara says, "Please have a seat. Would you care for coffee, tea, or something else to drink?"

"No thanks."

Barbara leads the way into the living room taking a seat on one of the two soft chairs while Henry heads for the other chair thus leaving the couch for Lilli and Natalie. Lucky follows Henry to plop comfortably on the carpet that seems from the dark stain is where her body typically rests … her usual spot.

Lilli smells the aroma of previously cooked food and thus concludes that someone, other than Lucky, must be a great cook.

There is silence for a short time until Lilli speaks. "Again, I'm so sorry for your loss. While Camille and I hadn't really stayed in touch after high school, we were each other's best friend during those years." She smiles as genuinely as she can muster up at the moment, hoping it comes across as authentic.

"I must say, Lilli, you and Camille were at times inseparable." Henry now remembers who Lilli is. He chokes a wee-bit after finishing his thought.

"And that's why we contacted Patti Iverson," adds Barbara.

Henry asks, "It seems Patti knew how to reach you. You remember Patti ... don't you?"

"Oh yes. She did contact me, although since I moved away I really haven't stayed in touch with any of my high school friends," Lilli admits. "And I assume she told you we had talked about ... uh ... the situation." Lilli thinks each of them is having a hard time remembering things since Camille's death.

"Yes," softly answers Henry. He continues. "And how about you ... what's happened since then?"

Lilli pauses, only willing to be short and to the point ... no sense getting into any detail ... the meeting is not about her. "I got into property security, although I never thought about that kind of line of work when I was younger. Go figure."

Barbara's forehead frowns quickly and then fades away. "Oh, so you're not a criminal investigator?"

Lilli clarifies. "That's right ... I mostly supervise safety patrol officers in a property security firm." Keep it short, she tells herself. "I don't know why you thought I was a criminal investigator."

Barbara ignores her comment. She gets personal. "So you mentioned you're a single mom." She frowns.

Lilli has taken a few courses in reading body behavior along with tone and inflection of words ... *every body talks*. She also understands the age generation thing. So, she's determined to keep it short. "Yeah, I'll do anything for Natalie ... my pride and joy." She smiles with obvious affection at her daughter sitting quietly next to her. Then she turns to look at Barbara and then Henry. "But I'm really here at your request ... about Camille, not me." She pauses just long enough for the message to sink in. "I can't guarantee I can help you until you tell me what specifically you want from me. I'm not a criminal investigator." Her grin now is more solemn than before, and yet still sincere.

Barbara turns her head to glance at Henry signaling to him it's his turn. She shrugs her shoulders.

Henry clears his throat. "The police say she committed suicide. Barbara and I know better. In fact, anyone who knows … knew … Camille understands that she would never do that, never. She might have been going through some difficult times … hell, we all experience that in our lives … but no way would she take her own life. We want to know the truth." Henry ends with an abrupt and firm nod of his head. Then he looks at Barbara.

Barbara agrees, "Definitely … the truth."

Lilli lets out a breath of air before she says, "This could take some time. I'd have to give up my paying job and maybe, although not definitely, move closer to you. I'd need someone to care for Natalie while I'm working on it. I don't know any of the details until I do some preliminary digging myself. Then I'd be better prepared to tell you more definitively, but I want to be clear that I'm not a criminal investigator."

Henry once again glances at his wife and then back to Lilli. He ignores Lilli's last comment. "We're not wealthy. I'm still working but at a middle income level, and Barbara stays at home and does volunteer work at Father DiZunzio's second-hand retail store."

Barbara adds, "All the workers are former felons who have turned their lives around … at least most of them have while others are still a work-in-progress. We pay them a little over minimum wage with minimum benefits. I, in a way, am the store manager."

Lilli takes in a deep breath of air and slowly releases it into the room. She glances at Natalie who remains quiet during all of this, and then Lucky who seems content just hanging out. Lastly, she looks first at Barbara and then Henry. "All I can promise you is that I'll spend a couple of days talking with the local police and anyone else who might be helpful. That's what I can do, at least for now."

This prompts Barbara to offer an idea. "You and Natalie can stay with us during that time." She does her best to put on a convincing smile … it works.

Lilli returns Barbara's smile with one of her own. "That'll work." She adds, "I'll need all the names of the law enforcement people who were involved in the situation and how I can reach them. Also, anyone else who you think might have something to say … positive or negative, that doesn't matter … understand." She sees affirmative nods from Barbara and Henry. "I'll need that information before I can do anything." She decides to stop emphasizing her lack of criminal investigative experience.

Henry reacts with, "We'll start on that right now."

Barbara asks, "Did you bring clothing and hygiene basics for the next couple of days?"

Lilli affirmatively nods her head, "Yes, Natalie and I are good for a few days."

Barbara beams with joy. "Any favorite food you'd like for dinner tonight?"

Early the next morning Barbara, Henry, and Lilli sit at the kitchen table drinking the last of their coffee. Natalie is a few feet away from her mother comfortably sitting in a chair playing with a doll while Lucky is finishing off her food from her personal bowl. There is a slice of peacefulness among the adults and the dog that permeates the air they breathe.

Then Lilli breaks up the mood. "Last night's conversation was helpful but I've got more questions that need answers to. I'm going to call my boss about helping me get access to the local authorities since I'm an outsider here and I may be considered too _unofficial_." She emphasizes _unofficial_ by imitating quotation marks with the index fingers of both hands. "Law enforcement people are a strange breed. That's not to imply they're weird in a bad way, but, well, they stick together and are very protective about what they do and say." She speed dials John.

"Hey, what's up?" He sounds surprised to hear from her and at the same time glad she's calling.

"I'm with Henry and Barbara Conroy at their home. They offered me the chance to stay at their home for a few days." She then explains to John more fully the situation as she steps away from the Conroy's.

John says. "Oh ... there's a lot of work ahead for you ... more than a few days."

Lilli agrees, "Yeah, I suspect that. I still don't know why they thought I was a criminal investigator but I'm going to see what I can do, and that's why I've got to ask you for a favor."

Before she can ask, John interrupts again. "Sure."

"I want to talk with local law enforcement here in Belview who were part of the team involved in their daughter's ... uh ... situation. I'm really not one of them ... you get my drift ... and well ... I just thought that you and/or Jeff could ... you know ... facilitate a meeting for me with someone."

"Do you want me and/or Jeff to join you?"

"Oh, that's a nice offer but I think that might be interpreted by them to be pushy. I feel comfortable in handling the meeting myself ... no offense ... but thanks for the alternative."

"Sure ... no offense taken. I've got some unplanned time right now to make a few calls myself. If I get resistance I'll bring in Jeff, but like you just said, no strong arming required, at least for now. I'll call you back when I've got something."

"You're great, John. I mean, I REALLY do appreciate everything you're doing." Lilli steps closer to Barbara and Henry as she nods her head a few times while looking at them.

The phones disconnect. Lilli turns to Henry and Barbara who stare at her to say, "This is all good."

Two hours later as Lilli sits in the Conroy's living room playing with Natalie, while Lucky remains close to them, Lilli's phone buzzes. She quickly answers, "John."

"That wasn't as difficult as it could have been. Your contact person is Detective Hoskins. He says he remembers the case and will answer any questions that are not otherwise sealed. He seems to be just the right guy you need. Call the

Belview Police Department and ask for him directly. He's expecting your call now. Do you have the number?"

"Sure do. You're the best."

"Yeah, yeah."

As soon as the phones disconnect she makes the call.

A male voice answers, "Belview Police Department. How can I direct your call?"

"Detective Hoskins, he's expecting my call. I'm Lilli Jackson."

"Please stand by."

There is a short interval before she hears, "Hoskins." His voice is coarse.

"Detective Hoskins, this is Lilli Jackson. I understand you and my immediate supervisor, John Walker, have just talked and you've agreed to meet with me about the Camille Conroy case. Thanks for your help."

"I haven't done anything yet."

"You agreed to talk with me and you answered the phone. You didn't have to do either."

He ignores her comment. "So you wanna meet regarding the Conroy case."

"Yes, what's a good time?"

"Tomorrow, nine sharp, here."

"Thanks again."

Before she can add anything else, the phones disconnect.

He was short and stocky even before he became a teenager … and much more inquisitive than anyone near his age and many adults, willing to ask all sorts of questions that popped into his head regardless whether the timing was right and even to the person or people he asked.

Additionally, his sense of humor made him the class clown not because he acted like one to get attention but rather because others thought of him as a weirdo.

Problem solving was his specialty and being a superhero was his dream. Sports, music, writing, or any other art form wasn't his thing.

One might think he was a lonely kid with an inferiority complex, but it was just the opposite. His imagination brought him as close to as many fictional characters as he wished for at any time.

Yeah, Hoskins was different from the onset.

He knew about John Walker … hell, Walker was the *MAN* at school in many ways … big and strong for his size and quite nimble. His classmates either respected him or feared him … a few did both. He'd get down and dirty if that's what it took to settle an argument, but he'd rather just intimidate you through his eyes that he'd place inches in front of your face. That's not to say he wouldn't talk things out … he had tremendous practical sense and even at his young age understood that each body talks. He stood out like a blade of grass in a manicured lawn.

Hoskins and Walker knew of each other, but never really spent any quality time together. They were often in the same classroom taking the same subject at the same time until one day when they were both eleventh graders something occurred. It was during a lunch recess in the school's playground.

A shout came out of nowhere, or so it seemed to Hoskins … "Gangpile!" He knew exactly what it meant and he looked around … fright was in his eyes.

All of a sudden a group of eight eleventh-grade boys appeared alongside him. He sensed he was their prey … he had been chosen.

One of the boys tackled him and he found himself flat face-down on the playground with the tackler on top of him. Then everyone else piled on top. He began to feel as if he was suffocating as everyone in the pile, except him of course, kept yelling, "Gangpile!"

He tried to shout to get them off of him, to leave him alone, but he didn't have sufficient fire-power in his voice. But then it quickly changed.

"Cut it out!" The voice seemed to come from nowhere.

Then there was silence.

The same voice made a second command, "Get off of him, now!"

One by one, each boy obeyed Walker's order. No one wanted to take him on by himself or even collectively.

Once all the boys were standing, except for Hoskins who was still face down on the playground, everyone heard something. "He's a pussy." The rest of the boys laughed.

"Shut up," Walker ordered. He walked to the kid who said it, stopped inches from him, and drove his index finger several times into his chest. "You wanna pick on someone your own size?" Walker's grin was fierce and taunting. "Here I am."

The kid clenched both fists of his hands that hung by his sides, thinking for a split second to follow through.

Walker kept staring at him, not moving, not even raising his hands. His body was saying … "Give me your best shot and then we'll see what happens next."

The kid's lips trembled a bit, not noticeable to those watching the square-off, except for the kid who felt as if his entire body was trembling and of course for Walker who was reading every word the kid's body was communicating.

There was complete silence. Not even the vehicle traffic alongside the playground was audible.

Then, the tension drained from the kid's entire body as he took a step backward.

By this time Hoskins had turned his body around to sit on the ground, watching it all. He couldn't believe the kid's behavior until he postulated that the kid and Walker might have been in a similar duel before and Walker had been the victor.

"Not worth it," the kid mumbled. "Come on, let's get out of here," he said to the others as they all walked away.

Walker turned to Hoskins who remained sitting on the ground and extended his right hand. "Here, let me give you a hand."

Hoskins, still a bit stunned by it all, nodded and grabbed hold of Walker's hand. He felt a strong grip. "Thanks."

Neither boy realized at that time that they would become good friends and later on in life would each work in law enforcement.

CHAPTER 15

The next morning as Barbara takes Natalie to work at Father DiZunzio's second-hand retail store and while Henry is at work, Lilli talks with Detective Hoskins in a conference room.

Hoskins is a big man. Some might consider him to be overweight but would never mention that to him face-to-face, not even as a silly joke. He has a big jaw and his thick neck necessitates the top button of his blue long sleeve shirt remain open. He is tieless with black slacks, black shoes, black socks, and black hair with obvious traces of gray. His black suit coat is flung over a nearby chair. He wears a blue-stoned pinky ring and a plain watch around his left wrist. There is no wedding band but in law enforcement that doesn't necessarily mean anything. He has a distinctly hooked nose with a bump in the bridge area as a result of a fight with a suspect who got the worse of the confrontation. His smile shows teeth that seem to curve away from one another. He doesn't bother to stand when Lilli enters the room, but he points to a vacant chair across the table.

Lilli is the first to talk. "I know you don't think you've done anything yet for me ... actually for the Conroy's ...

to thank you, but just having this opportunity is ... well ... great." Her smile is sincere.

Hoskins grunts something that is not coherent to her. He doesn't seem interested in hearing the niceties, probably because those particulars are uncommon in his profession.

"Barbara and Henry Conroy contacted me through a former high school friend of Camille Conroy's death. You see, Camille and me were best friends in school. I agreed to meet Barbara and Henry so get a better understanding of what they wanted me to do ... I'm not really a criminal investigator."

She sees Hoskins frown without speaking, so she continues. "I agreed to take a look into the situation anyway ... you know ... like with stranger's eyes."

Again Hoskins keeps quiet, so Lilli continues. "You probably know from John Walker that he owns a property security firm, and I'm one of his employees ... a Supervisor and Lead Public Safety Officer." She hesitates to see if Hoskins is now interested in saying anything.

He does not speak but he makes a circular motion with the index finger of his right hand for her to move on.

"The short-of-it is the Conroy's said to me that Camille told them she was going to spend the weekend with her _new love_." She uses the index fingers of both hands to indicate quotation marks around the phrase _new love_. "Five days passed and Camille hadn't returned. Her parents called the police. Then, later, the police told them that their daughter was dead, with no suspects. They said the cause of death was suicide. Although her parents knew Camille was going through some tough times, they did not believe ... and still don't today ... their daughter would take her own life." Lilli puckers her lips waiting for Hoskins to comment. This time he does.

"Is that it?" He twists his nose and frowns.

"That's all I know, for now. Mr. and Mrs. Conroy gave me some family information about their daughter, nothing that surprised me since Camille and I were best friends in high school. Camille was definitely a sensitive and insecure person. She rarely dated, not because she didn't like boys or because she didn't want to date, but because she was rarely asked. She didn't have beauty-queen looks but she wasn't unattractive. She didn't attend her Junior Prom or her Senior Ball because no one asked her and she was too bashful to ask a boy. She wasn't into drugs. I never saw her drink alcohol. And her parents confirm this. She had a minimum wage retail job, the best she could get with only a high school education and no particular skill set. She wasn't into sports or the arts. But when we were together she was a blast … funny … very funny. She moved out of her parents' home a year after graduation into a small studio apartment in town. The apartment manager said she was a quiet renter … no problems. She paid her rent on time. So, you see, she doesn't fit into the mold of someone who would commit suicide." Lilli nods her head to indicate she's finished talking for the time being.

Hoskins places his hands together to from a pyramid. "What is the mold of someone who commits suicide?"

Lilli now realizes she shouldn't have talked like an expert in suicide. "OK, I don't know scientifically, but I knew Camille pretty well, and I don't see her fitting into that category." Oops, she does it again.

Hoskins puckers his lips before he gives her a short tutorial of the types and causes of suicide. He clears his throat and then slightly leans over the table in her direction. "A French sociologist is often credited with identifying four main categories of those most likely to commit suicide and their causes. His name was Émile Durkheim."

Lilli's eyes almost bulge out of their sockets. She figures it's best to now listen.

Hoskins notices her surprise, but isn't interested in pointing that out to her, at least not now. "First, there is egoistic suicide. These are individuals who are unable or unwilling to form substantial bonds with other individuals or institutions. They have low levels of social integration which means they don't integrate well into society. Second, there is altruistic suicide. These people are so strongly bonded to social groups that they lose their own sense of individuality. They can become a tool of groups or institutions. Next, there is the fatalist suicide. They believe they are overregulated and don't believe they have enough freedom to act and say what they want. Lastly, there is the anomic suicide. These individuals believe that traditional norms and patterns of society have been abandoned. The bottom line here is that suicides occur when these individuals can no longer cope. Based on Camille Conroy's life experiences she can easily fit into egoistic as well as fatalistic categories. But, we'll never know for sure, will we." He waits for Lilli to ask a question but when she remains silent, Hoskins continues.

"After her parents called us, we found a car at the edge of Crossturn River. It appeared the vehicle had veered off the bridge into the River. There was a female in the passenger seat not wearing a seat belt, but there was no driver of the vehicle inside or out of the car. The female was dead. She was wearing a high school class ring with the name Camille Conroy inscribed inside the band. We felt we had found the Conroy girl, so we notified the parents. They were horrified as you might imagine. We sent the body to the morgue for identification. Mr. and Mrs. Conroy said their daughter had a permanent bridge back left upper tooth. The dead woman didn't and the morgue was unable to identify the dead woman and we weren't able to determine why the dead female was wearing the ring. We tried tracking down the new love, but that went nowhere. The vehicle was a stolen car. We pounded the pavement looking for Camille, the new love, and the identity of the dead girl, but the search went cold. Camille was still missing ... alive or dead ... we didn't know. Then 27 miles from where we found the dead girl, two months later, at the edge of the same River, we found another dead female. Her body was decomposed beyond recognition but she had a permanent bridge back left upper tooth. This was Camille Conroy. The autopsy results, minimal as they were due to the condition of the body, identified the cause of the death as suicide." He pauses. Still there are no questions from Lilli.

"So, we didn't know then and we still don't know today if we have a killer on the loose. As time passes, it comes more difficult to solve the unknown female's death, although Camille Conroy's death is still classified as a suicide."

Lilli now asks, "If the killer turns out to be a serial killer then would that change the suicide classification to murder?"

"That's possible, I guess." He shrugs his shoulders and now leans back in the chair. Then he grins. "Let's be Sherlock Holmes ... what do you say?"

Lilli frowns, initially unsure of the relevance, but she goes along just the same. What does she have to lose? "OK."

"You know who I'm talking about, right?"

"Yes, the fictional British detective." She puckers her lips beginning to feel annoyed and being dismissed by Hoskins.

"Yes. He was able to solve complex mysteries using precision. First, he focused on observation. By that I mean he discovered clues that others overlooked. Then, through logic, he comes to a solution. The man could cut through the confusion and uncertainties." He pauses to take a read of Lilli's attention. He surmises impatience in the woman. Her otherwise soft rounded cheekbones with gentle curves seem to have tightened.

Lilli notices a flash of hesitation on his face, brief yet noticeable, perhaps thinking about whether to pick up the pace, move on to something else, stop, or something else entirely. Telling the truth shouldn't take long to say, but she thinks he's taking a long time. She believes he is holding back something ... either intentionally or instinctively but has no idea what that might be ... nada.

Hoskins picks up again, speeding it up somewhat. "Holmes was also accurate. He not only valued the truth but he had a passion for accuracy and timely information, something, I might add, that was missing in our involvement in Vietnam. But that's another story at another time." He swallows as if something is stuck in his throat, but manages just the same to resume. "Relevance ... staying focused ... need I say more?" He's not looking for an answer as he takes up again where he left off. "And then there's consistency." He clears his throat maybe because the same whatever that was caught in this throat has returned. He finishes. "Each event has a cause. There are no such things as coincidences … they are merely causes and events hiding until revealed." He now leans forward towards Lilli.

She looks directly at him with a mixture of some impatience and a little confusion, but definitely otherwise impressed with his knowledge of and passion for critical thinking. "How do you explain Camille's school ring on the other dead girl's finger?"

"Great question!" He smiles for the first time believing the woman sitting across the table from him has a passionate drive for critical thinking standards. "That's a fact … it's not a coincidence. The truth is we don't know. Could Camille have given the ring to the other woman in friendship?"

"Like they knew each other? Is that what you're saying?"

"Exactly, it is a possibility. What other possibilities might there be?" He stares directly into her eyes. He knows she's now engaged in the analysis.

"The other woman could have taken it from Camille, maybe through a fight or something else. The other woman could have been responsible for Camille's death. Camille could have freely given it to a guy or the guy could have forcibly taken it from her so that he could give it to the other woman." She pauses and then says, "That's what comes to mind right now. There could be other causes."

"Precisely. And we don't know."

"And we really don't know about the accuracy of a suicide conclusion. It could be based on false, misleading, and/or irrelevant information."

"Again, precisely. We don't know."

"The real cause of death could be drowning ... that simple!"

He nods his head and adds something else. "When a dead body is found in the water, the lungs may reveal ... I say may reveal but not always reveal whether the victim drowned or was already dead before entering the water. Further, the dead body in the water does not tell us the full story. We don't necessarily know what caused the body to enter the water in the first place. Certainly, a forensic team does its best to search for the facts ... relevant, clear and accurate facts that logically lead them to a logical conclusion. And, that's often times very difficult."

"So, are you saying you think the real cause or causes of the deaths of these two women are still unknown? Is that what you're saying?"

"I'm a detective, not a coroner, medical examiner, or other forensic specialist."

"But, you're open to the possibility. Right?"

He shrugs his shoulders. "Everybody knows the shortest distance between two points is a straight line. And in law enforcement we know that truth applies to murders ... the spouse, the ex-spouse, the ex-spouses, another family member or members, and the current and/or former lovers are the obvious suspects. I can't tell you or suggest to you what you should do next. If you pursue investigating the Camille Conroy closed case and/or the unknown female's death, you're going to need a lot of resources ... time, money, and people. Sometimes ... and I don't like admitting this ... but sometimes the bad guys never get caught."

Lilli's nod is intended for her, not for Hoskins. She tells herself that persistence is worth it ... that she has no other choice but to go through with it. She also knows that she'd be lying to herself ... make that betraying herself ... because she promised Barbra and Henry Conroy. "But it could be classified as a drowning or something other than suicide."

Hoskins considers himself a good ... make that very good ... judge of character. He just knows, almost instinctively, what a person is made of ... the risks they'll take ... what they'll back off from. In a way, he can read the *"tells"* that the other person signals, especially when they are trying to hide something from him. And now he's convinced she's a fighter, willing to get in the mud for as long as it takes ... the type of person who double-downs when you say it can't be done, even if it puts her in jeopardy and maybe even willing to break the rules. He says, "You mean not a suicide."

"Yeah," she agrees.

"Autopsies don't work that way. You've gotta follow the evidence."

She wiggles her nose a bit. "But it would help the parents deal with their daughter's death."

"Like I just said, it doesn't work that way." He glances at the wall clock behind Lilli.

She forges ahead. "A simple thing ... a second opinion." She cocks her head to the side.

"That would be expensive. Do her parents have the money?"

"No. I'm talking about a second opinion within law enforcement. You must have some degree of influence."

He grins, shakes his head to each side a bit. "I work within the law. I don't do special favors. I can't help you any further." He crosses his arms as if the discussion has ended.

His defensive behavior does not curb her. "All I'm asking ... suggesting ... is to re-look at the evidence ... you know ... with stranger's eyes. That's all."

Hoskins looks at the wall clock again and then gives her a no-headshake.

Lilli asks, "what about a legal challenge?"

"Attorneys are expense ... very expensive. And secondly, it could easily be interpreted as taking-on local law enforcement ... a good way to alienate."

Lilli is about to reply but Hoskins holds up both hands, palms facing her. "Miss Jackson, I compliment you for your passion in wanting to help the Conroy's. I'm sure they appreciate it more than I can imagine. I'd probably act the same way if it was my child. But unless you, yourself, are willing to commit a huge amount of time and money resources yourself, I suggest you tell them nothing else can be done. You've already told me you're not a law enforcement criminal investigator, so already you're behind. I don't know what else to say. I'm sorry, but I've got another meeting in five minutes."

As Lilli walks to her car, she thinks about what's next. For starters, the return drive to update the Conroy's on her conversation with Hoskins will be depressing to say the least. The face-to-face with Barbara and Henry is not something she's looking forward to, but must. She isn't about to misrepresent or lie to them nor is she willing to accuse someone of incompetence. But she knows that the Conroy's will have to somehow deal with the suicide autopsy conclusion. There's nothing else she can do.

If she could see her own face at the moment, she might not recognize who she was looking at ... someone filled with stinging pain and heartache.

Then she begins blaming herself for the situation she's in. She shouldn't have visited the Conroy's in the first place, and then once she met them agreed to take on the task of meeting with Hoskins. Aren't the Conroy's counting on her to correct what they believe is a wrong?

Hell, she isn't Captain Marvel! She's got to be totally honest with them.

At the same time ... right after Lilli leaves Hoskins ... he calls John to give him an update.

John picks up on the first buzz. "Hey."

Hoskins gets right to the point. "She's sure something."

John knows who he's referring to. "Lilli can be a little persistent at times, but we've all got our strengths."

Hoskins starts smiling to himself. "Women will never be equal to men. You wanna know why?"

"I might not, but you're going to tell me just the same, so I'll say it. Why?"

"Until they can walk down a street with a bald head, four-day old unshaven face, and a beer gut and still think they're sexy." Hoskins lets out a rowdy laugh.

John joins in with an unruly laugh himself, and then says, "I'm never too old to learn something stupid." He laughs again.

Hoskins quickly replies. "Every joke brings you closer to the truth, at least that's what they say, whoever they are." He chuckles.

John asks, "What did you two talk about ... anything I should know?"

Hoskins clears his throat, a sign that he's now down to something serious. "I listened to her reason in wanting to see me. You've got one hell of an employee. Confident, caring, smart ... just to state the obvious, but I'm sure you recognize those qualities and surely more."

"Oh yeah, I'm lucky, and I mean that seriously." John pauses and then is about to say something more but Hoskins wants to continue.

"I gave her a rundown of how we operate here, and probably overdid it with a lecture on critical thinking and the four main categories of suicide. I just got carried away. She seemed interested and was attentive."

"So you mentioned Émile Durkheim and probably just had to bring in Sherlock Holmes." John snickers just loud enough for Hoskins to hear.

"Like I said, she seemed interested and was attentive. She also asked some relevant questions. Anyway, I told her that the documented cause of death was going to stay until there was new credible evidence to prove otherwise."

"How did she take that?"

"She asked about a second professional opinion, a legal challenge, and if I could pull a few strings to have the case reopened."

"And ...?"

"I said no to everything, but if she wanted to pursue anything on her own she'd need money, time, and competent professionals. That's entirely her and the Conroy's decision, not mine."

"Well, I don't think the Conroy's are wealthy, and Lilli isn't competent as a criminal investigator herself … she might have mentioned that to you."

"Yeah, she did."

John continues. "But she is a very caring person and will have to tell the Conroy's what you and her discussed. I think it would break her heart to have to walk away from going further, but that might be exactly what she'll have to do. I definitely can't give her any paid time-off to work on it, and my Company doesn't have the professional resources she'll need."

Hoskins agrees, "I follow you on that score."

"Anything else I should know?"

"Did you hear about the guy who walked into a bar on a Friday night with a parrot on his shoulder?" Hoskins snickers.

CHAPTER 16

Jeff talks into his cell phone, "Where does he wanna meet?"

"The cemetery." His voice is coarse. He's the go-between guy connecting Jeff with the source.

"The what?"

"The cem – e – tery. Are you hard of hearing?" The go-between guy yells.

"No, but why there?"

"The dead don't hear and they don't tell." He chuckles. "And, that's what he wants."

"What?"

"I thought you said you're not hard of hearing!"

"I did, but the cemetery. That's a strange place."

"You've talked with people in confidence, haven't you?"

"Sure, many times."

"He's just covering his bets. Make sure you bring something to drink … for him."

Jeff hesitates in moving ahead with the meet, but he knows the Centro Rail Service platform case definitely is not going anyplace and this source might have some useful information. His thoughts are interrupted when he hears the go-between guy ask a question.

"Hey, you still there?"

"Yeah, yeah, I'm just thinking."

"This is your last chance. The cemetery at six tonight or forget about it."

Jeff breathes out a frustrated puff of air. "OK, OK, six tonight."

"And don't forget something to drink ... for him."

Before the phones disconnect, Jeff asks, "Where specifically in the cemetery?"

"Just walk down the main path at the entrance. He'll spot you."

The phones disconnect.

It is 6:00 pm as Jeff slowly walks down the main path of the cemetery. He looks to his left and then to his right hoping to spot this source. In his left hand is a brown bag containing a pint of bourbon, the cheapest he could find in the liquor store, given the short notice. He doesn't spot anyone as he continues slowly walking another few yards. Then there is a voice behind him.

"Hey, my man. I wasn't sure you'd come."

Jeff turns to confirm the source.

Hands are the second best "*tell*," just following behind the eyes ... the greatest "*tell*" of all ... not to dismiss nervous behavior, lies, and inconsistencies ... in that order. Sometimes it's the small things that bridge the big parts.

He can't clearly see the man's eyes but his hands, both of them, are shaking by his side. Either the source is reacting to the need for alcohol or he's set him up for physical harm, if not death. Jeff takes his revolver out of its holster and points it at the man. "Stop right there! Are you alone?"

The man's hands stop shaking … he stutters, "Wh – what you doin'? You gonna shoot me? Please, don't shoot me. I done nothin' wrong."

Jeff slowly steps forward. "Just be careful … don't do anything stupid. You alone?"

"Ye – yeah." He swallows deeply.

Jeff takes a quick 360-look around to feel confident there's just the two of them. "OK." He returns the revolver to its holster.

"You … you scared the hell … hell out of me." The man's breathing returns to a normal pace. He looks at the brown bag in Jeff's hand. Then he grins. "You brought me somethin'?"

Jeff hands over the brown bag with the pint of bourbon. "It was on sale."

The man takes the bag and hurriedly pulls out the bottle, stares at it for only a second, and says, "Don't know the brand."

"Like I said, it was on sale."

He unscrews the cap off the top and takes a long swig. Then he grins towards Jeff showing off his yellow teeth. "You wanna drink?"

"Not really."

"The more for me." He takes another gulp and then coughs. "I've tasted better turpentine than this."

"Like I said, it was on sale. I didn't say it would taste good."

"Yeah." He coughs again.

Jeff wants to get down to business now. "Let's talk. What have you heard?"

The source twists his nose to each side a few times. "The boys at the rail service platform are part of a larger gang that sells drugs and crap to teenagers." He takes another gulp from the bottle. "They're gonna find the kid who got away and kill him ... can't let any witness live. It's just a matter of time." He blinks a few times and coughs again. "One gangbanger ... don't know if he was part of the two at the platform ... tried to hook up with a girl out of high school to get her into drugs and other crap. Don't know a name."

Jeff's mind flashbacks to an off-the-record conversation he had with John about Lilli's involvement with the Camille Conroy death, and so he asks, "Camille Conroy ... could that be the name?"

"Like I said, I don't know the name. But she got somehow involved with one of them ... said he was her lover or some crap like that. This dooshbag was pissed when she wouldn't do drugs, so he killed her, just like that ... couldn't leave alive a witness ... know what I'm sayin'?" He pauses thinking Jeff would have something to say, but when he only gets silence, he continues. "Heard he took a ring or some other bling stuff from the dead girl to give to another girl he was tryin' to get hooked on drugs. But the second girl also turned down drugs so she gets killed." He pauses and then continues. "What the hell is goin' on ... killin' for no good reason when you can drink and screw all night! Know what I'm sayin'?" He doesn't wait for Jeff to answer ... rather he takes another gulp from the bottle. Then he raises the nearly empty bottle level to his weary looking eyes. "This is really bad, man. You gotta do better next time." He coughs again and turns his look towards Jeff. "You gonna take a drink or what? Last chance."

Jeff extends his hand to take hold of the bottle. He puts the bottle to his lips and takes a small sip. He immediately frowns as he looks at the bottle again. "This tastes like turpentine." He coughs. "Here, take this." Jeff hands back the bottle to the source as fast as he can.

Chapter 17

Prairie cycles into the town's only park ... happy and playful during the day when children chase each other playing tag as their parents or babysitters talk about whatever they talk about. But now it's getting dark and the only ones within the confines of the park are people like him ... homeless, alone, and living one day at a time.

Most of those whom he comes across are much older than him. And, most of the time everyone stays by themselves, not interested in sharing what they've experienced earlier in the day, how they got to arrive at where they are today in their lives, their political view, or anything else. Why would it matter?

Prairie continues to have flashes of his old man coming at him in his predictable drunken state, yelling in loud and incomprehensible words and a harsh tone so that the message was totally unclear. And then, predictably, a slap on the face.

He remembers his old man's face full of anger and out of control.

His mother would try to intervene but she was no match to her drunken husband who she still loved in spite of this. She had faith in him and was a saint to Prairie's way of thinking, but he wonders if she ever tried to find him when he just left, or maybe she just gave up any hope.

He slides his .38 caliber gun from his backpack to tuck in between his pants and waist. You can never be too cautious of what the night might bring you. They're all coyotes in the park, one way or another.

He wonders if somehow he's responsible for the way his parents treated him. In other words, the fault entirely rests with him. He's thought about this notion many times before, and each time his reaction is the same … he feels as if his entire body is going to explode.

He'd love to have heard from his mother, at least just once, that she's sorry she wasn't there for him, that she should have stood up to her husband more forcefully. But, that thought is simply a pathetic notion.

He continues with his inner dialogue as he touches the gun to make sure it's still secure. Why didn't he do something, anything during the times his father walloped him. He is on the verge of tears, but he holds back. He's not someone who cries. He'll try to fall asleep, but this is the toughest part of his day, falling to sleep isn't easy.

Sometimes Prairie feels like a normal guy wanting normal things, feeling in a normal way. And then they're times when he's not. Things that repulsed him no longer do. In a way, it's become his new normal … he's become more of the *not* as years have passed, and only those whom he's around have kept the same pace. They all believe that they have the power of life and death over everyone else, which means that nobody has any exclusive power what-so-ever.

Life is all full of coyotes. It's a good thing he's not a juror on a murder trial voting whether to acquit the alleged murderer or set him free.

What he's experienced since he ran away many years ago can't be taught in school. He knows things, places, and people he'd never know if he was a family man. There are the so-called good guys and bad guys. He wonders how long it will be before somebody wants him to disappear, or even dead.

He can't afford to lose control of his life any more than he already has because he has no plan to handle that. He'd like to get drunker than a skunk or stoned from drugs. Either would work just fine at the moment. Somebody always has to pay. He wishes for less than a nanosecond that somebody, anybody, would ask him, "What's wrong … I'm listening."

It's darkness once again. At least that's something he can count on. He's moved to a place at the park's fringes far away from where children happily play during the day. It used to be a parking lot but now dead roots from formerly living trees are everywhere. There are no signs that tell you parking is not allowed or you can't sleep, eat, drink, or smoke week. Trashcans can still be seen around but they're uselessly damaged. There's a designated place off to the side where everyone has agreed to pee and take a crap. And then there is another spot where his type sleep the best they can, but they always have one eye open in case somebody loses it. Once you fall asleep, you can lose everything because there's always somebody out there who will take everything you have. Fortunately, he still has his gun and a pocketful of bullets.

There are some guys standing together, smoking something. The smell of weed is in the air. There's no music, nobody's shouting, singing or dancing. There are just lonely coyotes waiting for tomorrow to happen. This is the right place for him right now.

CHAPTER 18

There are 10 sentencing options used by jurisdictions across the United States that starts with *Probation* and ends with *Prison and Jail Time*. *Probation* offenders are required to report to a *Probation Officer* in a clearly defined timeframe, such as once a month, based on the offense. There are also scheduled and impromptu visits by the *Probation Officer* with little to no notice to the offender at his/her home, work, or other location where the offender has reported to be present. At this end of the scale, *Probation* is applied to misdemeanors and felony offenses. This is the least restrictive type of probation.

Lee "Bud" Moore has been a *Probation Officer* for 11 years, having chosen the profession due to a personal experience several years ago ... he was an offender of a misdemeanor and he claims that the hardworking and conscientious *Probation Officer* working his case saved his life. Bud loves his job in spite of the disappointments he experiences on a regular basis. It just takes one success to equal 100 setbacks.

It's Thursday morning as he finishes the last of his administrative tasks in his small work-place, mentally reviewing his schedule for the day. He suspects it will be another hot day. Bud is divorced … his often times regular planned out days were … and still are … so interrupted with unexpected emergencies at work that his wife couldn't take it any longer. They had been married for one month short of two years. They're still friends … distant ones … but every time they agree to have dinner together or just a drink in the evening one thing or another always seems to get in the way to dampen their plans. Maybe it's for the better, he concludes, because he thinks she deserves someone better than him. But it isn't easy to distance himself from thinking of her … he's still in love with her and probably will be forever.

Bud's first meeting is with a teenager and his mother in Ashton. The father/husband of the family left a while ago leaving her alone with her son. This visit is a scheduled one, but only he knows what's going to be covered during the meeting.

Ashton is the next town to the south of Belview, a dull looking place that is most of the time avoided by non-residents. Most of the population of Ashton is first to second generation immigrants from various countries … mostly legal but it has a good share of illegals hiding below the Immigration and Customs Enforcement radar. Usually, groups are formed with people of similar interests, but that's not always the case. The locals are aware of each other's way of life and try not to interfere with each other.

The teenager Bud's about to visit has had some problems with drugs and alcohol. He's been arrested twice and now is on *Probation* with Bud visiting him on a schedule once a month.

Bud pulls up to the side of the street that is badly in need of repair … not uncommon in this part of town. The homes are run down. He walks towards the home. In his left hand is a briefcase containing his working tools. He knocks on the door to wait a few moments before she answers. It's the teen's mother. She wears a kitchen apron over her loose fitting gray dress. She forces a smile that fools no one, but there's no sense in being hostile to someone who's just trying to do his job in spite of her being ashamed with the circumstances of the meeting, but it's the better option than having her son spend time in jail. She steps aside to let him in, "Welcome."

"Good morning," Bud says. His smile is more authentic than hers.

She grunts something in return that is not recognizable to him, yet he doesn't ask for an explanation. That's not why he's here. After she closes the door she raises her voice as she looks to her left, "Now. Get over here."

The teenager has been purposely waiting in the kitchen putting off the meeting as long as possible. Reluctantly, he appears without any comment. He's a good looking kid, seems to be in good physical shape, and definitely by the look on his face quite unhappy with Bud and the interview. His eyes are bloodshot, and his fingers move as if he is playing the piano that makes the ring on the index finger of his left hand obvious. There's a tattoo of a coiled snake ready to strike on his left arm just above his wrist.

His mother points to a place on the worn-out couch for him to sit as she moves to a nearby chair. Bud takes the remaining chair nearby.

Bud looks at the kid who, at least preliminarily, does not seem to be doing OK … the shaking fingers and his bloodshot eyes are obvious "*tells.*" "How's everything?"

The kid nods his head a few times keeping it tilted down all the while believing he can hide his eyes. He covers his right hand with his left hand to steady them. He hasn't fooled anyone.

"No alcohol or drugs?" Bud knows this is a laughable question to ask considering the physical state of the kid, but he's got nothing to lose and everything to gain.

The kid shakes his head no.

The kid's mother looks at her son. "Talk to the man! He's trying to help you!"

The kid's embarrassed realizing he hasn't fooled anyone. He mumbles, "Clean … no more." His partially hidden face and hands tell a different story.

Bud continues. "Only a few more months and we'll be ending our meeting." He tries to sound uplifting. He waits for a response that does not come, so he asks a direct question. "Anything I should know about … want to tell me? I'm here to help you … I'm listening."

Still no response from the kid, just a head shake no.

Bud looks at the kid's mother for a little help. "You OK with everything? Anything you want to say? Anything I can do? Just tell me, and I'll try to get it done."

She says, "Everything's fine."

Bud puffs out a breath of air, obviously not convinced of the mother and son's conclusions, but what else can he do. He also has a full schedule of similar interview meetings as well as a revocation hearing in Judge Noble's court that will take time, a swing by the County Jail regarding one of his clients who was arrested last night for DWI, and then back to his work-place to write up separate reports for each of the cases. He figures he can't squander time where it's not wanted.

The mother and son might be feeling happy that the interview was short, but Bud has a surprise in store.

Bud reaches into his briefcase to pull out a capped plastic bottle with a label on the outside indicating the kid's name, today's date, and the case number. As he hands the bottle to the kid he says, "Go to the bathroom and fill it with your urine. Keep the door open so I can observe."

The kid looks at Bud, bloodshot eyes widen in surprise and anger. Then the kid looks at his mother for a little help.

"Do what the man says! Go!" There are angry burrows on her forehead.

The kid wants to resist but his mother's stern look tells him he should reconsider.

"Go," she repeats more loudly than the first time. There is a noticeable spot of annoyance in her eyes that does not go away.

The kid grabs the bottle with an equal mark of anger in his eyes. He stands and heads for a nearby bathroom.

Bud shouts out, "Keep the door open so we can both observe."

There is a sound of urine filling the bottle and then some urine into the toilet bowl. The kid turns around, about to rejoin his mother and Bud but his mother interrupts him.

"Flush the toilet!"

He turns back to comply and then back again towards the two adults watching his moves. He hands over the bottle to Bud as if to get rid of something rotten. He knows what the results will be well before the urine analysis takes place.

Bud conceals his grin, "Thanks."

He turns to the mother, "Thank you."

Then Bud heads for the door to leave. He doesn't realize the kid's mother is close behind. He opens the door to step outside. She follows him.

Now outside, she stares fondly at him to say, "It's the little things that matter. Thank you." There is a small tear at the corner of each of her eyes. "I pray each day."

It's a typical summer early evening on the same day ... still a little too hot and humid for most, but it's about 10 degrees cooler than it was at mid-day ... no sense of complaining since it won't matter.

There is a normal group of teenagers from Ashton, male and female, hanging out together at the edge of the main park doing what teenagers do when adults aren't around to supervise their actions. While there is no sign indicating its existence or name, each group has its own label ... an example of equal opportunity.

At one corner of the park there are kids getting drunk on beer combined with some dope. The guys often get a little too friendly with the gals but no one seems to mind being touched in places usually reserved private. It seems to be everyone's right-of-passage. The beer and dope aren't free ... somebody's got to pay for it. And that's when a few of the males exercise their freedom. They either steal the alcohol and dope or get the money from unauthorized sources to buy it. These guys are unofficially the leaders and nobody in the group messes with them … <u>nobody</u>.

These evenings begin to form shortly after they've had dinner with their parents, and either sneak out of the house or fabricate an excuse. Their parents know all too well what's happening, but they figure their kids are better off not being cooped in a run-down non-air-conditioned place where sometimes a family feud can be dangerous.

Once or twice during the evening a clearly marked cop car might patrol by, but that's not always predictable. The cops figure that since there's not been any recent shooting, fighting, or stabbing the best tactic is to leave them alone.

While there are both males and females hanging out together, respectable girls and for that matter boys wouldn't in their right mind go anywhere near the park at this time of evening. They know better.

One of the unofficial leaders struts around drinking a beer. The dope he recently took hasn't made its full affect now but that isn't obvious by the way he's dressed … jeans only, barefooted, and shirtless. There is a high school ring on the index finger of his left hand that was given to him by one of his many girlfriends to show him how much he is loved. He's not counting the number of high school rings from girls he has. He's not a big kid but his upper torso looks well-conditioned from regular push-ups, and his stomach is flat from sit-ups without any sign of fat. There's a tattoo of a coiled snake ready to strike on the inside of his left arm just above his wrist. His brown hair is the color of wet dirt haphazardly loosely drooped to almost touch his ears. He doesn't notice a car that's been circling the park a few times.

Suddenly everyone is taken by surprise at a noise that sounds like a firecracker on the 4th of July. They jump and for the moment are rendered speechless and motionless.

At the edge of the park, a middle-aged couple walks their dog. They hear the sound as well and decide to call 911 on their cell. Then they hurry away not interested in getting further involved in whatever just happened. Better to be safe than sorry.

The jeans only, barefooted, shirtless guy with the tattoo wearing the high school ring holding a beer falls to the ground. The beer can falls from his hand while the contents spill alongside of him. Quickly, there is a stream of blood flowing from his head that without delay mixes with the beer on the ground. He feels dizzy and his head begins to suddenly hurt.

Everyone else simply stays motionless for a very long few seconds as the car disappears out of the park.

Then the crowd quickly begins to disperse looking for a safer place.

The guy on the ground yells, albeit subdued, "I've been shot!"

There are sounds of screaming yet nobody really knows what just happened.

The guy on the ground somehow manages to stand, albeit wobbly. He tries to yell louder the second time but that too is weak. "I've been shot!" He reaches for his head feeling moisture. He can't catch his breath. He has difficulty hearing. His heart beat picks up. He feels cold and clammy, and then he falls to the ground with a thud. He's dead.

There are only a few teens left in the park. Nobody is nearby the dead boy to witness the situation. But those still around hear a siren. They then disappear as quickly as possible leaving no one to be interviewed.

It's a little past 7 pm the same evening … still not a rain cloud in the sky but still with the some of the remnants of humidity from earlier in the day. Eric Jackson is returning to his pathetic studio apartment, still cluttered to the gills with all sorts of debris but feeling higher than a kite having consumed sufficient beer to fill a keg and sniffed enough weed as well. He considers it to have been a successful day … selling to stupid-ass teens alcohol and drugs at the Park. He smiles, proud of his knack to have successfully disappeared once he heard the gun shot, yet having no further knowledge of what happened next. Hell, why would he care? He's got a hundred or so dollars in cash bulging out of his pocket. Yet, considering his past experiences in similar situations he pretty much accepts the notion that competing gang-bangers were pissed off at somebody in the Park and took out their anger at these teens. He also is quite sure the cops would arrive, and that's not where he'd prefer to be. He blinks his eyes a few times to clear up the debris that seems to have found a home, distorting his vision. Suddenly, he spots a **YIELD** sign up ahead, close-by. He slams on the breaks of the Chevy that belonged to the big guy he hitched a ride with, although there is no other vehicle or pedestrian he can see. Then he switches his foot to the gas pedal to accelerate at a high speed. He doesn't spot a Police vehicle off to the side.

Immediately there are flashing lights and a siren from the Police vehicle right behind him.

Eric considers for a quick moment that he might be able to speed away, but that stupid idea is brushed off quickly. He nervously pulls over to the side of the road. He's not happy.

The female Police Officer remains inside the Police vehicle while the male Police Officer steps outside to walk towards him.

The driver side window of Eric's car is already down as the Officer comes closer and then says, "Can I see your driver's license." It's clearly not a question. Eric doesn't have a personal driver's license, only the one that belonged to the big guy he hitched a ride with who died. And he can't show that one because the photo on it doesn't come even close to looking like him. Before Eric responds the Officer smells alcohol from within Eric's car. Then the Officer orders, "Please step out of the vehicle."

Eric stumbles out of the car and soon is told to go through the steps of walking a straight line, touching his nose, and turning around. He fails miserably. Then he is given a breath test that shows blood alcohol content to be at a dangerously high level.

The Police Officer turns to motion to his partner still in the Police vehicle to join him.

"Search the car," the Police Officer says to his partner.

She finds inside the Chevy a small amount of marijuana, an opened can of beer, and two empty beer cans.

Without provocation, Eric gets violent and tries to throw a punch at the male Police Officer. The struggle between the male Police Officer and Eric ends quickly as Eric is, without a doubt, in no condition to be a threat. He is placed in constraints by the male Officer as the other female Officer reads him his Miranda Rights.

CHAPTER 19

Jeff walks into the restaurant ... more like a watering-hole for serious beer drinking fans who eat meat, fried foods with lots of hot gravy. While it's late at night, the place is packed. Loud music is blaring through tired speakers that makes it impossible for him to understand the lyrics, but that doesn't seem to bother the regulars who seem to have the music memorized. While most of the regulars are sitting at tables littered with beer bottles, there are a few seated in booths with plates of their favorite fat-loaded cholesterol-extreme meals.

To his right is the bartender who signals him to a small private room in the back, reserved for those who don't want to be disturbed. Jeff follows his signal and soon spots the man he's looking for, his head tilted down towards a full plate of pork ribs, eating as if he hasn't had a bite of food for weeks.

Next to the plate of food is a glass of clear liquid, not what he'd prefer. It's tap water. His left hand is missing the pinky and ring fingers, but that doesn't stop him from moving the ribs into this mouth. His hair is long with the beginning streaks of gray that is parted in the middle and is more than obvious needing a wash. The front of his otherwise dirty shirt is stained with barbecue sauce from the ribs. He avoids using a napkin, preferring to employ the usefulness of his shirt instead. His senses pick up someone's presence. He lifts his head to spot Jeff. His smile is more vampire-like than anything else.

"Hey, Prairie," Jeff calls out.

He stays quiet, yet there is noise coming from his mouth from chewing on the ribs.

As soon as Jeff sits in a chair, a waitress comes by.

Without looking at her, Jeff says, "Draft beer."

Prairie asks, "What about me?"

Jeff frowns, "Not while you're on probation."

"Not anymore." He pauses and then he says, "I ordered."

"I hadn't noticed." He looks at the plate in front of Prairie. "Eat as much as you want. It's on me."

"Take out too?" Prairie's grin shows off his decayed teeth.

Before Jeff can nod yes, his glass of draft beer is delivered. And before Jeff takes a sip Prairie drools with envy.

"Drink your water," Jeff orders.

"Yeah," Prairie says, shrugging his shoulders. He continues, "You know, it was all a mistake." He looks ragged as if he hasn't slept for days. His eyes are almost swollen shut and the skin on his face is drawn tight as a drum. He may have been in control of his fate at one time, but not now.

"How so," Jeff says with a frown. His hand stills holds onto the glass of draft beer.

"I wasn't involved. I was set-up to take the fall."

"Really, is that so?" Jeff replies as he takes a sip from the glass of draft beer.

Prairie wipes his hands nervously on the front of his shirt. The sauce blends in nicely. He cleans his mouth with a swipe from his left shirt sleeve and then says, "Yeah, a mistake, a big one."

"I wish I could have helped you out, but that happened out of my jurisdiction. Sorry." Jeff doesn't try to sound sympathetic because he isn't.

Prairie shakes his head and grips his mouth shut, but only for a second or two. Then he says, "They thought I was a snitch." He looks at Jeff squarely into his eyes.

"Like I just said, I wasn't any use." Jeff shrugs his shoulders wanting to move on to another topic.

"But you want something from me." Prairie's eyes open wide, thinking he's now got leverage.

"That's why I'm paying for your meal." Jeff pushes his beer in front of him. "And the beer."

Prairie grins as best as his face allows like a surprised boy who just got his first kiss from a girl. He quickly drains the glass of draft beer empty.

Jeff raises his hand to alert the waitress he wants another beer. Then he continues, leaning toward Prairie. "I'm working on a case … not important for you to know anything specific about it, but what I need are a few names." He pauses to watch Prairie take it in. Then Jeff repeats, "Names."

Prairie frowns, not keen on giving up sources. He's walked past gravesites many times just whistling that he's not 6-feet-under, and he doesn't want to push his luck. "Ahhh." He strings out the sound as long as he can to get his point across.

Jeff reminds Prairie of something important. "I've kept a few of your secrets hidden … you know what I'm talking about."

He stares directly into Prairie's eyes and then continues. "Crossing the line once never seemed much of a big thing to you. You promised yourself, and me, that you'd never do it again, but that's when it got a little muddy. You betrayed yourself and did it a second time. Hell, you thought, what harm would that do? And then you repeated it again and again." He pauses to make sure it's all sinking in before he continues. "It's the slippery slope phenomenon. You kept repeating, or in this case, kept sliding down the same slope again and again until you never saw the line that you crossed because now there wasn't a line at all. At first it was distinct … then it got blurry … and now it's disappeared completely, totally vanished, gone someplace. You've put yourself in a world of hurt."

The second beer is placed on the table by the same waitress and then she leaves the two men alone again.

Prairie's eyes drop to the glass of draft beer.

Jeff pushes the glass of draft beer towards Prairie. "On me, since you're not on probation."

Prairie's eyes light up like fireworks on the 4th of July as he quickly takes hold of the glass of draft beer for a quick gulp before Jeff can take it back.

Jeff says, "Here's what I need. I'm looking for locals who sell alcohol and drugs to teenagers. One particular male wears a high school ring on the index finger of his left hand. He could be a serial killer … but I really don't know. I want to find this pathetic scum."

Prairie leans back in his chair. The plates in front of him are now completely empty and could even summarily be thought of as washed since they are clean. He keeps a firm grip on the glass of draft beer as he takes another sip … this time slowly. "Did you hear about what happened in the Park in Ashton?"

Jeff frowns. "That's not my jurisdiction. But no, what happened?"

Prairie says, "Now, this is only what I've heard … understand … I can't prove anything."

Jeff quickly answers, "Go on."

"Teenagers in the Park doing whatever they do during the summer." Prairie grins and then continues. "Cops patrol the Park but not on a regular basis … know what I mean?" Prairie doesn't bother to wait for Jeff to answer because it wasn't mean to be a question looking for an answer. "Anyway, a kid got shot and died." He pauses. "But I wasn't there … understand?"

Jeff clarifies, "So the kid was murdered."

Prairie answers as he shrugs his shoulders, "If you say so. I wasn't there."

Jeff is getting impatient. "What else?"

Prairie takes a slow sip from the glass of draft beer. "The kid was supposedly one of their leaders."

Jeff asks, "Leaders of what?"

Now it seems to be Prairie's turn for impatience. "How the hell would I know?" He takes another sip of beer to calm down. "He was on probation … at least that's what I heard."

Jeff asks, "For what?"

Now, more calmly, Prairie says, "I don't know. I'm not his probation officer."

Jeff takes in a deep breath of air before he continues. "What else ... got any names?"

Prairie shifts in his chair needing to take a pee, "That's it."

Jeff learns over the table towards Prairie, "Was the kid wearing a high school ring?"

Prairie looks away quickly and then back to Jeff as he shakes his head sideways, "How would I know?" His head jerks back.

Jeff lets out a noticeable amount of air from his nose and mouth that can't be misinterpreted, even to Prairie, as frustration.

He knew that talking with the guy in front of him, who often in the past was a useful source of information, is now questionable. I guess guys like Prairie will agree to meet with anyone who's willing to buy a meal along with a few beers.

Jeff continues to stare directly at Prairie, but now his thoughts go elsewhere, if only temporarily, to something seemingly unrelated ... his former military career in the United States Air Force. He was stationed at an *Air Force Base* just outside of Cheyenne, Wyoming, the capital of the State. That particular Base was dedicated to maintaining over 100 InterContinental Ballistic Missiles (I. C. B. M.) in underground silos scattered in the States of Wyoming, Colorado, and Nebraska branded *The Minuteman* whose purpose was to reach as far away as Asia and Europe with a payload of a nuclear warhead.

He was a Target and Alignment Officer whose mission was to verify *The Minuteman* was correctly targeted, as well as reset *The Minuteman's* coordinates when ordered. When either of those two goals was achieved he inserted a large key into *The Minuteman's* computer within the Missile and turned the key 90 degrees to the right until he heard a click sound that confirmed *The Minuteman* was fully ready to be launched by a *Launch Officer*, miles away, in an underground *Launch Facility*. A daunting task, for sure, with no room for error.

However, during the long drive between the *Air Force Base* and each *Missile Site* in a 5-ton military truck that contained him, two Airmen, and duplicate pieces of equipment available to him and his team, he often noticed large areas of private land belonging to ranchers. He remembers thinking at times what it would be like to be a rancher with all the land … cattle, horse, whatever. His Airmen would often joke with him that he'd get bored-stiff.

Yet, today, with the stress of law enforcement and no one as his wife or anyone in line that he knows of, he wonders if that situation might not be so bad today. He's got a bunch of money stashed away that he could buy a rundown ranch, maybe one through an auction, and stay busy renovating it. He's pretty good with his hands and isn't afraid to get his hands dirty, literally. He could hire a few hands to help run the place. And he could live out the rest of his life there in peace and tranquility.

But unfortunately, today is today, and he has a full workload. And then, he thinks of Lilli. There's a risk for him to think too long and hard about her, especially her eyes. To him, Lilli has those kind of eyes that you never forget, even if you want to erase them from your memory.

But now isn't the time to get in touch with his feelings … it's not who he is. It's got to be about the mission, objective, goal or whatever someone may label it. His only concern now is to focus on what he agrees to do … to the best of his ability, nothing less … because nothing else matters.

The ranch and Lilli will have to wait a little longer. He's not sure how long that will be, if ever.

CHAPTER 20

Lilli drives headed to the Conroy's to update them on her meeting with Hoskins. They're not going to like it, but it would be worse if she lied … and she couldn't live in peace even if it meant they weren't going to hear what they desperately want to hear. She automatically blinks a few times and then notices in the rearview mirror a highway patrol car with lights flashing red. She figures the driver must be chasing someone ahead of her so she slows down to pull over to the side of the road.

When the driver of the highway patrol car mimics her actions, Lilli realizes she's the one being pursued.

Both vehicles idle for a few seconds and then a female highway patrol officer approaches her.

Lilli lowers the driver side window.

The female highway patrol officer is the first to speak. "You sure seem to be in a hurry."

"I – I didn't realize it. Was I speeding?" Lilli's voice is thin and weak sounding. She barely hears herself talk. It seemed to come from some faraway place.

"Fifty-five is the maximum. You were clocked at sixty-seven. Let me see your driver's license and vehicle registration."

Lilli's face looks vulnerable, and if she could she'd prefer to pull her knees up to her chest like a child. She feels embarrassed and drained of energy. She hesitates.

The highway patrol officer frowns. "Are you OK?"

"Ye – yes, I'm sorry." Lilli reaches into her jacket on the passenger seat to get her wallet containing the two documents.

The highway patrol officer, smart and a good judge of character, cautiously watches Lilli wondering what's really going on.

Lilli hands over the two documents. "Here they are."

The highway patrol officer takes the two documents. "Wait here." She returns to her vehicle to further confirm their authenticities.

Lilli feels her eyes swell. She uses the corner of her sleeve to dab at the now randomly falling tears.

A few minutes pass until the highway patrol officer rejoins Lilli. "Here." She returns both documents to Lilli. She continues. "So, you too are in law enforcement working with *Verity Security*." She now is smiling.

Lilli is surprised at first, but then quickly understands. "Not in your capacity, just a Public Safety Officer ... not as dangerous or as important."

"Doesn't matter ... it's nice to meet a sister." The highway patrol officer hesitates as if she is questioning herself on whether to ask something else. She decides to do it ... nothing to lose. "But you're not in the field now, are you."

Lilli feels somewhat more settled down. "That's right. I'm doing something for a friend ... actually for her parents ... and now I've got to tell her parents something they're not going to want to hear about their daughter ... but I'm not going to lie to them. I guess my mind was too distracted."

"No problem. I'm sure you'll do the right thing. Be safe. You're good to go. Watch your speed." The highway patrol officer turns to return to her vehicle.

Lilli realizes she's been given a free pass. She grins and mumbles softly, "No complaints, sister."

The highway patrol vehicle pulls onto the highway first, and then Lilli carefully follows, holding back a wave of her hand from one sister to another.

Before Lilli realizes, she pulls the car to the side of the street to park ... in front of the Conroy's house. If she could see her own face ... which wouldn't be all that difficult ... she could look into the rearview mirror ... she probably wouldn't believe her own eyes. She looks both sad and tensed.

Lilli sits on the couch with Natalie in the Conroy's living room facing Henry and Barbara.

Lucky rests on the floor alongside Henry at her usual hang-out spot on the carpet spot.

Lilli swallows and looks at Henry and Barbara, eyes alternatively fixed on each of them. She says, "I met with Detective Hoskins of the Belview Police Department. He's veteran law enforcement and very well respected." She clears her throat. "He shared with me information about Camille's situation, taking me precisely step by step of the investigation. I asked him many questions and he provided me with credible real evidence. We even argued at times. But, it is in my judgement, from what I now know, that the case is closed. There is no reasonable doubt to believe otherwise." She pauses to clear her throat again and hoping she comes across as honest, sincere, and thorough. She continues to keep her eyes focused on Henry and Barbara whose eyes now seem to be in pain. "You could hire a private investigator to find credible and relevant information that could be used to reopen the case, but that will be expensive and time consuming … and it could create misleading hopes from you as well. I'm not qualified to be that investigator." She leans towards Henry and Barbara. "I'm sorry, but there isn't anything more I can do. I wish there was." She pauses and then softy adds, "I really am sorry."

The quietness of the silence permeates the room … not even their breathing is heard. It seems each one of them is waiting for someone else to break the ice.

And then Barbara starts wailing and shedding tears.

Henry quickly moves close to her, wraps his arms around his wife, and says something in private that is kept between them.

Next is Lucky, who starts barking. She stands to face the Conroy's.

And finally, Natalie begins to cry as well. Her hands wiggle in the air.

Lilli moves closer to her daughter to wrap her arms around her. "I'm sorry I couldn't do more."

There is nothing else anyone can do, except to grieve, yet no one knows what it all means.

It's well past Natalie's bedtime before Lilli arrives back at her apartment, but her daughter, like most kids her age, seems to be able to sleep at any time, at any place. Carefully, she takes hold of her daughter, locks the car, and slowly walks towards her apartment. She knows it'll be empty and in many respects a lonely place. She looks again at Natalie, sound asleep in her arms, to say, "I love you and always will." She kisses her daughter without a peep from her daughter.

Now inside her apartment, Lilli carefully undresses Natalie for bedtime and then places her in her crib. She leans over to kiss Natalie, and then heads to her own bed to prepare for sleep, difficult at this time.

A little earlier the same day, but some other place, Vincent is talking with his grandson, Joey, inside a hospital room where Vincent was admitted a day ago due to symptoms of a heart attack that eventually was confirmed. Joey and his father, Louie, are the only family members who seemed to have any interest in seeing him. Vincent suspects his grandson somehow convinced his father to visit him. It's hard to turn away from such a plea. Otherwise, there most likely would be no one within or outside of the family by his side at the moment. It's sad, but it is what it is, and not so uncommon these days.

Vincent turns to his grandson. "Joey, you're a good boy. I'm proud of you. I'm sure you've got dreams … you know … what you wanna do in life." His voice isn't as strong as he'd like but that's to be expected … influenced by his medical condition. He looks at the boy for some sort of acknowledgement but all he sees is a young kid's blank stare. So, Vincent continues. "We all have dreams … you know like an imaginary tomorrow that can come true. And, what I want you to promise not only me, but to yourself, is to dream your future and then create a plan to get there. Would you do that … huh?" He waits for a reaction that doesn't take place, not even a little something that crops up … nothing. Vincent closes his eyes and softly says, "I pray to God that Joey will create his future before his youth passes away." He reopens his eyes to look at his son. "Louie, come here closer to me." He motions with his hand for his son to move nearer to him.

Louie moves his chair to touch the bed. "Yeah, Pop."

Vincent says, "Give me some water. I'm thirsty, and I've got something to say to you in private."

Louie hands over to his father a glass of water with a drinking straw. He helps guide the straw to his father's mouth as Vincent starts to take in some water. When he's satisfied he moves his lips away from the straw to motion to Louie that he's done.

Louie places the glass with the straw on a nearby table adjacent to the bed.

Vincent clears his throat. "This is between us … you and me."

Louie nods his head. "Sure, Pop. Just between us. What is it?"

"First, thanks for bringing Joey to see me. I wish it was under better conditions. I miss the family."

Louie remains quiet and motionless as does his son sitting in a chair a few feet away.

"I know you and Annie are … well … having some problems. It happens in every marriage, even with me and your mother. But we always worked it out, and so will you."

Louie frowns, straightens his body in the chair. "What are you talking about? Everything's fine." He seems surprised but down deep inside he knows how intuitive his father has been, something he admits is missing from his skill set. There's never been anything he's been able to hide from his father.

Vincent waves his a hand in the air as if to dismiss the argument, but he's really more interested in talking further. "Listen to me. I want to give you something." He pauses again and then restarts, "This is only between us … you and me … OK." He coughs but waves his hand toward Louie to ignore it.

Louie shakes his head, "Sure between us, but Pop, you don't have to give me anything."

Vincent waves a finger in the air in disagreement. "I know I don't have to, but I want to. Just listen." He pauses and then continues. "I got a pistol locked up in my apartment. You'll need to get the key to open the safe. I'll tell you where it is. It's the same pistol I had during the military."

Louie reacts, "But, Pop, I really don't like guns." He frowns. "You know that."

Vincent counters, "So, you'd want a Rolex watch instead ... is that what you'd want?"

Louie nods his head, "Yeah. That would be better. But do you have a Rolex watch ... really?"

Vincent shakes his head, "Hell no ... never had one ... never wanted one. But shut up and listen." He pauses to take in a needed breath of air before he continues. "Someday, you're gonna come home early from work and maybe find Annie in bed with another man."

Louie interrupts, "That'll never happen!"

"Listen to your father, will you!" Vincent pauses again for another breath of air. "What are you gonna do when you see Annie with another man but all you got is a Rolex watch? Huh? Answer that. Huh? I'll tell you. You'd point to the watch and say, hey buddy, your time's up?"

For a short time the room is silent, but is interrupted by a Nurse who walks into the room. She looks at Louie and Joey, and at Vincent. "Excuse me, but visiting hours are up. He needs some rest and some instructions about tomorrow's stress test."

Louie stands to reach over to his father to kiss him on the cheek. Then he motions to his son to join him. "Say goodnight to Grandpa."

In a soft sound, Joey says, "Goodnight Grandpa."

They leave him alone with the Nurse who starts a new conversation.

"Tomorrow is your stress test. I want to review what's going to happen tomorrow. OK?"

Vincent says, "Yeah ... yeah."

"This is a specialized test for diagnosing heart abnormalities. We'll start at 9:00 am tomorrow morning.

An IV will be started in your arm to allow the injection of medicine. Then an isotope will be injected through the IV and special pictures will be taken of your heart shortly after the injection and during the test. Do you understand what I've just said?"

Again, Vincent says, "Yeah … yeah."

"OK. For the next part wires will be attached to electrodes that will be placed on your chest and then connect the leads to an EKG machine that will monitor your heart rate and rhythm. You'll be injected with a medication named lexiscan through the IV. You might feel a little flush, but that'll be temporary. Then we'll wait for a short time for the lexiscan to absorb into your heart muscle so that we can take a second set of pictures of your heart. Do you understand what I've just said?"

This time Vincent says, "Yeah … yeah, but I'll forget about it by tomorrow."

"Yes, that's understandable, so we'll give you the same information again tomorrow morning before the stress test. The total time should be about 2 hours. You'll not be allowed to drink any caffeinated beverages or eat anything for the next 12 hours, only water that will be provided to you. Do you understand what I've just said?"

Vincent repeats what he's been saying all along, "Yeah … yeah."

"OK. Have a good night's rest. You'll be waken-up at 7:30 am tomorrow morning." She shuts off the room lights and leaves him alone.

Vincent will not experience the stress test tomorrow morning because he will peacefully pass away early tomorrow morning before the 7:30 am wakeup.

CHAPTER 21

The next morning, after an unrestful sleep, Lilli decides it's time to get up just the same. Her thoughts off and on during the night were about angst that Henry and Barbara must still be feeling. She doesn't hear a peep from Natalie, and thus assumes her daughter is either still sleeping or just quietly playing with her favorite fluffy toy that looks like a Panda.

Still stretched out flat on her back in bed, Lilli stretches her arms over her head. Her neck muscles, shoulders, and upper back are stiff. She takes a final yawn and then swings her slender legs from underneath the blanket to reach the floor. Then she finally stands as straight as possible to finish off the last of her typical maneuvers before she heads to check on Natalie. She slowly walks towards the crib to see her daughter content with the fluffy Panda in her grasp. "Good morning sweetie."

Natalie ignores her mother's morning greeting ... too infatuated with another discussion that she seems to be having with the fluffy Panda.

"It's time to get up." Lilli reaches to pick up Natalie and the fluffy toy to head towards the small kitchen to prepare breakfast.

It takes her less than 20 minutes to get Natalie's breakfast prepared while the coffee machine finishes off its task. She steps back to look at Natalie and her friend. "I'm so blessed."

A little more than 30 minutes later she finishes cleaning up from the breakfast and sits in a chair in the kitchen to finish off the last of her coffee that she'll have for the day. Then, for some reason, she thinks of Vincent. A frown casts over her face. She turns to Natalie. "Let's visit Vincent. I don't want him to be mad at us, but, well, what he proposed was ... ah ... a marriage proposal ... and I turned him down. I feel like I need to explain further to him."

Natalie doesn't seem interested in dialoguing with her mother ... the fluffy Panda is more important to her at the moment.

Lilli takes a firm hold of Natalie and her friend. Then she calmly walks to the apartment door to head towards Vincent's place on the next lower floor.

Lilli knocks on Vincent's apartment door, but without a response, she says, "Vincent, are you home?" She waits for a response that doesn't come. She knocks again, this time with more force and repeats the same call-out, but only gets the same no response.

She tries the door knob, expecting it to be locked, but surprised when it easily turns with only a single twist. She hesitates for a second or two and then steps inside, keeping the door open. "Vincent, are you here?" All she hears is Natalie still communicating with her friend.

Lilli has never been inside Vincent's apartment. Why would she? He had always come to her place to take care of Natalie, and on occasion enjoy a meal or two.

The interior layout is relatively simple, similar to her place. The first room is a small living room with a worn-out couch and a single chair. There's no television in sight but there is a radio resting on an end table along with a lamp. Across the room is another lamp ... a floor lamp. The kitchen is visible over a waist-high wall. There's a small electric stove, a refrigerator, and a basin but without a dishwasher. A few cabinets are attached to the wall and some are at ground level. She assumes they contain dishes, cups, knives, spoons, and forks along with canned food. The bedroom is to the back of the apartment with an unmade double-size bed and an alarm clock and landline resting on a small table. Across from the bed is a closet, presumably filled with clothes and shoes ... the closet door is closed. Off to the right is a small bathroom containing a wash basin, a small cabinet, a mirror, a shower-tub combination, and a toilet with the cover opened. There's a hamper at the entrance to the bathroom that is used for dirty clothes to be washed. The coin operated washers and dryers for all apartment renters are at ground level in a dedicated room. There are no photos of any kind inside Vincent's apartment ... old ones or new ones ... of family or friends.

Lilli wonders how lonely Vincent must feel, but where is he? The place is tidy. She turns to leave the apartment, now headed for the on-site-apartment manager who might be of some help.

Betty Manners is about 55 years old … that's just Lilli's guess, but the manager isn't talking about that metric. She's been the on-site-apartment manager for the last 10 years, much longer than Lilli has been a renter. It's a job Betty's happy to have based on her outdated skill set. She's single, never married but engaged several times, and at one time had false hopes to be a professional singer. Her specialty was blues. While dreams are important in everyone's life, the more realistic they are the better chance they have of coming true … at least that's the conventional wisdom. Betty lacked one key ingredient to be a professional blues singer … she couldn't carry a tune, always out of key. Maybe it had something to do with her hearing. The backup unmet requirement for singers is to remember the lyrics … another strike against Betty. And the third strike for her was she was frightened to perform in front of a live audience.

Her current job offers her a free apartment and utilities along with a small monthly stipend for food and incidentals. What else could she want? She's happy, or perhaps she's simply not unhappy.

After the first knock on Betty's apartment door it opens. She smiles, "Hi Lilli." She looks at Natalie and her friend, "And of course to you and your friend." She switches back to look at Lilli. "What's up? Anything broke in the apartment?" She slightly twists her head to the side to hear Lilli better.

"No, nothing like that … but there is something you can help me with."

"Sure, come on in. That's why they pay me the big bucks." Betty grins, thinking the comment to be funny. Then she laughs at her own corny joke. "No loud music coming from another renter?"

"No, but it's about Vincent."

Betty's face gazes at Lilli, "Vincent?" Her head remains slightly turned to the side.

"I – I wanted to talk with him about something, so I went to visit him. He wasn't in, but the door was unlocked." She decides it's not the time to tell her about the tour she took of his place, if ever.

"Yeah." Betty's face saddens. "I hope he's OK."

"Oh, what happened?" Lilli frowns in concern.

"Evidently he called 911. He thought he was having a heart attack. When the paramedics arrived I directed them to his apartment, and unlocked the door to let them in. I guess I forgot to relock the door … stupid of me." She shakes her head to the sides. "Don't tell him, OK."

"Oh, no, you've got my word." Lilli pauses. "How is he?"

"I don't know. I didn't check up on him. I mean, well, his rent is paid up to date. Why would I check up on him?" She frowns in confusion.

Lilli frowns with annoyance. "What hospital is he in?"

"I don't know for sure, but I suspect it's the Ellis Hospital. It's the city's largest public hospital."

Lilli, now back at her apartment calls the Ellis Hospital.

The woman who answers sounds like a robot … no emotion. "What department are you calling for?"

One word is sufficient, "Admissions."

Another robotic sound, "One moment please while I connect you."

A third time isn't the charm in this instance. There is another robotic sound, "Admissions. How can I help you?"

Lilli doesn't sound desperate to herself but she is. "I'm calling about a recent admission ... an elderly man who allegedly suffered a heart attack. EMT responded and he was admitted just recently."

"Are you a family member?"

"Well, no, not exactly."

The robotic sound is either extremely well programmed to now sound human, or else she is. "What do you mean? You're either a family member or you're not. But if you are law enforcement working on an active case, then I need to transfer you to another department."

Lilli thinks fast. "I'm his sister ... we actually haven't been close for a long time, but I just got word from my ... uh ... brother ... older brother ... that Vincent has been admitted."

"What's the last name ... Vincent who?"

"Vincent Doni."

"And your name?"

"Lilli Jackson ... I'm married ... Jackson is my married name."

"One moment please."

Lilli hears silence, and then the sound of music of some sort ... instruments ... as if children are each practicing something different from one another.

"Mrs. Jackson?"

"Yes, what can you tell me?" Lilli sounds anxious.

"It's not smart to lie … to misrepresent yourself as a family member. In fact, it's illegal."

"What do you mean? I am his sister, Lilli Jackson!"

"Not from our records. I suggest you reconnect with your … brother … older brother."

The phones disconnect.

Lilli frowns, figuring the only way she'll find out about Vincent is to reach out to John, who knows where all the strings are to pull. She calls John.

After one ring, she hears John's voice. "Hey, how did it work out?"

She knows what he's referring to and feels sad all over again just thinking about it. "Not like they wanted it to turn out … nor me. It must be a terrible feeling." She sniffles.

"But you did everything you could have done. Sometimes, it's the gesture that really matters … the little things." He pauses … waiting for some response but all he hears is her sad breathing. He decides to change the topic. "You're calling to tell me when you're returning to work?"

She pulls out of her funky feeling, but not completely. All she's able to say is, "Yeah."

He knows something else is up. "But there's something else bothering you. You wanna talk about it?"

She grins at his intuitive prowess. "I've never figured out how you know things that are not obvious."

"Some people are easier to read than others. What else is bothering you?"

She decides to tell all. "There's a man … elderly in a way … wife passed on a few years ago. He lives in the same apartment building as me. I met him one day in the laundry room. Natalie was with me. And honestly, John, I was surprised at how the two of them took such a quick liking to each other. He volunteered to babysit in a pinch. And he's been very good to Natalie." She pauses, now considering whether to go on or not.

"I'm listening," says John. His voice is comforting.

She clears her throat. "So, I just figured it was nice of him to be so gracious with his time. It seems his family has distanced themselves from him for some reason. That's something I'm not going to get involved in. Anyway … and this is now going to sound weird, crazy … a few days ago he proposed marriage to me. Can you believe that? I was shocked … and sure a little flattered … but hell, John, he's old enough to be Natalie's grandfather and my father! I told him thanks but no thanks … that it wasn't anything personal … but I'm sure he picked up on what I really meant. Then I left to meet the Conroy's." She takes a breather.

John takes advantage of the pause. "So, are you reconsidering his offer … is that why you called me … to get my sage advice?"

"Actually … no." Then Lilli moves on. "For some reason, this morning, thinking about the Conroy's, Vincent popped into my mind."

John asks, "That's his name … Vincent?"

She's quick to answer, "Yeah, Vincent Doni."

"And so, what happened next?"

"I thought that maybe I should explain in more detail why marriage is out of the question. I guess I felt that the conversation needed a better ending, so this morning I

knocked on his apartment door ... but no answer. I turned
the door knob and it was unlocked so I walked in. He wasn't
there, so I asked the on-site-apartment manager if she knew
anything. She said he was taken to the hospital ... it turns
out it was the Ellis Hospital ... in an ambulance because he
felt he was having a heart attack. So, I called the Hospital to
confirm, but they said only family members have the right to
know about patients, except, of course, for law enforcement
if it is an active case." She pauses to catch her breath giving
John an opportunity to ask a question.

"So let me guess ... you want me to find out the status
of Vincent Doni ... is that it?"

"See, John, you are psychic." She smiles.

"No problem. Give me an hour. I'll circle back to you."

"Thanks John, I owe you."

"You don't owe me a thing. If I can help, I will. Talk
soon." He doesn't pursue when she'll return to work and she
doesn't volunteer that information.

Lilli decides the best way to pass the time is to get busy
with cleaning her place.

Thirty minutes later, she picks up her cell. "John?"

"Vincent Doni passed away early this morning, 2:17
to be exact, in his Hospital room, from a heart attack. He
couldn't be revived. Next of kin have been notified."

Lilli cups her mouth with her left hand, remaining silent
and lost for words, just feeling rotten. She feels her eyes
moisten. Then she whispers, "Oh."

"Nothing you can do. I didn't ask for the names of
the family because that's way out of line ... an abuse of

the family's privacy. You might keep an eye on funeral announcements in the paper and online if you're interested, but there's nothing else I can do." He doesn't ask when she's returning to work.

"Yes, yes, of course, I understand. John, again, thanks." She forgets about saying when she plans to return to work.

She disconnects and thinks out loud. "First it was the Conroy's and now it's Vincent who I've let down."

Later the same day, Detective Hoskins of the Belview Police Department places a call to John at *Verity Security*.

"What's up?" John is surprised by the call … no pending business between him and Hoskins … must be social … but it isn't.

"I don't have what's her name contact information or else I would have made contact with her directly, and not have to bother you. Sorry."

"Who's what's her name?"

"If I could remember I'd tell you. It's one of your employees who was helping the Conroy family … you know, about their daughter's death."

"Oh, you mean Lilli Jackson. I was talking with her earlier today."

"Bingo … that's her."

"She's off today but I can pass on the info to her myself. Don't think she'd appreciate me giving out her personal cell number. You know."

"I get it … I wouldn't want that to happen either. Here's the update. Evidently, before the deceased was released to Land's Funeral Home, her body was reexamined. Don't know why, but it's not unusual … could have been just a precaution. Anyway, this second examination included detailed probing of her head. There was an abrasion a half inch above her left ear. I honestly don't understand how the M. E. didn't pick up on that the first go-round … maybe the responsibility was delegated to someone junior with less experience and insight. The abrasion could have been inflicted by someone … the deceased herself or someone else … either intentionally or by accident … or it could have been the result of falling on a solid item like a rock just below the surface of the water. However it happened, blunt force trauma to the head almost leads to a finding of death by homicide … but not this time. And without noticing the bruise during the preliminary examination I suspect it must have been concluded that the deceased killed herself and drowned, and therefore, strangulation, smothering, or trauma to the head were ruled out. But now, the cause of death is being changed from suicide to asphyxiation … water in the lungs. But still they don't know what caused the drowning. There were no other physical signs on her neck, face, or other parts of her body. She wasn't raped. No defensive wounds, no ligature marks, no other bruising that would suggest she was attacked. So, was her drowning an accident, was it self-inflicted, was there someone or more than one person involved? They don't know and with this new information I have no idea. Therefore, we can't say for certain it had to be suicide." Hoskins takes a second off from talking that gives John an opportunity to say something.

"Accidents do happen, but it doesn't make it any easier for the loved ones to accept someone's passing."

"Agreed."

John adds, "I'll pass this onto Lilli and then she'll figure out what to do next. I don't want to nose into this situation. She has your number, so she might call you directly. How does that sound to you?"

"Fine with me … and I agree with your personal judgement of not getting involved any further."

Once the phones disconnect, John makes a call to Lilli to pass along the update.

She listens without interruptions, but once John is through she comes to a conclusion. "You know what I'm going to say before I say is … don't you."

"Yeah, you wanna meet with the Conroy's to tell them in person."

"Once again, spot on. I'll take Natalie with me."

No one mentions to the other anything about her return-to-work plans, which seems to be just fine with each of them.

CHAPTER 22

The area looks like it has been abandoned for a while … that's because it's been empty for about the last 10 years. The politically correct politicians prefer to say that it's just in a transitional stage … they're looking at several proposals to convert the vacant property into something respectable. But, of course, those are simply politically correct statements and blatant lies to the citizens who voted them into office in the first place, something too common these days. There are no plans to do anything with the barren land. What most agree on is that it's probably not the type of place you want to go at night … alone or with someone else including your pet … and some say to avoid it even during the daytime. The things that happen here aren't reported to law enforcement. But it wasn't always like that.

For several years this abandoned area was the site of a local school … Alexander Schools … named after the first Commissioner of Education of the State. It had been built, like many other schools during that time in the country, to accommodate a rapidly rising birth rate where the young kids would need to go to school at one time … from K to 12th grade.

The rectangular brick building itself, when it was completed filled one city block. At the southwestern corner was where kindergarteners started, and as they graduated to the next grade, they moved northward, then eastward, then southward, until they moved westward where, next to their classrooms were the kindergarteners. In a way, students would consciously or unconsciously remember where it all began for them.

The teachers were competent and strict … you had to do your homework and be polite or else feel the "paddle" … something you never told your parents about because it showed disrespect to a teacher, most of whom were married women with an occasional single female, as well as a splattering of men.

The students knew each other very well since their families lived in small houses close by each other in a variety of small neighborhoods. This meant that your classmates in K were most likely the same classmates in the 12th grade.

If you had an older sibling who was part of the student body, there was a good chance you'd have the same teacher. And if your older sibling was academically high-quality and well-mannered that teacher would remind you of those facts, putting the pressure on you to step up your academic rigor and politeness.

In addition to the academic courses such as English, Writing, Math, Sciences, Foreign Languages, Social Studies, Shorthand, and Typing, there were Physical Ed, Shop, Speech, Music, Art and Sports. The building was large enough to easily accommodate a cafeteria with staff, and on-site custodians. There were several formalized Clubs such as a Student Council, Red Cross Council, Future Teachers of America, International Foreign Relations Council, Hi-Y, Key Club, Tri-Hi, Ski-Hi, Blue Triangle, Girls' Athletic Association, Boys' Athletic Association, Booster Club, and Audio-Visual Club.

And, as many good things often come to an end, Alexander Schools faded away. The nearby Army Reserve Base closed, the city's largest manufacturing company relocated out of State, and funding for Alexander Schools disappeared. The once prosperous town also faded. Locally owned businesses went belly-up and young adults moved to other more potentially prosperous communities while the homeless who lived on the streets substantially grew.

Alexander Schools building was torn down and what replaced it was this abandoned area.

Yet, he parks his vehicle to the curb across the street directly under a flickering street light that needs to be replaced … but that won't happen at any time.

He spends a few minutes while sitting in the vehicle sizing up the area … definitely not remotely close to being as previously mentioned, and there have never been mansions with pools or high gated fences to keep out undesirables. He doesn't see anyone walking by. He looks at his watch. It is a few minutes before midnight. There's a full moon that as best as it tries cannot breakup the otherwise gloomy atmosphere.

He gets out of the vehicle, locks the doors, and stands still for a while … like a statue … rechecking the environment. There are no prying eyes he can see, but that does not mean anything.

"Hands up high where I can see them!" She suddenly emerges out of nowhere, like a ship appearing from the fog of the sea.

He obeys the order, but doesn't recognize the female voice. Male or female, it doesn't matter in these situations where someone else has the upper hand. He resists turning around … it just makes sense to follow orders under these conditions … no sense in provoking unsuitable behavior that could cost him his life. But, he thinks, it might surprise her … he could pull out his weapon from the holster, turn, and duck as he fired at her. He wisely hesitates to make any move unless directed by her.

"Spread your legs!"

She sounds like law enforcement so he decides to follow her command as he says, "I have a revolver in a rear belt holster. And my badge and creds are inside my front left pocket of my coat."

She circles him and eventually ends up face-to-face.

He looks at her … the size of a pixie, smooth face and seemingly on the younger side. She is slender looking but her appearance might be camouflaging her strength and ability. He can't make out what's underneath her uniform in terms of muscle and flexibility. He resists smiling with pleasure at the uniformed female police officer … no sense in provoking her at this moment in time. And he's definitely not going to compliment her good looking appearance. He finds female cops attractive, very attractive, in fact hot.

Then, still holding her gun at him she gives him a quick and efficient pat-down. Then she removes his pistol from his rear belt holster and badge and creds from his front left pocket of his coat. She steps back. "What are you doing here?"

"Beautiful moon." The phrase slips out too quickly before he can retrieve it. Dumb! But it's in his DNA. He knows better than to alienate people, especially during those times when he is dependent on someone for his life. And further, for that matter, on those who count on him.

"Cut the crap. This isn't a safe place to be, especially at night." She is old enough to suspect most things told to her, yet young enough to want to believe. But one thing is for sure, she's learned survival skills. She stares directly into his eyes.

He isn't surprised at her lack of humor, but he can't resist saying, "Are you going to arrest me, or just keep talking away?"

"We can go down to the station to figure this out, or we can do it here and now."

"Do you really want to arrest me?"

"No. Too much paperwork."

"OK, at least that's something we can agree on. I'm here to meet someone who supposedly has some information that I need. But, I'm sure he's gone by now once he spotted you."

"You wanna tell me about it?"

"Yeah, but I'm not gonna. You understand."

She takes a look at his badge and then his creds. "Detective Jeffrey Abrams, hmm."

"That's me." He smiles for the first time, believing it's now safe. He notices her last name on her uniform, *Kipling*, wondering if she is somehow related to Rudyard, but decides now isn't the time to ask … maybe never.

She returns his badge, creds, and gun to him. "This is not your jurisdiction."

"I go where the leads take me. Think I should have informed your Chief?"

"Your call … not mine to make." She continues to stare at him and then says, "You're good to go. Be safe." She turns and walks away, irritated at having to deal with him, hoping never to see him again, and definitely not having to ever work with him.

Jeff stays put as he refocuses on the vacant site, the place where his School once prominently stood, the School he attended from K to 12th grade.

He had been well liked by other students and his teachers, but shy around girls, dating only a few times … if you can believe that, which you should because that is the truth. He was a little above average academically, went onto College, then into the U. S. Air Force as an officer, and then enrolled in the police academy where he believed he found his niche. And, as they say … whoever they are … the rest is history. Relentless law enforcement work gave him a sense of duty and pride thus without any significant time for a family. He still wonders if it's now too late.

He takes himself out of the self-imposed recollection, hesitates before leaving and then grabs his phone to call his Chief to talk about an idea … a long shot for sure but what the hell, when they pay off they really do. His Chief isn't pleased at the midnight call, yet he listens, none-the-less. After the talk, he waits to be joined by others although not exactly sure who specifically they will be, especially at this hour.

Beauty is an eighty-pound gray and white German-Shepard, beautiful to look at and exceptional at what she can do. She enjoys her job more than most animals, including humans, because it's like play. This time it is searching for a suspect without an identifying name as of now ... but most likely a male not a female ... and no other visual characteristics yet known. A K-9 Officer named Wayne Wake is Beauty's handler ... also one of the best.

Her ID number, B527, is tattooed inside her right ear, but she doesn't know that. She only knows what she needs to know ... she and Wake are a pact ... each will protect the other at all costs. She feels in scents which trigger her emotions that lead to her actions. She's able to run long distances at a steady and unwavering pace without complaining, a trait passed down from mountain wolves who hunted their prey, to protect their pack.

Beauty is the only dog released for this particular hunt. The territory to be covered is not populated at this time of night ... deserted actually ... which means there's no need to alert residents to remain in their houses or apartments, lock their doors, and remain quiet while the hunt takes place. There's also no broadcast in multiple languages ... no helicopter overhead with high-magnification cameras and heat sensitive equipment that operates with x-ray vision. In other words, there is no eye-in-the-sky ... just Beauty.

Wake is backed up by Jeff and Officer Kipling who isn't happy to have been called back. That's the life of law enforcement ... take the good with the bad and don't complain.

Beauty is trained to source for both a specific scent from a human as well as a non-specific human scent, a rare set of skills among her breed. The non-specific human scent hunt takes much longer and is very methodical. During this hunt Beauty will be slow and methodical.

Wake has already been fully briefed by Jeff without a peep from Kipling. He shouts to Jeff and Kipling, "You ready?"

Jeff grins at Kipling who doesn't reciprocate the gesture and then turns his head towards Wake. He yells back at Wake, "Bring it on! It's time to rock and roll!"

Kipling mumbles, "I can't believe this guy." Her head nod is only noticeable to someone looking directly at her, and in this case, there isn't anyone.

Wake slaps his knees and when he rubs Beauty's head he hears a squeaky sound from Beauty meaning she's ready to rock and roll. "You wanna find him?" he says, all the while looking directly into her eyes.

Beauty wiggles her body and rubs against him. She's ready to rock and roll.

Wake stands straight and lowers his voice to sound deeper, "Down."

Beauty positions her body flat on the ground as her ears slant forward all while keeping a well-honed eye-to-eye contact with Wake.

Wake points ahead with his hand. "Beauty, smell him ... find him ... go."

Beauty begins her job as she sniffs the ground and anything on its top like leaves, twigs and the like to find the strongest human scent in the area. She moves forward, cautiously and methodically for a few minutes while Wake follows close-by, and then with Jeff and Kipling picking up the rear in silence but now they have drawn their guns and flashlights lit. Beauty moves from one area to the next, slowly and deliberately all the while storing in her brain what she smells. She goes to any place where the smell takes her … where a person could hide or otherwise be immobile.

Then Beauty flattens her tail and stops for a few seconds as if she is thinking about something. She's really processing the information quickly to arrive at a logical conclusion as to what to do next. Then she slowly trots forward, again with Wake close behind, both of them realizing she's picked up a non-specific human scent. Beauty picks up her pace. Then she starts barking.

Wake keeps up with her pace as he calls back to Jeff and Kipling, "She's onto something!" He grins.

Up head Wake sees Beauty circling something on the ground, still barking but this time much louder and with greater fervor.

Wake draws his gun at this point as he more carefully advances towards Beauty. The grin has vanished.

Now with a lit flashlight, he spots a motionless body, flat on its back, eyes closed, legs slightly spread and arms by its side with the palms against the ground. He yells, "Suspect down … not moving." He then waits for Jeff and Kipling to join him.

Once Jeff and Kipling arrive at the scene Wake backs away with Beauty. He says, "All yours."

Kipling speaks for the first time, still looking at the motionless male body on the ground. "Do you recognize him?"

Jeff stares at the motionless body on the ground, mumbles to himself but also just loud enough for others to hear. "Prairie, the guy I was gonna talk with. He said he had some information for me." He pauses to look away and then returns staring at the dead man. "What the hell! What did you want me to know?"

Prairie doesn't answer.

Prairie is dressed in faded dark colored pants with a long sleeve shirt that is tattered at the cuffs and collar. He wears a pair of worn down running shoes of unknown make, model, color, and design. The shoe laces are close to tearing apart. There are no finger rings or a wristwatch on his hands. His messed up black hair that contain a few signs of graying needs to be cut … it's way over his ears and too long in the back but that can't clearly be seen due to the position of his head … face up.

Underneath his fingernails on both hands are ample deposits of dirt. His left hand is still missing the pinky and ring fingers, while his right hand looks like it has been in a recent fight … bruises and a crooked index finger.

There appears to be two wet spots on the chest part of his shirt that indicates wounds of some sort. Later it is confirmed that two stab wounds to his chest was the cause of his murder.

The air temperature at this time of the night is around 58° to 59° F. Prairie's body temperature to the touch seems to be around normal which suggests he's only been dead for a few hours, at the most, but sufficiently long enough ago that he would never have been able to meet up with Jeff.

He was obviously murdered, but why and by who still needs to be answered. What did he know that he was about to tell Jeff? It's safe to assume that someone didn't want that information revealed.

CHAPTER 23

John hears his phone buzz, takes a look at caller-ID, and makes the connection. "Hoskins, what did I do to deserve this?" He chuckles.

Hoskins's voice is nowhere close to expressing amusement. "Between us only ... OK?"

John frowns. "Sure, if that's what it's gotta be ... sounds important."

"Yeah, very important." Hoskins hesitates before continuing. "What do you know about Detective Jeffery Abrams?"

Another frown from John. "Jeff?"

"Yeah, you've worked with him ... Detective Jeffery Abrams."

"Can I ask what this is about?"

"Sure, you can ask all you want, but you go first. I'm listening."

John shrugs his shoulders. "OK. He's former military, Air Force Missile Officer. Left the service with an honorable discharge. Became law enforcement by choice ... his. Promoted to current position. I've relied on his expertise a few times. Always delivered. What else do you wanna know?"

"Personal life … marriage … bad habits like drinking, gambling … you know what I mean … anything and everything."

"You really wanna go there?"

"Definitely."

"OK, well as far as I know he was married for a few years, not sure how many … got divorced, don't know the reason… no kids. Parents are gone. Hard worker … loves his job. Adopted a dog just recently from a homeless guy who died … nice gesture. Oh, yeah, I think he's got the hots for Lilli, but that's just a hunch … never asked. Ah, that's about it."

"So, you've never socialized with him. Is that right?"

"Correct."

"But you haven't mentioned any bad habits … whether or not they're expensive or not."

John lets out a breath of air, "Don't know of any … maybe he has them, but I'm not aware … none of my business."

"Ever been arrested … felony pops … interfering with an investigation … obstructing justice … collusion with the wrong people … anything like that?"

"Are you thinking of tapping him to join your Department?"

"No."

"Are you on an eval committee of some sort … you know for a promotion or an award?"

"No."

"Then what?"

"Between us only."

"Yeah, I've already agreed to that. What's up?"

"He's under suspicion for involvement with the bad guys ... speculated of having a stash of cash hidden away just waiting for the right time so he can disappear to live the good life."

"You can't be serious!"

"Oh, I am and so are the Feds. If he's been dealing with at least one of the bad guys, why not two, or even more."

John's face looks shocked, perplexed and worried. He doesn't believe any of this for a second, but he also knows better than to dismiss it completely. He remains quiet. Hoskins isn't someone who draws irrational conclusions using skimpy and/or false information.

"Point being, he's under surveillance. I won't ... make that I can't tell you by whom. And I don't want to waste your time getting you involved any further at this point. Just keep it between us."

"I'm just having a hard time wrapping my head around this. I mean, he's a Vet ... Air Force. Maybe he's had too many close calls and PTS is kicking in. If that's the case he needs help, an intervention immediately."

"Yeah, he is a Vet and his record is clean ... no misconducts or warnings. If he had an assignment in battle it must have been highly confidential because there's no record of that, but it wouldn't surprise me ... a lot of guys took on off-the-record assignments from a sense of their duty and obligation. And, as to PST kicking in late ... my old man who served in WWII always appeared level headed and mentally stable. But during his last eight hours before he left this Earth, he had an unexpected and extreme series of flashbacks in the hospital while I was by his side. It scared the crap out of doctors, nurses and me ... ordering us to take cover, to drop to the floor so he could protect us from the enemy."

John's mouth opens and remains that way for a few seconds with nothing coming out. Then he says, "Hell, seeing what he was seeing through those flashbacks had to have brought back awful memories. I'm sorry for him."

"I'm not too sure of that. Maybe those memories never left him, but he couldn't keep it to himself any longer. I don't know." Hoskins sniffles.

John knows he's got to wade through this information to figure out a truth or two. Deep in his gut he wants to dig as deep as possible and in as many places as he can find. Rule 1 ... there isn't anything that's not unimportant. Rule 2 ... suspect everyone. Rule 3 ... small observations lead to large and unexpected revelations. Rule 4 ... compartmentalizing comes from not giving a crap. He pauses to take it all in. Then he asks Hoskins a question. "How do you know so much about Jeff?"

"Can't talk about that. Let's just leave it there. OK?"

John doesn't push it any further for now, but this business about Jeff seems more than a stretch. "OK."

Hoskins says, "Oh, one more thing."

"Yeah."

"Work under the assumption that Abrams is not what he claims to be. He could be dangerous."

The phones disconnect.

John still can't believe any of this. He, himself, has been in security work for a very long time, and has seen it all ... at least a substantial amount ... drunks, drug addicts, killers, liars, just to name a few ... but nothing like this. Sure, he's heard of cops gone to the other side through temptations, compulsions, retributions, revenges, and paybacks, but those were in large metropolitan cities. This is different. He's worked with Jeff … closely enough to know when someone isn't what they claim to be. And Detective Jeff Abrams doesn't fit that profile.

This might be the last time he and Hoskins speak of their conversation about Abrams … but then again life has a way of changing things.

Great!

CHAPTER 24

In Jeff's nightmare he's again confronted by a person of unidentifiable gender wearing a mask, ski cap, gloves, and dark clothes carrying an AK-47. There is a continuous drum noise that makes it difficult for him to understand anything else.

The person with the AK-47 points the weapon at him, and says, "It's your turn."

There is a loud explosion with an assortment of colored flashes all around that throws him back a few feet. Then, everything suddenly goes silent and fades out.

He wakes up, damp with a cold sweat, and trembling. His mouth is dry.

Lady, his adopted dog, is now only a few inches away from him. Her ears are folded and her eyes are worried, just like all the other times. She seems to understand something.

"Sorry it's happened again."

Lady squeaks out a sound of understanding and sympathy. Then she finds a good spot to lower herself onto the floor alongside the bed.

Jeff gets up and heads for the bathroom as Lady follows close behind as if she loses eye contact with him something awful will happen.

He takes a long look at his face in the mirror. He doesn't like what he sees but he's seen it so often he's not surprised. He washes his hands, neck and face.

Lady, now in the doorway keeps watching him as he opens the medicine cabinet that is lined with a row of brown, green, and yellow bottles ... each separately for anti-anxiety, painkiller, and anti-inflammatory. He selects the ones he thinks best fit his current needs and then swallows them, followed by a glass of tap water. He turns to Lady, "I wish I didn't have to."

Lady lets out a squeaky sound of understanding and at the same time disapproval, but she can just do so much.

Usually, there's only a little margin of error when someone does a wrong ... legally and/or morally. You've got to be exact at the right time. Crimes of any sort are not done in a vacuum. There's always some evidence left behind ... as well as stupidity.

Jeff is determined to find out who put an end to Prairie's life and why, although he has some ideas as to the reason. The situation is not simple, rather quite complex, and for the most part anyone else who'll investigate will probably give up early and let the case run cold ... but not him ... not a chance in hell that happening. Yet he needs help from someone he can trust ... totally ... an outsider ... maybe even trade one help for another ... off duty.

Jeff stands outside Lilli's apartment building feeling anxious for some reason, but not really ... he knows why. He doesn't know her all that well but for the short time with her and listening to John rave about her, he figures she's his best bet. He could even help her out in the Conroy case if she asked … maybe.

She isn't the woman in his life that he's never had … make that loved … nothing like that, or to the best of his knowledge she isn't currently married, engaged or living with someone as an inseparable couple … no nothing like that. But he's talked with buddies he's known over the years after a few beers … make that several … and they've all said the same thing. There is always one woman you remember the most that made your hormones boil and you lusted after her. Not like all the other women who were simply fun to be with, made you laugh, and feel good … end of night. It's the one you never forget, and it's the one you lost because it was your sorry ass fault … you were stupid, inconsiderate, insensitive, and selfish. In other words, you let your ego get in the way. And then when you think about her, it's painful.

But for Jeff, it's not that personal with Lilli … or so he wants to convince himself but obviously not successfully at the moment. So why is he thinking about it right now? Is he lying to himself to protect a fragile ego and his past mistakes? He's still in love with his divorced wife and will forever, he's sure.

His thoughts and feelings pass. He's onto another mission. He now feels the effects of the capsules he swallowed earlier this morning … prescriptions from a medical doctor, not someone else with a loose hand eager to support an expensive life style … or from a drug dealer.

He presses the button to Lilli's apartment, but there's no response. He tries a second time and then a third time with the same result. He hesitates, turns and is about to walk away when he turns around again. He notices the name

Betty Manners, Apartment Manager, on the directory. He presses the button to Betty's apartment.

"Yes, how can I help you?"

Jeff recognizes a female voice. "Yes, I'm here to see Lilli Jackson, but no one is answering. Do you know when she'll return?"

"Sorry, I don't keep track of the residents." There is a pause. "But I got a nice one bedroom that's for rent … just became available. Move-in condition. I can show it to you now if you want. Huh?"

Jeff doesn't think, even for a split second, as he stays quiet. Then he hears a click from the speaker indicating the short conversation has ended. Then he turns and walks away.

It only takes him less than fifteen minutes to get to his parked vehicle … actually an unmarked police vehicle issued to him by the City. He notices how dirty it is … dark colored vehicles tend to show off the grime more noticeably than light colored ones. He makes a mental note to get it washed soon.

On most days, after his meds kick in, he feels pretty good about his life, but this isn't one of them. There are too many ideas bouncing around in his brain that seem to be determined on colliding with each other. He could use a drink of bourbon right now, but he knows better … don't mix booze with work with meds … a dangerous trifecta. He decides on a good cup of coffee … not what he gets at work.

He unlocks the dirty car's door with one efficient press of a small button attached to the ignition key. He heads towards an independently owned and local coffee shop …

not the franchised ones with fancy-smancy ludicrous names of coffee drinks with high prices and stupid music humming through ceiling speakers inside and speakers that are outside as well.

Traffic is light. He reaches *The Coffee Roasting Place* within fifteen minutes. The *Place* is located in a small shopping center containing a local grocery store, a women's clothing shop, a pizza place, and a movie theater that is across the street from a branch of the City's library. Parking is ample and it's free.

It only takes him five minutes to walk to *The Coffee Roasting Place* from where he parks.

Once he steps inside the *Place*, the aroma of freshly roasted coffee beans fills his nostrils. He knows exactly what he wants … a large dark roast coffee with no room for milk, cream, or sugar. It costs him $3.50. He leaves a $0.50 tip in a tray next to the cash register, turns, and spots an empty seat outside. He feels good.

Next to his seat is a woman-man couple, about his age, talking and drinking their beverages. He suspects they're not married since he doesn't see any wedding rings on either person's hand, but in these times that's not necessarily a factor. He sits down without acknowledging them, as they remain focused on each other … fine by him. He has other things to think about.

The first sip is usually the best. This time is no exception. Then, the couple's conversation drifts to his ears, so he listens. So much for the other things he intended to think about. That'll just have to wait a while.

The man says, "Both of my parents were heavy smokers … Camels all the way with mom but dad preferred

Marlboros. The house smelled of smoke all the time, even times when my eyes would tear and burn. The only worse place was inside the car, especially when the windows were closed."

She nods and says, "Same here, but I don't remember the brands. My father loved the pipe as well as cigars. I sort of enjoyed … only occasionally … the smell of the pipe." She takes a sip of coffee.

"Did you ever smoke?" He asks and then mirrors her taking a sip of coffee.

"No way, I never had any desire whatsoever. That's not to say there wasn't pressure from my high school friends." She pauses and then asks, "And what about you?"

"I wasn't a smoker in high school either, and like you there was a lot of pressure from my friends to be cool, but when I went away to college that changed. I not only started to smoke but drink. Hell, I got caught up in fraternity life." He shakes his head and shrugs his shoulders for emphasis.

She curls her nose in disapproval, but doesn't verbalize anything …she doesn't have to … it's obvious.

He continues as if he didn't pick up on her behavior or else he just didn't care. "Cigarettes, coffee, and beer … I kept it up throughout four years in college. Somehow that combination made each taste good to me. Crazy … huh?" He laughs.

She frowns and her back stiffens. "I really can't imagine that … it sounds so disgusting."

"Well, everyone has pleasures." He pauses, "What's yours?" He grins as he takes another sip of coffee.

She crosses her arms and tightens her lips. Then she speaks, but not as a response to his question. "Smoking is totally unhealthy … and only moderation in alcohol and coffee is OK."

"Oh."

She slightly leans towards him. "I know you drink coffee … that's obvious … but do you still smoke and drink alcohol?"

Jeff is now totally into listening to their conversation and he suspects they don't even realize it. He glances at the man while he prepares his answer.

Most people don't know how to lie effectively. Only a few are experts at it. The experts don't mess up with the big thing, but more importantly, they're also experts with the small things. You've got to be an expert with both the big and small things. Most people fail at the small details.

Jeff takes in a slow but deep breath of air. The man sitting next to him smells of cheap tobacco. Jeff watches as the man tilts his head backwards showing a shortened and upturned nose. Then he tries to smile but it is more like a nervous quiver of his lips and fast blinking of his eyes. The man glances away for a slit second to surprisingly catch Jeff's stare.

Jeff shakes his head sideways … don't do this … you'll only get one opportunity … but it's your choice to make.

The man says, "I never again want to be trapped …." He is unable to continue with the lie, so he tells the truth. "Bars aren't the same without them. And the hell with vaping … that's probably worse. I enjoy smoking and drinking alcohol … beer, whiskey, wine, whatever." He grinds his teeth together. "That's who I am."

She stands, grabs hold of her coffee cup and squarely looks into his eyes. "That's what these speed-dating meet-ups are all about. Thanks for your honesty. Unless I personally inform you otherwise, I'm looking for a different kind of guy ... not you." She walks away leaving him alone with his coffee.

CHAPTER 25

The good news is that Lilli's return drive back to update Camille Conroy's parents on the final determination of her death might bring some closure, but the bad news is that it most likely won't. They'll want to know more specifically as to how … and therefore more unanswered questions for them. Further, they'll probably never know enough specifics to ease their pain.

The sun is into Lilli's eyes as Natalie peacefully sits in a designed backseat for children, secured safety. But in a short time the moon will appear as the sun will disappear.

Lilli keeps the air conditioner off, even with the outside temperature coaxing her to use it. It's all a matter of saving a few dollars … less miles to the gallon when the air conditioner is on … it's that simple, and she's got to find as many ways to keep expenses as low as possible until she finds the right high paying job … if ever.

She figures she's about half way to the Conroy's place when she spots ahead a flashing signal along with two construction workers with flags slowing down traffic. She has to stop the car and wait for one of the workers to tell her something.

Now close enough to recognize the worker approaching her as a female, Lilli takes a deep breath of air, preparing for the worse.

"Two car – two truck accident ahead. This road will be closed for a while … not sure how long. Your best bet is to turn around … I'll direct you across the median." She waits for Lilli's response as she looks up ahead to see vehicles already making the U-turn.

"OK, I'll take you up on the turn-around."

Within a few minutes Lilli waits in line for the vehicles ahead of her to head back to wherever they came from. Now her turn, she complies with hand instructions from the female construction worker to do the same. She is waved through.

Lilli's thoughts jump back to the Conroy's wondering if she should update them by making a call instead of in person, face-to-face. What choices does she have … call to update them, call to tell them of the traffic delay, or don't call at all. Most people want to know what's going on.

She drives a few miles when she spots a rest stop … truckers mostly, but occasionally a few cars as well. She pulls off the road, parks her car in the designated *Cars Only* section, and then turns to Natalie, still secure in the back seat, and still asleep. How wonderful if everyone could sleep as soundly as children … many, but not all.

Then she pulls her cell out to talk with the Conroy's. She hears Barbara's voice. "Hello?"

"It's me, Lilli. I was on my way to talk with you and Henry about an update on Camille's situation, but there's been a multi-vehicle accident that closed down the highway.

Don't know when I'd arrive at your place to talk face-to-face, so I thought the next best was to call. OK to talk now?"

"Sure." Her voice sounds a bit shaky, but expected under the circumstances.

"OK, here's what I've been told." Lilli clears her throat. "The case of death has been changed from suicide to asphyxiation. In other words, water in the lungs."

Barbara asks, "You mean drowning?"

"Exactly, but they still don't know what caused the drowning … an accident maybe, or self-infliction is a possibility, or was there another person or other people involved. I wish I had more definitive information. I'm really sorry." The pause in the conversation provides a short time for her to think to herself … "Even though the cause of Camille's death is now known … drowning … the parents will still be living with not knowing who specifically was responsible. To them this unknown will continue to haunt them, she's sure." The private thought now passed, Lilli only hears the sound of silence. "Hello, are you still there Barbara?"

A weakened and soft voice says, "Yes, thank you."

Then the phones disconnect.

Lilli continues to sit in the car unsettled, wishing she could have done more to comfort Camille's mother, and once her father is told, him as well. Not much of a comfort for anyone.

Suicides are more difficult to deal with than homicides … the family of the deceased as well as the investigators. When someone is murdered by another person or persons, there is someone else specific to blame. But with a suicide the victim and the murderer are one in the same.

Lilli steps out of the car, reaches to the back seat to take hold of Natalie, locks the car doors and slowly walks into the rest stop area, tightly holding onto her precious child in her arms.

The rest area is identified as *Jaso Rest Area*, named after Master Sergeant Stephen Jaso of the United Stated Marines who had lived in the area before volunteering in the military, only to lose his life during a brutal war. There are signs explaining in more detail about the Marine, his military service, and his family.

There is a stream behind the bathrooms with a few Adirondack-styled wooden tables and chairs for travelers to rest as they listen to the even flow of its water … peaceful and comforting. Lilli takes a seat holding onto Natalie.

At night time, this place is also a popular spot for teenagers to party, usually leaving behind empty beer bottles and cigarette butts … and occasionally used condoms.

Wild animals like deer, bear, and rabbit have never been reported, but that's not to say they could have been present but not spotted.

They're never been any dead human bodies found at *Jaso Rest Area*, but that fact is about to change.

Lilli checks her wristwatch and is surprised she's been sitting in an Adirondack-styled wooden chair for a longer time than expected. She probably needed the rest and solitude. The sun has just set as the moon winks its appearance. The peacefulness is about to be cancelled.

An ambulance is the first to arrive, followed by a clearly marked Schoharie Emergency Management Authority vehicle containing one State employee with several civilian volunteers.

The ambulance doors open before the vehicle is at a complete stop. Then EMTs jump out and then roll out a gurney with amazing precision and speed. Their faces, male and female, are serious looking ... all business. They rush to a slant by the stream where a victim lies still, not going anyplace except to the morgue.

Lilli stands up, holding onto Natalie with even greater intensity, to get a better look. But she is quickly halted by a female civilian volunteer, and thus is not able to walk closer to the body yet she is still able to recognize some of the characteristics ... a Caucasian female, average height, slight build, brown hair, and probably in her early twenties. Lilli can't see a watch around the wrist of her left hand, and an engagement and wedding rings on her delicate fingers. Dirt covers most of her body, but it looks as if she is dressed in blue jeans, a dark colored shirt, and sneakers without socks. But that is just one of the victims.

A child, no more than two or three years old, lies beside her. There is so much dirt covering the second victim that is takes a closer examination to determine the child is also female.

Lilli shivers involuntarily as the two bodies are moved into the ambulance and then it drives away.

As if things couldn't become stranger, the unimaginable becomes the reality. Lilli hears her cell phone beckon.

"Hello?"

"I know you don't know me, and I'm sorry to be calling you like this, but your boss, John Walker, said it'd be OK. I'm Detective Parsons with the Green Island Police Department."

She's sure she doesn't know the man nor has John ever mentioned him to her. "I'm having a little problem in hearing you." She walks away from the Adirondack-styled chair with one hand holding the phone and the other hand holding onto Natalie to see if that improves the connection.

"I can hear you fine," Parsons says.

"OK, now's better. Who are you again?"

"Your boss, John Walker, and I go way-back. He said it was OK to call you directly. I'm Detective Parsons with the Green Island Police Department."

"Oh." That's about all she can think of to say.

"I'll get right to the point. It's about Eric Jackson. You know him … right … married for a short time."

"Yeah, my ex. … something he's done … in some sort of trouble? How did he know where I worked?"

"He told us you worked in a security job, but didn't know the name of the company. That's why I called John to see if he had heard of you. Just lucky I called John. And yeah, he's definitely in trouble, and he's asked to speak with you face-to-face about it."

She feels her heart rate accelerate, angry and confused. "What did he do?"

"He's confessed to killing someone … walked into our Police Station and gave himself up."

"Why talk with me?" She feels herself getting angrier. She knows somewhere in the back of her mind that her anger is reasonable, that it's coming from a dark place that she's still trying to ignore.

"He said you're the only one who will listen and understand."

"I'm not a psychiatrist or social worker. We split. And I want to forget about him." She closes her eyes, wanting to shut out the conversation.

"Well, I understand. He wrote out a confession, but there are chunks of missing information he says he can't remember about what he said he did."

She quickly moves into law enforcement talk. "Isn't that called guilty knowledge?"

"So, you are familiar with people like him."

"I'm a fast learner and John is a great coach." She gives a slight nod of her head. "Has he lawyered up?"

"No."

"But he confessed … isn't that what you said?"

"He laid it all out. He made a confession to me saying he wanted to have sex with her, but she didn't, so he killed her."

She pauses, unable to process that information. Then she asks, "How long did it take for him to confess?"

"He screwed around for an hour or so, and then I turned up the conversation to find the truth. So many people have this sense of hubris … that they can get away with committing a crime. Killings of passion are compulsive and uncontrollable."

"So, his reasoning for killing her was what?" She still can't believe it.

"Reasoning … hell, he's a whacko!" He takes off his glasses to clean the lenses as if that will make it more clearly for him to understand her question.

"And then what happened?" She shakes her head, still in disbelief.

"I read him his rights again. He said he understood. Then, I formally accused him of the crime and put him in a holding cell."

"When did he ask to speak with me?" She frowns.

"On the way to the cell."

"Did you get his confession on tape?"

"Oh, yeah, the entire conversation was recorded … audio and video. He was a compelling witness against himself."

"So, everything makes sense to you?" She's still in disbelief.

"This kind of crime never makes sense."

"No anger during the interview … interrogation … conversation … whatever it is called?"

"Not usually a trait from whackos."

"Can I see the interrogation video?"

"Nope … you're not law enforcement with a need to know. Sorry."

"Do you know the identity of the victim?"

"We're working on it."

"So, you haven't found the body … is that what you're saying?"

"Like I said, we're working on it."

Parsons is very certain Eric Jackson committed the crime but Lilli isn't. He might have been a dip-head to her, but killing someone is ruthless.

She finds herself breathing rapidly and heavily on the phone. Then she says aloud, "But you don't have the victim's body!"

"That's correct. We don't yet."

"So again, why does Eric want to talk with me?"

"I wish I really knew that answer. He seemed quite awkward … and, excuse me for saying this, but scared witless. I'm just trying to make sure his legal rights are not violated, so that's why I called you … nothing more. Just following the rules."

"Maybe he wants to use me … to take back what he confessed."

"Most do … he'll say he was confused …that he didn't do it." Parsons pauses. "Listen, I'm sorry for having to had brought you into this, but it's entirely your decision on whether you'll see him or not. You don't have any legal requirements."

"Detective Parsons, I appreciate hearing that. Right now, I'm not in a good place in my life to even spend one tiny second with him. So, what I'm saying is tell him a big nope. He's on his own."

"I understand. Sorry again to have brought this to you. Good-bye."

The phones disconnect before she can reply.

While Natalie slept straight through the night, Lilli couldn't get half-way close to that herself. The phone conversation with Barbara Conroy, the death of a mother and her baby daughter, and then the talk with Detective Parsons about Eric were too much for her brain to process.

After making breakfast for Natalie and herself the next morning, she makes an unexpected decision to visit Eric. Maybe the gesture, as small as it may seem, will have a positive effect. She calls Ginger hoping the teenager is free to babysit Natalie on such a short notice. Bingo, wishes sometimes do come true.

Lilli decides not to contact Parsons about her change of mind, yet instead calls John for the specific address of the Green Island Police Department. John doesn't press her for any information, yet acknowledges he spoke with Parsons yesterday and admits he probably should have reached out to her directly rather than giver her number to Parsons. He asks when she'll return to work. She promises he can count on her for the upcoming Monday but doesn't comment on him giving her number out.

To a surprised Detective Parsons, Lilli offers a firm handshake with little more than a few words in a greeting that he seems to gladly reciprocate.

Then she follows him and a uniformed police officer down a long and narrow hallway where there are five steel doors with iron bars on each side. The bottom half of each door is metal while the top half of each door has iron bars. At the bottom of each door is a slot to pass through a food tray, and each door has a key-locking mechanism at waist high.

Lilli keeps her focus straight ahead without looking to her left or right, yet she can see out of the corner of each eye male prisoners glaring at her that almost creeps her out.

Halfway down the hallway the uniformed police officer stops. "Wait here."

Parsons and Lilli stop on command as they see the uniformed police officer take out of his pocket a large metal key. He then glances between the iron bars on the top half of the metal door to make sure the prisoner isn't preparing to make trouble. The breakfast food tray is still lodged in the slot at the bottom of the door … something isn't right.

"Oh crap!" The uniformed police officer inserts the large metal key into the lock, turning the bolt to open the door. Then he murmurs something as he pulls open the door.

Eric Jackson lays on the floor of the cell with, most likely, more blood on the cell floor than inside his motionless body. He is dead.

A few feet away on the cell floor is a six inch long ballpoint pen that, after investigation, is proven to be Eric's weapon of choice. Why the pen wasn't taken from him from the onset is unknown.

Parsons moves quickly to the side of the uniformed police officer. He rubs his face with both hands. "Damn." He motions with a straight-arm pointed at Lilli. "Don't come any closer."

On the drive back she stops off at a restaurant, but not for the food. It's late in the afternoon.

Lilli is the only one at the restaurant's bar. She's drinking a Chardonnay that tastes bitter, not the flavor she's looking for … make that she needs … at the moment. Too many events happening too fast, none of which are what you'd call pleasant.

She finds herself just gazing straight ahead at no one or nothing specific, something that is quite the opposite of her typical behavior. She favors direct eye contact because she's learned that she could often learn more about a person by how they behave than the words they use … not always but definitely enough times.

The bartender disrupts her inner thoughts. "How's the Chardonnay?" Her name tag reads *Stella*. Her eyes are magnetic, not so much beautiful, but rather powerful, balanced, composed as if she is someone you could trust, to talk to, without hearing any critique or judgement … ideal for a great bartender. About the same statue as Lilli … and even about the same age … someone you feel comfortable with.

"Haven't really fully decided."

Stella says, "You don't like it."

Lilli is surprised, but shouldn't be. Hell, the woman is a professional bartender. Duh! "You're good." Lilli nods a few times to compliment her words.

"Here, let me replace it with something a little sweeter." Stella reaches for the glass of wine between them and moves it away. Then she turns to a bottle labeled *Venache'*, and fills a fresh wine glass with it. She smiles and places it in front of Lilli.

"You didn't have to do that."

"I know, but I did." Stella lifts her head slightly upward as she says, "Try it."

Lilli takes in a quick breath of air and then lets it drift away before she takes a small sip. Her voice is almost intimate in sound. She tries to separate from Stella's gaze, but that seems to be difficult. "Yes, much better."

"You wanna talk about what's bothering you? You can always trust a bartender." Her voice is steady and calming and her smile appears sincere. Further, Lilli is her only customer at the moment.

Lilli doesn't hesitate. "I think I'm supposed to find the truth."

Stella doesn't move, blink, or seem to breathe. She just listens.

"My only marriage ended in a no-fault divorce. I have sole custody of a beautiful daughter, Natalie. I work my ass off in a job I don't really like that much but my boss is a gem … one in a million. I get paid enough to cover my bills and put a few dollars aside just in case. My best friend from high school recently died … circumstances very weird and her parents asked me to find the truth about her death. Then my ex who was in jail for something asked to talk with me about something. For what reason, I have no freakin' idea. I initially refused but then on my own without telling anyone, I went to the Police Department where he was jailed. He was dead in his jail cell." She pauses to take another sip of wine, but this time more than a tiny sip. Her eyes stare into the glass.

Stella keeps her position in silence. But when Lilli blinks a few times, now looking directly at her, Stella slightly nods her head as if to say, "I understand," without uttering any words.

Lilli continues, yet her right hand remains clasped around the stem of the wine glass. "Hell, I'm not an investigative detective. I just work for a property security firm as a Public Safety Officer." She takes another taste of wine this time returning to a small sip, places the glass on the top of the bar and removes her hand away. She puffs out some air through her nose. "But I've got to find the truth."

"Find the truth to what?" Stella doesn't think the question is unfair, but it's her first instinct.

Lilli frowns and shrugs her shoulders ever so slightly. Then she says, "To what the real cause of Camille's death."

"Camille is your high school friend?"

Lilli's fingers start to tremble, "Yeah." She takes a breath of air, nods and says, "I'll take another one." She quickly gulps the remaining wine and then slightly slides the empty glass towards Stella.

By the time Lilli gets back to her apartment she finds both Ginger and Natalie sound asleep. She nudges Ginger just enough to wake her on the couch. They talk for a very short time when all of a sudden Lilli feels exhausted, something that Ginger easily recognizes way before Lilli does. After being paid, Ginger leaves, and Lilli trudges to bed but without first checking her cell for any incoming calls. If she had she would have known that Barbara Conroy had called twice.

Early the next morning, but after Natalie has awaken, Lilli's cell buzzes as she lays in bed feeling somewhat rested, but not entirely. She almost decides to let the call go to voicemail, but then decides otherwise. She reaches for the cell without checking caller-ID. "Hello." Her voice is soft and almost inaudible.

"Lilli Jackson?"

She recognizes the voice. Now she is suddenly fully awake. She sits up in bed. "Barbara, is this you?"

Her voice was typically musical sounding … not suggesting any pain or discomfort … unless … of course … she talked about her daughter, Camille. But why is Barbara calling her now? She sounds troubled.

"Yes, it's me. I'm sorry to call you, but … well … I thought you'd want to know." There's nothing musical about the voice.

Lilli hears a broken-sounding voice accompanied by sniffles. "Barbara, what's the matter?"

Barbara Conroy cries for a few seconds, and then managers to say, "Henry had a heart attack that …." She isn't able to finish the sentence.

"Is he in the hospital? Is that where he is?"

Barbara's sniffles subside and the crying stops. She manages to say, "He was the love of my life. I already miss him."

Before Lilli can stop herself she asks a question that she's quite sure she already knows the answer. "What do you mean?"

Barbara's voice stutters, "He – he's passed away." The crying restarts.

It's not only her daughter but now her husband. Lilli wonders how she will be able to find a way to stay composed. She closes her eyes, nods her head to confirm what she's about to say. "Barbara, listen to me. Natalie and I will leave immediately. We'll be there as quickly as possible. OK?"

Barbara's response is delayed for a few seconds while the crying settles down to nothing. "Oh, Lilli, you don't need to … really … please … you don't."

"Not only do I need to but I want to. Stay strong. We'll be there as soon as we can."

"Bless you, my dear."

Lilli hears Lucky barking in the background. She smiles.

Today's the day she promised John she'd report back to work, but things have unexpectedly changed for the worse. John's a great guy, and she doesn't want to take advantage of him. She hopes he'll understand what she has to do.

She wonders to herself ... "What is love? It this thing called love attainable or is it essentially irrelevant. For those up in age it means a few days, months, or a couple of years at most. But really, what is this thing called love? Is it totally and eternally truth even if the truth hurts? Or, is it a version of truth to protect the one you love ... even yourself? Is it worth it? Who cares ... anybody?"

She holds onto her cell phone, firmly in her hand's grasp. She knows what she has to do and she's willing to accept the consequences. She calls John, although she's not sure if he's at work yet. If not, she'll just leave a voice message saying she's got to talk with him about something very important ... something quite unexpected has come up that needs her undivided attention. Also, she's hoping that Ginger is able to help her out again.

Gray skies have opened up as Lilli drives to meet with John, but this time it starts to rain. She wonders if the weather may portend some kind of omen.

She faces John at his office, each holding a cup of coffee ... some of the worse tasting stuff you'll ever drink. He sits behind his desk while she sits in front.

"You sounded concerned about something on the phone. Natalie OK?" He takes a sip of the nasty tasting brew, but doesn't seem to care one way or another about how it tastes, or maybe he just likes the taste.

She mimics his action, but unlike John, she grimaces at its taste. Her mouth then sets in place as if it's from years of reactions to terrible things she's seen or been through personally in life. But the truth of the matter is that she feels terrible about what she's about to tell him. Then, slowly and clearly, Lilli tells John as he attentively listens without a miniscule of reaction.

When she finishes John takes his turn. "People in general, not everyone, have a sense about things, not everything, but you know what I mean. Anyway, most do ... both cops and civilians. Sometimes it's the way they say it, sometimes it's what they specifically say or don't say, and sometimes it's all of that. I guess what I'm saying is that you had a talk with her ... she called you ... acted at first a little strange and you thought it was odd. But you waited 'til she told you everything. You listened."

"Yeah, she told me and I just listened." She begins to fell a bit more settled. She lets out a breath of air.

"And you did the right thing."

Lilli feels relieved. "So, you understand why I need to be with her right now. I've got to be by her side ... I don't know for how long, but I ... uh ... well ... just feel I must. You understand ... don't you?"

"Believe me ... I completely get it."

Lilli's eyes look relieved. "Thanks, I appreciate hearing that from you."

"Sure, not a problem." He waves his hand towards her as if to dismiss what he's just said but they both know he supports her. He pauses and then his eyes light up. "Here's a crazy idea." He sees her eyes mimic how he feels.

She learns forward, "OK, I'm all ears."

"You're gonna have a lot of time with Mrs. Conroy and Natalie ... time to help her heal ... to recover ... if she can ever. Anyway, I know you're not satisfied with the official cause of Camille's death. You could, on your own, investigate it further. You're smart, strong, and sensitive. But I'd be very careful who you talk with. Know what I mean?"

She nods in agreement. "But I can call you for advice ... right?"

"Definitely." Before he can stop himself he unintentionally ignores the advice Hoskins recently gave him, although he personally doesn't buy Hoskins' assessment. "And you probably could call Jeff ... maybe even convince him to help you on the case." He shrugs his shoulders. "I really don't know if he'd be interested or if he has any jurisdiction, but if you don't ask you'll never know." He shrugs his shoulders again. "Just an idea that popped into my mind ... take it for what it's worth." He tightens his jaw now wondering if the idea of contacting Jeff is really a good idea, but he keeps that thought to himself.

Lilli ignores his facial change. "I know my pay will end. I've got a small savings I can tap into. And, staying with Barbara won't cost me a thing.

"So, you'll give up your apartment to live with her. You think that's a good idea?"

"I've paid for the full month in advance, so I've got a few weeks remaining. I'm not going to give it up or pack everything to take with me. I'll see what happens."

"You know you can always come back here. I know it's not your dream job, but they'll always be a place for you here."

She feels her eyes moisten and can't hold back extending her arms to wrap around him. "I owe you so much." She starts to cry.

"Now, now, you don't owe me anything." He keeps his arms wrapped around her. "Call me once in a while ... just stay in touch. OK?"

She sniffles. "I promise."

Now alone, John turns to the Felix-The-Cat clock on the wall that always looks happy to see him, regardless of what he says or what he does. Felix always seems to be smiling at him, reminding him of his own father named Felix Walker, whose love and devotion to him was amazing and constant.

Lilli steps outside after talking with John. The rain has ended for the time being and the streets and sidewalks seem to be drying up at a remarkable rate of speed. Her car, while needing a good wash-job, seems cleaner now than before she entered John's office. The colors of the buildings, vehicles, people's clothing and everything else that she sees are now some of the most beautiful colors she ever remembers seeing. She smiles.

Everyone needs someone like a lighthouse that ships see on the sea.

The return drive to her apartment seems quicker than the trip from it to see John.

She informs Betty Manners, the on-site-apartment manager about her plans, confirms that she's paid-up for the entire month, and asks Betty to hold onto her mail until she returns. She gives Betty her cell phone number just in case they need to talk for some reason.

Then she returns to her apartment to explain to Ginger what she's up to, although it's really unnecessary.

Once Ginger is paid and after they hug to say goodbye, Lilli starts packing a few things as Natalie watches her with great curiosity.

"Everything is just fine, honey. We're helping out someone who really needs help at this time. And ... we'll see Lucky again ... won't that be great." She reaches over to kiss Natalie. "I don't know what I'd do without you. I love you so very ... very ... much."

Natalie somehow gets the gist what her mother is saying as she moves her arms and giggles with pleasure.

"Just a few more things to pack ... and we'll be on our way."

Natalie restarts moving her arms around as she giggles again.

In a few minutes less than an hour, two suitcases and three boxes are stuffed with items Lilli thinks she and her daughter will need during the stay with Barbara, although presently no one really knows how long that will be. She takes one last tour of her apartment just in case she might have missed something … nothing is obvious.

Now standing in the small living room with Natalie still playing on the floor, she decides to inform Barbara of her status and ask a few questions. It takes only one ring before she hears Barbara's voice.

"Hello?"

"Barbara, this is Lilli. Natalie and I are about to leave my place, but before we do, I have a few questions to ask you. OK?"

"Sure." The sound of her voice however, is less convincing than the one word answer.

"It's about Camille. I've just been wondering about a few things, and I might have time to check them out."

There is a delay in Barbara's response, except for the breathing that Lilli easily hears on the phone.

"OK, what is it you want to know?" Barbara's voice is stronger than just a second or two before.

Lilli asks, "Did Camille have any boyfriends during or right after high school? I've been thinking about that for some reason and I don't remember her dating much in school, but then again, although we were friends, she never mentioned boyfriends to me, and honestly, I never asked."

Barbara asks, "Boyfriends ... why's that important?"

"Motive includes people ... family ... friends ... lovers ... that sort of stuff."

Barbara thinks for a short time. "Not during high school that I remember."

"Oh, so after she graduated ... is that what you're saying?"

"Jack ... oh what's his last name?" Barbara notices her own fingers tightly clenched together. "I only met him once or twice and we ... he and I ... didn't hit it off very well ... didn't approve of each other. Oh, what's his last name?"

"Why was that ... didn't approve of each other?"

"He treated Camille as the flavor of the month ... no one really special, just someone when he was bored. I think he got arrested for something or the other ... more than once I think. I tried to convince her he wasn't good for her ... that he didn't really care one penny's worth about her ... but he seemed to be the only one who gave her any attention at all. I didn't know anything about his family ... if they were local or not. But him ... no way Henry and I were going to let him get close to our baby." Her eyes tear up and Lucky jumps on her lap.

"So, I think I hear you saying that he had a reputation ... but for what?"

"Weird, eccentric, looked at people in strange ways. And honestly, never came across as having any sense of courtesy or respect for others. I don't know what others thought of him." She pauses, looks at Lucky still on her lap who returns a stare of her own to Barbara ... love. "Glass, that's his last name! His name is Jack Glass ... G L A S S!"

"Did he drink alcohol or take drugs that you were aware of … and what about Camille?"

"Definitely not Camille, neither drugs or alcohol, but him, I wouldn't put it past him if he did both… but I really don't know." She repeats for emphasis, "But definitely not Camille, my daughter. I'll swear on a stack of Bibles."

"Anything else about Jack Glass," Lilli asks?

Barbara hesitates, thinking about something, and then says. "He had a scar on the tip of his nose and just above his right nostril. Not noticeable at first, but it was there. Don't know how it happened, but it wouldn't surprise me if it was from a fight or something like that."

Lilli wonders if this guy named Jack Glass is still around. It might be useful if she could talk with him … to get his take on the situation. But how does she do that? She's got no professional investigative background, reputation or license to investigate, but she could make a few phone calls, namely John and Jeff. Which one should she try first? She hesitates to think about it. She's already talked with John so many times, so she figures it's time to give Jeff a call. She's got nothing to lose and John mentioned he might help her.

She ends her conversation with Barbara. "I'll see you as quickly as I can."

"OK, I'm so happy you're going to spent time with me … drive safely … love." Lucky barks.

As soon as the phones disconnect, Lilli calls Jeff. He picks up after the first ring, "Detective Abrams."

"Jeff, this is Lilli Jackson. Do you have a few minutes to spare?"

Jeff is taken by surprise in spite of hearing from John that she might call him for some help. He clears his throat. "This is a surprise … a nice one. How are you?"

She's happy to have caught him so easily, and apparently by his voice and words he's happy she called. "Fine … thanks … and you?"

How bland can you get?

He's sure the pleasantries are over with. "Good." Now he's ready to get down to business. "How can I help you?"

She picks up on his change to a professional tone. Maybe that's good … just keep everything professional. "Did John update you on what I'm up to?"

He keeps it professional, "Yeah … but only briefly … that you'd be with Mrs. Conroy to help her out during her grieving stage for the loss of her husband. That's awfully nice of you."

"Yeah, I don't know how well I would have handled it myself if I were in her shoes." She pauses. "But there's more to it, and John mentioned that you might be willing to help me out."

"And what's that?"

"So, John didn't tell you everything."

"Like I said, it was brief. He might have but why don't you tell me."

"I'm gonna try to help Barbara Conroy find out what really happened to Camille … more specifically her death by drowning. And I've got a name to give you … if you could and would get me some details about him … a boyfriend of sorts. You've got access to arrest records, convictions, prison time and so forth that I don't have." She waits for his response that seems to be delayed in coming, or maybe it's just her high sense of urgency.

"Sure, give me his name."

Relieved, she says, "Jack Glass. That's G L A S S. He dated Camille a short time after high school but her parents were always suspicious of him … his motives and interest in their daughter … acted in a weird-type of way according to Barbara."

"Sure, shouldn't take me long … less than an hour is my bet. I'll get back to you. How does that sound?"

Lilli is more than pleased. "I owe you big time … maybe I can buy you a drink at some time."

He says, "I'll keep you to your word," although he'd like more than a drink … way more.

"I'm headed for the Conroy house now, so I'll be driving. Don't want to drive and talk at the same time so if you get a voice just leave a message and I'll pull over to stop and call back. OK?"

"Sounds like a plan … an hour at most … drive safely."

The phones disconnect.

She's been on the road with Natalie for a little over an hour since talking with Jeff but no call yet. At least she's making good time in getting to Barbara's place. Up ahead the road looks clear with few vehicles traveling in either direction. At least she's thankful for no delays. Natalie is secured in her car seat in the back.

Up ahead is a slight downgrade where the road descends slightly but noticeably so that she can't see that far.

There is a **STOP** sign that she can barely make out, but what is readily noticeable is a **YOUR SPEED** sign that blinks when it electronically picks up the speed of a vehicle. There is another sign that indicates the **MAXIMUM SPEED** limit of forty miles per hour but it doesn't appear anyone pays much attention to either one … the blinking sign isn't close to the stated maximum sign of forty miles per hour. However, Lilli decides to slow down to the maximum speed limit to be safe.

Rapidly closing in on her is a Chevy Camaro that she spots in her rearview mirror. Quickly the Camaro passes her as if she is stationary. Behind the wheel seems to be a youngish looking male with a female passenger sitting in the front passenger seat. Both of them seem to be talking, or maybe they're singing, as their bodies bounce around effortlessly.

The **STOP** sign that she could barely make out a short time ago is now quite noticeable, but the Camaro doesn't seem to be interested in obeying its command.

Then, suddenly, a Toyota Tundra Double Cab truck sluggishly shows itself to the right, just about one hundred yards ahead, moving onto the highway. It is carrying several different pieces of equipment like an electric leaf blower, an extension ladder and a lawn mower along with rakes, shovels, and tree clippers. A man dressed in his outdoor work clothes is in the driver's seat while a younger looking male … more like a boy … sits in the passenger seat dressed similarly. The truck has oversized tires.

The Camaro and Tundra meet. The axels of the Camaro corkscrew and the front end of the Tundra partially collapses into the Camaro. The sound of the crash is deafening as horns of both vehicles blare. Both vehicles rest in front of the **STOP** sign with black streaks of parched rubber on the highway.

All other remaining vehicles on the road near to the crash scene pull over to the side of the road, including Lilli. She reaches for her phone to call 911, as do others in a few of the other vehicles. No one leaves their own vehicle to offer help to the drivers and passengers of the Camaro and Tundra, and there are no sounds of humans heard from within the two vehicles that crashed.

While it seems like forever for EMT and Police to arrive at the scene, the reality is that it took only eleven minutes for the first Police Car to appear and then another three minutes for the Ambulance.

Then Lilli's phone buzzes. It's Jeff.

"It's me." Lilli's voice and the color of her face are pale.

"You don't sound good. Are you and Natalie alright?" Jeff sounds sincerely concerned for their well-being.

"Yes we are. I just witnessed a terrible multiple vehicle collision on Highway 76 between two vehicles. I called 911 and they've arrived.

"But you and Natalie are OK … right."

"Yes … thankfully."

"Are you ready to listen to what I have, or is another time better? Just tell me."

"Now is good. Thanks for your concern."

"I know I've never said this before to you, and maybe now isn't the right time, but it's been eating at me to keep it inside." Jeff pauses, waiting for an interruption or even a signal for him to continue, but all he hears is Lilli's breathing.

Lilli is taken aback, wondering what in the world he's thinking about … what could it be?

Jeff decides to change the topic … better be safe than sorry. "Let me tell you what I found out about Glass. The other thing can wait." He's not going to let Lilli press him on the other subject. "This guy, Jack Glass, had his first encounter with the law when he was seventeen … arrested for possession of marijuana and driving under its influence. From that point forward he got into more trouble with increasing severity … drinking, disorderly misconduct while drunk, speeding, invalid driver's license, taking a punch at a police officer … just to give you a sense. He was mean tempered with the police … a definite no-no. But he seemed not to care much. His violence at this point in time was always with men … no women involved. But that changed once he was out of high school. He was charged with sexually assaulting a sixteen year old girl claiming it was only a game they consensually agreed to. I won't get into those details. Then, with another underage girl, a date rape … she was drugged. They found sufficient traces of zeteraine in her body. In small doses this drug is medically prescribed to control tremor, but fatigue, weakness, and sluggishness also frequently result. It's also used to relieve symptoms of Parkinsonism. However, in large doses it can lead to mental confusion, disorientation, agitation, hallucination, and psychotic-like symptoms. The drug can last for up to five days in humans. In larger doses it can cause death. It has been shown to be used to control women's behavior leading to rape and a loss of memory of the event, meaning she has no idea she was drugged and what happened. The drug can be ground up into a white tasteless powder to place into any liquid."

Lilli interrupts with anger, "So the victim doesn't even fight!"

"Absolutely right. It's called conscious sedation … even if she knows what's happening she can't do anything about it. And, in the end, she most likely will not remember the event at all … her memory is blocked."

As Jeff talks, Lilli imagines what might have happened to Camille. Her eyes are sorrowful and angry as hell.

"Where's Glass now?"

"He's definitely not in prison, but where else could he be is anybody's guess. The other strange thing about this son-of-a-bitch's encounters with the law is that while he was detained by law enforcement, formal charges were never made by the women he molested, probably because he drugged them.

"Unbelievable." Lilli's clenches her mouth tightly to stay in control. "Do you know if there are family members living nearby or any other place?"

"Could be, but we don't know. Could have changed last names, but we don't know that either."

"Damn!"

"That's all I could find. I hope this helps." He pauses and then with more of a timid sounding voice he says, "I'll take you up on that drink whenever you want."

Lilli doesn't hear the second part, fully focusing on Camille even more now than before. And, she's even more convinced she'll not get any further along in helping Barbara find out what really happened to her daughter. "Thanks Jeff, I appreciate your help." She disconnects her cell but now feels even more in the dark.

CHAPTER 26

Later that night, Jeff sits comfortably on a red leather chair in a private room that is so dimly lit you can't tell if the carpeting is blue, orange, green or whatever color or texture. He really doesn't care at the moment. He's been here before. He knows exactly how the room is laid out. More importantly he's focusing on the "exotic dancer" named Pamela, completely naked, demonstrating her unusual flexibility skills in front of him. She is perfectly constructed … mostly natural parts while a few others have been altered. Her ruby red lips, long blond straight hair, and dark blue eyes are mesmerizing. He can't imagine being anyplace else at the moment … it's his birthday … and Pamela is his birthday gift to himself.

Pamela reaches for an opened bottle of Champagne to refill his almost empty glass and pours the bubbly liquid into it, but Jeff is more interested in focusing on her two large exquisite perfectly shaped breasts. She's the hottest "exotic dancer" at this particular "gentlemen's club." She rhythmically moves her gorgeous body to the background music, and then settles to straddle him.

"You are amazing." He says feeling his body mid part respond, not looking for a verbal reply from her.

Some guys join a tennis or golf club, others do the racetrack scene, and some like to hit the gym to work out. Not Jeff ... he loves it at *Ambasciata* ... where he is treated first class all the time.

A few hours in a private room at *Ambasciata* usually costs a patron a minimum of one thousand dollars for the entertainment, food, and drink. But Jeff has a special deal ... nothing ... since he looks the other way when there are infractions of the law. And for the first timers, they are pleasantly surprised that such an establishment could be located in a second-rate city, but this location is intentional.

The rest of *Ambasciata* contains a first class dining area, a top-end bar, and a full stage where the entertainment is usually geared for the male customers, but not exclusively.

Wealthy businesspeople, their clients, and often celebrities from the sports, music, and movie sectors are frequent customers, often flown in by private planes to a nearby private airport.

Jeff is about to take another sip of the Champagne when his cell rings. He looks at the phone resting face up next to the red leather chair to check caller-ID. "Hell," he says. He hesitates, not wanting to be distracted from Pamela's slow moving body, still straddling him, not wanting the out-of-this-world feeling to stop.

Pamela leans closer to him so that her breasts are less than one inch from his face. She continues to work her body, graceful and with just enough pressure.

She's always been the type of woman who prefers five-card stud poker that her Uncle Sal from New Haven taught her around the kitchen table, not bridge. Staying at the lowest rung of the career success ladder wasn't fun or helpful in advancing her career, so she had to find another way … another career, if necessary, that would use her God-Given attributes.

So, she lied for a living, a good one at that. It was about telling the client what they wanted to hear, which may or may not have been the truth. She was so good at it that she fooled the best of the best. She still does. She's cultured and tri-lingual. Men want her. And, for the right price, if you can afford it, she is willing to make a deal. To her, it is that simple and that powerful. It's always about making the right deal that gets both parties what they want so that they come back for more.

Jeff smells her delicious body … he's in a trance, but not for much longer.

The cell rings again. "Damn it," he says … "I gotta take this." With obvious no enthusiasm whatsoever he reaches for the phone. "This better be important!" He listens and then with huge displeasure he says, "I'll be there in twenty minutes." He shakes his head … he's not happy to leave Pamela.

Most people have little to no personal experience with nicknames. Within the Italian-American culture, nicknames have importance. To others those nicknames may seem harsh but to the insiders, whether they are biological family, friends, business associates, and the like, they identify a sense of community, a belonging, and they distinguish one person from another.

Often, nicknames are named after godparents, the order of birth, saints, appearance, behavioral trait, favorite food, and even a memorable incident.

Using one's nickname is contained within the "family." Thus people outside of the "family" aren't even aware. But remember, the "family" can include biological linkage with one another as well as very close personal ties.

Mickey Zitano is the only child of Italian immigrants, Frederico and Katherine Zitano. His father had been a successful undertaker while his mother stayed at home to keep the home pleasurable. They were unsuccessful in having more children. They figured it wasn't God's will, so they focused on Mickey, born Michael Anthony Zitano.

Due to Mickey's early life experiences he developed a reputation outside of his own home. Soon those who knew him outside of the home referred to him as "Terror," which became his nickname.

Within Mickey's team of protectors are, "Bull," "Fist," "Wolf," "Skull," "Scowl," and "Stone."

It's a few minutes past midnight when Jeff knocks on the door of an exclusive private suite that consumes the entire top floor of *Ambasciata* ... a few minutes quicker than the twenty minutes he committed to. There doesn't seem to be any signs of life anywhere but the cameras, noise and motion detectors, and hidden human protectors for Mickey Zitano are abundant.

The door opens after all the precautions have been taken to make it safe for the man inside, the man who is being protected. Jeff is face to face with one of the protectors ... a large man six feet two and one-half inches tall weighing in at a compact muscular body of two hundred and thirty-three pounds. The large man's face seems as if it was carved out of solid rock … not a movement, a blink, or a crack from his mouth, nothing, except for the solid hard stone stare. His nickname is Stone.

Jeff inhales deeply and slowly lets the air escape into the air. He waits for a signal to step inside the room.

Stone, the protector, nods his head ever so slightly as he barely steps aside to allow Jeff to enter, and still the maneuvering space is quite cramped due to the size of the protector.

"Un-believable," a voice deep within the room is heard, a voice that Jeff recognizes. "You're early!" There is a guttural laugh that would frighten most people, but Jeff has heard it many times before. If the sound had been anything different he'd be scared to death. It's Mickey.

The suite is chocolate-themed. The living room, master bedroom, three guest bedrooms, kitchen, and four bathrooms are considerably flavored with chocolate dispensaries. If you don't like the sweet flavor of chocolate then you're out of luck.

Mickey used to be muscular but too many niceties in life have fattened him. He's just short of five feet eleven inches with a full head of gray hair combed straight back to reveal his now pudgy face. There is one noticeable scar just below his left eye and a few less noticeable scars on his chest. Otherwise his skin is surprisingly smooth looking. He is dressed in a white linen bathrobe with full length sleeves and long enough just to fall an inch below his knees. Part of his hairy chest is exposed. His feet are covered with soft velvet red slippers. It doesn't appear he is wearing anything underneath the bathrobe, but that's not certain and nobody is asking. He is fifty-nine years old. He is sipping *Sambuca Anisette.* There is a plate of biscotti on a nearby table.

He's always lived for action, even as a kid, playing any sport possible, although he was only average at best in all of them. The activity refueled him, and he loved it. He was born in Schenectady, New York. His two year older cousin lives in Florida with her husband … they have three adult children. It's been many years since he's visited them … he doesn't like the guy she married. That does it for his living biological family. Unfortunately, for him, he got into a lot of trouble with a few of his buddies on the street. Nothing ever involved taking someone's life. Stealing what didn't belong to him and reselling what he had stolen comprised most of his young life. He continued to be a mass of explosive energy.

Unable to enter the military due to his criminal activities, he left home after getting kicked out of high school because the football coach who desperately wanted him to play the game called him an ugly name based on his Italian heritage in front of his classmates. Mickey knocked out the coach with one well delivered punch to the coach's nose. And that was the end of that.

He still carries a photo of an adult male holding a baby. He claims the adult male is John Gotti and the baby is him, but there's not been anyone who's been able to support the claim or challenge him.

He eventually developed a reputation on the street as the guy who could make things happen. His only flaw and still is when he's overly passionate about something and he tries to convince others to be as passionate … that's when, if he is sitting, his left leg bounces almost out of control, a signal to others to just back away. His current team of protectors are highly committed to him as he is to them, just as if they were all in the military during battle … protectors just like a pack of wolves … a united family.

Jeff walks towards Mickey who remains seated, and bends over to embrace the man. Words are not exchanged because that's not necessary. They both know that something important is about to be discussed, and there's no time for exchanging pleasantries.

Mickey nods to an empty chair that has been placed a few feet away from him so Jeff can take a seat. Jeff complies.

Mickey leans over to the small table next to him. He grabs one biscotti that is on top of the plate. He doesn't ask Jeff if he wants anything, because he wants to get to the point quickly … in other words to do what matters and to ignore the rest. After he finishes chewing the biscotti he says, "Look, I need some information, and I'm not sure who else can get it. So, it's you."

Jeff shifts his weight in the chair from one leg to the other. "I'll help out anyway I can."

Without a glint of a smile Mickey says, "Good to hear. I know I can count on you."

"What is it?"

Mickey shrugs his shoulders as he simultaneously reaches for the partial glass of *Sambuca*. He takes a small sip. "Maybe it'll take care of itself. I don't know for sure, but I don't want any loose ends out there."

Jeff feels the tension heighten. "I understand."

"Oh, yeah, I don't want to forget." Mickey reaches for another biscotti on the plate. "You want some? I got more."

Jeff raises both hands, palms facing Mickey. "Oh. No thanks."

Mickey takes a bite and chews as he shrugs his shoulders again. "I'm sorry 'bout what happened to Prairie, but it was unavoidable … for the best … for everyone. Believe me."

Jeff tries to hold in his surprise, but his body jerks just enough to give away his thoughts … "How the hell did he know about my source … my former source?"

"You know, you gotta do what you gotta do." Mickey shrugs his shoulders again, and then pops the rest of the biscotti into his mouth, and chews until it's gone.

Jeff feels his body heat up as he waits for whatever is coming next. And he knows it's all been leading up to this. He's totally floored when Mickey speaks.

"Lilli Jackson … you know her … right."

Jeff isn't sure he can keep calm, but he has to. "Sure, I know her … not well though." He pauses not sure he should ask, but he does, "Why the interest? She's a Public Safety Officer or something like that … not real law enforcement. She works for John Walker … I'm sure you know him or at least have heard of him … who owns *Verity Security*. She's got a young daughter and she's a single mom."

"I know all of that." Mickey pauses. "It may just blow away. But if it doesn't it'll be more difficult … very difficult to deal with, but not impossible … know what I'm sayin'." He pauses again before he restarts. "You know, some people just don't know when to stop nosin' into other people's affairs. Know what I'm sayin'?" He's not interested in a response from Jeff as he shakes his head sideways.

With that being said both men momentarily stare at each other. The only noticeable smell in the room is of chocolate. Neither man says anything for a few ... very long ... seconds.

Then Mickey says, "All right. That's it. But you might be back here talking to me about her, and even a favor I'll need." He nods to the protector who's been silently standing a few yards away signaling the meeting has ended.

Jeff says to himself ... "Hell!"

Jeff is escorted out of the room and into the hallway by Stone. He hears the door lock shut, and then he says to himself ... "What the hell is he up to? What does he want from me? What does Lilli have to do with any of this?"

CHAPTER 27

Regardless of whether you've ever lied, stolen, cheated, or killed someone, or if you've tolerated it among those who did, then it might be difficult to image what it's like ... how you would feel. It's really unexplainable in a way, the first time, but it never leaves you regardless of how hard you try to forget. Sure, you can try to put it aside as only a one-time occurrence, but that never solves your problem.

We're not referring to hard-core liars, robbers, cheaters or killers, who are typically psychopathic, because they can't stop even if they wanted to.

But we're describing all the others and their choices ... what clothes to wear, what college to attend if any at all, who to marry if anyone at all and how many times, if you should rent or buy a place to live, what to eat and drink, who to socialize with, and the myriads of other common choices we all make in life ... because we all have choices to make that construct who we are and will become ... unless you believe you have no choice whatsoever.

But even then, that belief of having no choice is something you choose to believe in, so that's a choice.

In a nearby State, three to be exact and to the northwest, the night is dry and cold, and the ground is hard and empty.

The days have shortened, waiting for winter to arrive and last for several months, and then back to the start of it all … the cycle … natural … predictable.

He pops a small white tablet into his mouth and swallows it. It almost gets stuck and he almost spits it out, but doesn't. He should have tried harder.

He sits on a bench in a park that is in need of repair, but funding is scarce, where usually few things of importance happen. He's been doing this for several consecutive nights … alone … not anxious to return to a place he doesn't even call home … why would he … where he'd be alone as well. He's now a drifter, wandering around like a rolling stone.

He continues to sit … feet beginning to go stale … numb to be more accurate … yet he closes his eyes for some degree of comfort, if that's at all possible. His body slowly tilts to the side as it carefully fully rests on the bench. He falls asleep, and he won't awake. The blow to his head by contact from a metal pipe ensures that.

The two male teenagers looking almost worse than him … run down and ragged … responsible for the murder search his body for money, drugs, or anything else they can use to finance their own drug addiction. They come up empty handed, so they simply walk away leaving the white male face up.

The scar on the tip of Jack Glass's nose and just above his right nostril is obvious … a remnant of an accident when a detached window fell over his head as he was trying to enter and burglarize a house a few years ago to pay for his drug habit. He was never captured. He made many very stupid choices in how he would live his short life.

The next morning a jogger discovers the dead body and immediately uses his cell phone to call 911.

Police officers arrive … not quickly, since there are limited law enforcement personnel in the area … another sign of inadequate funding. They preliminarily examine the body and the scene.

Then investigators are called in for a more detailed examination. No identification is found on the dead male body, but later an autopsy reveals sufficient traces of zeteraine are found … enough that probably would have killed him even if the metal pipe hadn't done its job. The forensic pathologist has little doubt in completing the death certificate with the cause of death as a fatal blow to the head of the unidentified white male with the scar on the tip of his nose and just above his right nostril.

CHAPTER 28

The vehicle accident between the Tundra and the Camaro is still vividly clear in Lilli's mind, no matter how much she wants to wipe her brain-disk clean. She thinks to herself … "This could have been Natalie and me!"

The passengers of both vehicles are transferred to ambulances … Lilli's not sure who survived and who didn't … and the Tundra and Camaro are towed away for further inspection. After the drivers and passengers within the vehicles who witnessed the terrible incident have been debriefed on site, each is permitted to leave the scene.

Lilli still feels rattled but it's ratchetted up another few notches when she slowly starts to drive away. She notices in her rearview mirror a few cars behind her a familiar looking vehicle although she's not sure from where or when. The black sedan has tinted windows so she can't possibly make out who is inside, nor is she any good at identifying makes, models and years of motorized vehicles. It's never been her thing. She wonders why she's even thinking about any of this now … too weird in a way.

She's now driving. She looks at the speedometer … she's already up to seventy. Then she slows down, breathes slowly and evenly. Her body, legs, and limbs feel heavy and a bit weak, probably, she assumes from witnessing the incident between the Tundra and Camaro.

Then she checks her rearview mirror again … the black sedan with the tinted windows is directly behind her, a bit too close for her comfort, so she steps on the accelerator. The black sedan with tinted windows mimics her action.

"Am I being followed?" she says aloud to herself, "And why?" She has no ready answer at this time.

Up ahead she spots a combination gas station and diner. She decides to pull in to fill the gas tank and then for her and Natalie to get a bite to eat and rest a while. She wonders what the black sedan with tinted windows will do next. She signals to take a right turn as she slows a bit. The black sedan with tinted windows stays the same distance behind but doesn't signal. She pulls into the combination gas station and diner as the black sedan with tinted windows continues on the highway.

She fills the tank and pays with cash. Then she moves her car to a parking space reserved for diners. Hers is the only car, the rest are trucks of all sorts, but she has no idea of makes, models, and years.

After locking her car she and Natalie enter the diner. No one inside looks her way … they're all busy eating and talking with each other at both the tables and the counter. There's a sign right in front of her next to the cash register that reads, **SEAT YOURSELF … TRUCKERS GET FIRST CHOICE**. She spots a small table near the doorway to the kitchen that under normal conditions she'd ignore because it's very noisy and busy. However, it's the only choice she thinks she has at the moment so she won't have to wait, so she heads directly for the spot.

An hour later she and Natalie have finished their meals. She ordered meatloaf, mashed potatoes and cream corn with coffee while Natalie ate a meal that she had prepared at her apartment before they left. She's delightfully surprised that the meatloaf, potatoes and corn was delicious, including the dark rich coffee. It's amazing how rest and food can replenish one's body.

Lilli looks around now that the meals are finished. She sips her coffee. She's not necessarily looking for anyone specifically, nor does she notice anyone she already knows. The customers are mostly large sized men dressed in loose fitting jeans, boots, and long sleeve shirts. Some have facial hair while others don't. Everyone seems to be in need of a good haircut. There are a few men-women couples sitting together that seem to be having a good time as well.

She remembers reading an article a short time ago in some publication she doesn't remember how truck driving, especially long haul drivers, are in high demand. Pay has reached nearly ninety thousand dollars a year with full medical benefits for some that also includes training. Married couples have jumped into the profession, and therefore their combined income is at one hundred eighty thousand dollars. A good gig if you and your mate get along well and there is no one else to care for.

The server, a female dressed in a brown nondescript uniform, stands by Lilli's table. "Anything else … she's a cutie."

Lilli knows the compliment is for Natalie. "Thanks, she's the love of my life."

"Keep her safe."

Lilli thinks that's an odd comment but ignores it. "I think we're good. Great food."

"Sure. Pay at the counter." The server hands over the bill and then walks away to attend to another customer not interested in carrying on a conversation.

Lilli now glances at the bill ... seven dollars and thirty-five cents! She blinks her eyes a few times because she can't believe the price ... much less than a comparable meal in town. At the top of the bill it reads in bold letters, **Pay the cashier ... Leave tip at table/counter.**

After paying the bill along with a twenty percent tip she and Natalie leave the diner to head for her car. Once inside with Natalie secured in the backseat, Lilli pulls out of the parking spot that is next to a truck to re-enter the highway, not noticing the black sedan with the tinted windows several spots away. That seems to be the last thing on her mind at the moment. She feels relaxed. She lowers the driver side door window a little for fresh air. Then she enters the highway towards Barbara Conroy's place unaware that a tracking device has been placed underneath her car while she and Natalie were inside the diner.

If she were more experienced in law enforcement with trained eyes and high suspicion, she would have profiled all the vehicles at both the gas station and diner parking spots. She also would have noticed two males about her age of average height but athletic looking wearing jeans, black t-shirts, and Levi gray casual shoes at the diner's counter after she arrived who were out-of-place because they are a surveillance team assigned by Mickey Zitano to follow her whereabouts.

But right now she's more interested in helping console Barbara … it's nice to be a friend when you can. She lets her mind reminisce about her own childhood, although it's usually not something she enjoys thinking about much of the time … not happy times. But she clearly remembers her childhood dream of wanting to be a model … not sure even today where that notion came from … she didn't even have anything close to Barbie-Dolls to play with, didn't know anyone who was a model, yet that's what she thought about as a child.

The odds of her succeeding in that career were slim to almost zilch. So many things could go wrong and she was risking her young life … not literally, of course … for a gamble that was more likely to fail than succeed. Right now the more she thinks about what she wanted to be seems more like a piece of wet paper starting to shred apart. But to do nothing at all at that young of an age seemed out of the question. It was her dream choice, and she always believed she had choices.

Just thinking about that time of her life gives her a few goose bumps. She smiles brightly as she glances at her daughter in the back seat. She thought back then that the whole idea would be incredible and irresistible although at that time those weren't the words she used to describe her emotions.

She imagined being driven in a fancy-smancy car to a photo shoot all dressed up in exotic clothes … Italian, French, Portuguese, whatever … it didn't matter. Her modeling name she assigned to herself was Lilli-Anne because she thought it sounded so pretty. She envisioned herself under lights with someone priming and fussing over her as cameras were setting up to take photos. She would giggle when she was a kid just thinking about it, except, however, when she offered her opinion about make-up, clothes, background music, and so on because she feared she's be told just to keep her mouth shut and look pretty. Her opinion didn't matter.

That was the critical incident, so she quit thinking about modeling because she always thought her opinion and those from others did matter.

We all make choices at each and every stage of our life, and we have to live with not only the choices we make but the consequences of those choices. Sometimes the consequences are not pleasant and sometimes the choices are difficult to make. However, when we make a choice we should not look back and say, "what if" because we'll be second guessing ourselves for the rest of our lives.

CHAPTER 29

"Yeah, whaddaya got?" Mickey recognizes the number from a member of the surveillance team.

"We're still following her … she's completely clueless, even at the diner. She's a real looker, but still a rookie when it comes to …." He's interrupted.

"Diner … what the hell were you doing in a diner with her! Jeez, you gotta act more responsibly. She could've spotted you two goons." Mickey is obviously furious.

"We were hungry. The place was packed. The food at trucker stops is always great. No way was she suspicious … no way at all."

Mickey has simmered down a bit, but not much. "OK. How close are you to the place?"

"We're about forty minutes away, according to our GPS. What's next?"

"Conroy and her freakin' dog have been taken care of. The house has been cleaned. And the rest is in place. This should end it for her, but in case you gotta do something about her and her kid, park where you can't be seen. She's gotta learn not to interfere in other people's business. I'll let you know. Anything else?"

"Sounds like a plan." The phones disconnect. The black sedan with tinted windows follows Lilli without her notice.

Just about forty minutes later given a minute either way Lilli pulls into the driveway of the Conroy residence. She frowns once she sees an **OPEN HOUSE** sign on the front lawn. After she shuts down the car's engine she opens the driver side door to get out so she can move to the back door to take Natalie in her arms, leaving the luggage inside the car for the time being. She approaches the front door, rings the door bell, and quickly a woman slightly older than her greets her.

The woman is dressed in a dark colored jacket with a light blue blouse and lighter colored loose fitting matching slacks, low heal shoes, no jewelry. She is tall and lanky with small eyes and a long and narrow face. "Hi, here for the open house?" Her smile is sincere looking. It should be ... she's part of the surveillance team ... she's a pro.

"Uh, where's Barbara Conroy?"

"Oh, I'm sorry, I don't recognize that name. Who is she ... another real estate agent?" She is very convincing ... she has to be ... she specializes in lying.

"She owns the house. Where is she?"

"I don't know anything about that. My company just assigned me to host this open house. The place is up for sale."

"That can't be. I spoke with Barbara earlier today. She's expecting me." Lilli begins to feel she's way over her head in something she doesn't fully understand.

"I'm sorry again, but I really can't help you. You wanna look around? Maybe you'll give an offer."

Lilli has a hunch, nothing definite or absolute, just a gut feeling, so she throws it out like bread crumbs to see what happens next. "Since I'm here, why not?"

"I'm Emma." She extends her right hand to shake that Lilli grabs hold of. Emma then steps aside. "Nice daughter, you must be proud."

Lilli, still holding Natalie but much tighter, steps inside the home she's visited before, but it doesn't look the same. It appears like it's had a make-over, and in a way it has.

After Barbara and Lucky were abducted a few hours ago, the entire place was vacuumed ... carpets, furniture, everything and anything. All personal items such as pictures, clothing, jewelry, dog items and so forth were removed. All of this was to ensure even the smallest amount of trace evidence belonging to Henry, Barbara, Camille, and Lucky disappeared forever. Even tiny bits of hair, fingerprints, anything that could be matched to the Conroy's ... nothing could match anything ... zero ... zilch ... even forged documents were created as to the current owner of the house.

Even the power of fluorescent print detection would not be useful in recognizing any finger or palm prints left behind.

And since the neighborhood has a reputation of rarely getting involved with their neighbors, if questioned formally or informally by anyone, everyone would say they hadn't heard or seen anything unusual from the Conroy house ... zip.

Lilli's head begins to fill with tons of confusion. She knows she's not dreaming any of this, but it's so unreal ... but it can't be true.

"Wanna look around?"

"Huh" Lilli didn't hear a word Emma said. She feels a little lightheaded so she sits in a nearby chair, still holding onto Natalie, putting off the decision to look around.

"Are you OK? You look pale. Maybe some water will help." She reaches into a large handbag to pull out a bottle of water, unscrews the cap, and hands it over to Lilli. "Take this."

"I – I don't know what to say. I'm so confused." That's all Lilli is able to say at the moment.

As if on cue … which it is … the doorbell rings.

"Stay seated while I see who's there." Emma walks to the front door already knowing who's there, opens it, smiles and nods to the young couple who are part of the team. "Welcome to the open house. Please come in and feel free to walk around."

Lilli is like most people … demanding at times to know what's going on in her life. But what's going on in her life right now is so baffling she's not sure how to even start demanding anything, and to whom.

A few more minutes pass as Lilli finishes off the bottle of water while the young couple continues to walk through the house, just as planned, exhibiting convincing behavior that they're the real thing. In a way, they are the real thing if it means professional cons.

Lilli stands and says to Emma, "We're going. I don't know what's going on here. It's not right. Something is very wrong." She turns and walks back to her car, even more tightly holding onto Natalie.

Lilli opens the car's doors, secures Natalie in the back seat, and settles herself in the driver's seat. She pulls out her cell to place a call to Barbara, waits, and then she hears,

"This phone number is no longer in operating service." She swallows deeply, and then starts the engine to get as far away as possible for the time being not sure, however, what to do next, if anything at all. Her face suddenly becomes impassive, but that won't last for long.

CHAPTER 30

After Jeff gets into his car, and before he fastens his seatbelt, he accidentally drops his keys on the driver side floor mat. His hands are trembling and his breathing is irregular. He sits in his seat for another few seconds or so before he slowly reaches down between his legs to pick up the car keys and then locks all doors. Then he fastens his seatbelt. He gives a look of himself in the rearview mirror. He looks scared because he is, but he's also proud of himself for standing up to Mickey in an attempt to look confident. But who's fooling who. Then he says aloud, "Who does Mickey think he is, Don Vito Corleone?"

His feelings for Lilli … the real ones … have been hidden, his typical behavior with everyone. He's been acting with her as if he's in some kind of witness protection program, keeping secret who he really is and what he's become. He prefers tinted windows in his car to prevent anyone from the outside recognizing him because he only shows as little of himself as he can, not because he's ashamed … OK, maybe he is a little or even a lot … or maybe he doesn't think much of himself or care about what others think of him. His mantra is something like, "Take me as I am or don't take me at all." Maybe he's just plain and simple conning himself. But regardless, he'll most likely remain unattached, except for those like Pamela, unless he's willing to show his weaknesses, or as he prefers to say his developmental opportunities.

Specifically, as for Lilli, sure, he's got the hots for her, meaning he'd love to have unrestrained sex with her. But if he's really … really honest with himself there's more to it. She's perfect for him and probably for almost any normal man, but he's not normal. She's sexy, interesting, smart, honest, caring and a great mother to Natalie just for starters. He wonders though, what she may see in him that could be appealing to her.

He now is settled down as he puts the key into the car's ignition. But he suddenly stops, not continuing to turn the key as he flashes back to the recent meeting with Mickey. He wonders if he appeared too much like a schoolboy who'd gotten in trouble and he was face-to-face with the School Principal … just the two of them.

Sure, bad stuff happens to most, if not all, people. Decent ones mess up … some get hurt … those wearing the black hat sometimes win while the ones wearing the white hat sometimes lose. And doing the right thing … whatever that means … may not lead to a reward, but to a punishment. Sure, he's screwed up many times, not always though. And yeah, he's currently walking the line between good cop and bad cop, but right now it seems different when Mickey asked him about Lilli. He tells himself this isn't the time to lie to himself … he's concerned for Lilli's safety.

Bluntly, he loves Lilli, but does she, or will she, love him, including all of his flaws and the bad things he's done.

Maybe he should just set the record straight with her … tell her everything … let her decide? She's a responsible adult.

Although Jeff moved up in rank to Detective, he still thinks of himself as a working man's cop from an average background. Most cops are from similar backgrounds as him starting at just slightly above minimum wage, working the worse shifts possible in the worse neighborhoods, seeing the worse of humankind. Statistically he should be married by now with two kids … married to a stay-at-home high school sweetheart … with what at times feels like a ton of financial debt. But that's not him … not even close. Yeah, he was married for a short time before they got divorced, and as painful as it is for him to admit, he still loves the woman.

His brain stops processing all of this information and then suddenly, almost out of nowhere, like a ship appearing from the fog of the sea, he snaps out of the past to the present. His hand is still on the car key. He turns it to the right and the engine responds.

He has obviously and conveniently set aside the oath he took when he became a law enforcement officer … the code of ethics: *I recognize the badge of my office as a symbol of public faith …. I will never engage in acts of corruption or bribery, nor will I condone such acts by other police officers ….*

He's not sure what he'll do next, so he drives off, but for sure he will not let Lilli face harm's way.

CHAPTER 31

Lilli wonders if she'll ever hear from Barbara Conroy again, directly or indirectly, even if she tries to actively look for her in order to understand what's going on. However, thirty miles away in a small town named Gazette, something new is taking place that Lilli, or for that matter most people, will never be aware of.

A demolition crew was preparing to bring down an abandoned three story building that is owned by the city of Gazette. The building had been in this condition for almost a full fiscal year, but just a few hours before the planned demolition there was an unexplained explosion that caused the building to burst into flames. Some were blaming it on a gas pipe that had never been turned off, but to others that notion was ridiculous ... something else caused the explosion and fire. There were no plans to construct anything in its place since the town was and still is financially strapped.

After it's determined safe to enter the building, a pair of insurance claim adjusters' walkthrough is almost complete before the building is totally leveled and the debris removed when one of the claim adjusters comes across what appears to be burnt remains of a human and some sort of animal.

Police investigators and forensic specialists from Green County are immediately called to the scene. The condition of the bodies prevents them from identifying whether the human body is male or female, the type of animal, approximate ages, or anything else via a visual inspection. The remains of both bodies are transported to the County morgue for further inspection.

The human body is X-rayed revealing a metal implant on the body's left arm just below the elbow. The implant is removed and found to contain a blurred partial serial number and unclear manufacturer's name making it impossible to contact the manufacturer for information about the name of the body, address, closest kin and anything else they might have on file. If the information on the implant was clear and distinct the name linked to the body would be Barbara Conroy. As to the other body, the animal, all they figure out is that it is a dog.

Chapter 32

Larry's not a big man by any stretch of the imagination. He's rather portly with excess fat apparent from the top of his head to bottom of his feet. His height of five feet three inches accentuates his appearance. As a kid he was called Fat Larry, something he obviously hated, but couldn't get away from. He had a good appetite for all the wrong foods and despised exercise.

He hasn't changed since then, now at the age of twenty-one, and he almost dropped out of high school but was so afraid of his domineering parents that fear was his sole motive. And after that he screwed around, not accomplishing much, while he continued to live with his parents. He was their only child … a big disappointment to his father and mother.

He figured that maybe, just maybe, college wasn't in the cards because he only thought of a four-year school. And, who would pay for the tuition and other expenses … not his parents or him. So, he entered a local community college without having the need to take any entrance exams, just to show his high school diploma. He lied on the application form about his ability to pay for the schooling. He still lived at home with his parents during this time.

It was in his second year, at Anzor Community College, when he met by accident Francesca, known as Frankie. If you took a look at them side by side, you wouldn't in your wildest imagination think they had anything in common.

Frankie has always been a full-size female, and according to her recollection, was feared by most of her high school classmates. At six feet even and one hundred eighty pounds she was intimidating. Word spread early in her teenage life not to mess with her. She still has a huge appetite for the wrong foods and like Larry hates to exercise. That's probably what their mutual attraction was and still is.

They met at a local bar only a few blocks from Anzor Community College one Friday evening … *The Library*. Larry took an immediate liking to her take-no-prisoner style when someone tried to take a cheap verbal shot at her. She decked the guy, and anyone else, who looked at her side-ways. And Frankie liked Larry's submissiveness to her as well as what seemed to be his admiration for her. He was easily controllable, something she loved. There were never any sexual overtones or actual sexual foreplay or activities between them … something that was also never talked about, but jointly assumed.

And then tonight happens … a real surprise because it was simply spontaneous. Each of them had too many drinks and a white colored tablet for each of them that set them off into an uncontrollable urge to do something crazy. That's what alcohol and drugs will do. Duh!

Without a vehicle either owned or a driver's license, they leave *The Library* on foot … staggering sideways, sometimes bumping into each other, as they clumsily walk to no specific place. They eventually wind up in a neighborhood of middle class houses needing repair, but who still have owners or renters living inside. One house in particular, however, catches the eye of Frankie, so she stops on the sidewalk in front of it, and steadies her body so she doesn't tumble over. There is a **FOR RENT** sign stuck in the ground in front of the place. The lawn is barely a lawn, pathetic looking, weeds everyplace, lots of dirt, and what's left of real grass needs a good cut.

Without a word, Frankie walks directly to the **FOR RENT** sign and with both hands pulls it out of the ground. She tosses it aside and turns to Larry, "Around back. Let's go inside." She is remarkably coherent in spite of her alcohol and drug condition. She knows Larry will follow her in full compliance as she waves him to follow her to the back of the house.

They walk in a single line, Frankie in the lead and Larry close behind.

He isn't feeling all that good, but he dares not complain to her.

Once both of them reach the back of the house they look at the backyard that seems to have been unattended for quite some time … a close cousin to the front yard. Frankie moves to check out each window and backdoor for a way in. The door is locked but the third window is a charm as it is unlocked. She easily climbs through it. Once inside the house, she yells, "Larry, come on in."

As Larry is partially through the now opened back window, a neighbor living in a house immediately behind them hears the commotion.

Antonio F. Vianna

The neighbor is an elderly woman living alone since her husband passed away a few years ago, and refuses to take up in a retirement place ... much too proud for that. She peaks outside her bedroom window to spot Larry climb through the window, so she immediately calls 911 to report seeing one person enter the house through the window.

Jeff Abrams is on duty tonight, alone, covering for the one who originally was scheduled, but got sick. He isn't happy ... he'd rather be with Pamela. It's been tranquil so far, and quite boring, but that's about to quickly change.

He receives a call from the Anzor Police Department, a few towns away that shares law enforcement services with other nearby towns that have small understaffed law enforcement departments. This sharing arrangement is common among many communities. Jeff is briefed about the 911 call made by the Anzor citizen living in the house next door regarding a probable house break-in. He immediately responds to head for the house in Anzor.

When he arrives, so far, there are no television crews or spectators, but that's all about to change.

Inside the house, Frankie is passed out on the bare living room floor, the effect of her prior drinking, one tablet, and then a second one.

Larry looks at her ... now scared more than he has ever been or remembers.

Jeff knows that he has to control his emotions and not panic if he wants the situation to end the right way. But that's easier said than done. He's not a hostage negotiator, but he's the only one at the scene. At least he's had some preliminary training in the area, but not much.

The call came unexpectedly and he was geographically the closest law enforcement professional to the scene, and there needed to be someone there as quickly as possible.

A Crisis Team usually includes several specialists working together, but Jeff is the only one presently ... that makes him a one-man team, and not even a specialist in any one area. Go figure, but he's got to do his best.

He knows how essential it is to concentrate and focus on the most basic things: secure the area, collection information, and keep the target calm and cool ... to prevent him or her from becoming irrational.

He doesn't have a number to dial into, so he uses a loud speaker that will ultimately wake up the neighbors. He has no other choice at the moment. "Who's inside? Identify yourself!" Jeff waits for the target to say something but when that doesn't happen he repeats. "Who's inside? Identify yourself." He remains calm yet his heart rate picks up.

"Who are you?"

The voice sounds younger than Jeff had initially expected, but its coarseness suggests heavy use of drugs and alcohol for starters. "I'm Jeff. I'm with the local police department." He knows best not to give his full name, rank, specifically identify the City, or provide any other specific information such as the number of other law enforcement personnel who are with him ... in this case zero. He needs to make the conversations simple, clear, and personal but appear to have ample on-scene support. If the guy makes any demands he wants to be able to stall him a while by, for example, having to check in with his boss, that way Jeff will appear to be the good guy by trying to help the person in the house get a deal. It's all about keeping tensions low and bonding with the target. "What's your name?"

Lights from nearby neighbors' homes light up.

"None of your business." The tone of his voice hasn't changed.

Jeff feels a wee-bit relaxed, not enough to sink his teeth into. "Well, OK. Are you alone or are there others with you?"

There's no answer, not even the sound of the guy's breathing.

Jeff continues. "Does anyone need a doctor or other kind of medical help or anything else? I can send someone in."

There's another round of silence.

Jeff picks up again, wanting to mention the guy's first name in as friendly of a way as possible. He doesn't want to set him off. "I'm just concerned about everyone who's there. That includes you, of course. I don't want anyone hurt. Know what I'm sayin'?"

"Everythin's cool." The tone maintains its edge.

"That's good to hear. You're doing OK yourself?"

"I said everythin's cool! Aren't you hearin' me?" His voice begins to sound anxious.

Jeff reminds himself to be careful not to press him much further. "I'm just concerned, you know, just worried about you and the others. How many did you say are with you?"

The guy doesn't answer.

Jeff believes this is a good sign ... the guy's thinking logically as he can at the moment, which probably isn't much, but you take what you can. And the guy's not thinking about making any emotional decision at the moment or doing something totally stupid that would escalate the situation.

Jeff nods his head, wanting to get the guy's first name at least as well as the last name at most ... and then the truth. "You sound OK. What's your name? I'd like to talk with you using your first name. Whatta ya say, buddy."

"Yeah ... OK ... I'm Larry."

Jeff needs to know if Larry is acting alone or if he has a team. "Larry, you come with anyone else?"

"You don't need to know that!"

"OK Larry, so you're saying you won't identify who else came with you. Is that what you're saying?"

Larry doesn't answer the question. "We're OK."

"OK, I hear that. You're not going to tell me the names of those who are with you ... I mean everyone. I understand and that's cool Larry."

"You're asking a lot of questions." Larry now seems more introspective than before.

"Well, Larry, that's my job." Jeff purposely chuckles just loud enough for Larry to hear, and then continues. "But I gotta tell you that the longer you stay inside, trouble lies ahead. That's the honest truth, Larry. It really is."

Silence again.

Jeff picks up. "But we still have time to work out of this. Know what I'm sayin' Larry?"

Larry's voice is about to explode. "Don't even think about rushing us!"

"Hey Larry, who said anything about rushing you?" Jeff wonders how many there are, specifically if there are hostages and who else is with Larry. "But I gotta be honest with you Larry. The longer this goes on the worse it'll get. So, I'm asking you to come out with everyone."

"No way!" Larry's breathing is heavy. "You'll kill me and Frankie!"

Jeff now knows the target consists of two people, most likely both are male, but he's uncertain of their ages. "I know you're suspicious right now, Larry. But I give you my word that we're not gonna storm the place and shoot you and Frankie. You got my word on that. I promise, Larry, really, I promise."

"You better not." Larry's voice suddenly is muted and sounds undemanding.

"I gave you my word, Larry. Do you understand?"
"Yeah."

"And you can't escape. The place is surrounded." Jeff lies. "The best thing is for you and Frankie to surrender peacefully. That way, it'll be better when you face a judge. You see, you'll have cooperated with us. And you can tell the judge that Frankie didn't want to cooperate but you did. You'll probably go free. Know what I'm sayin' Larry?"

The silence suggests that Larry is thinking about what Jeff said, about the deal.

Jeff then says, "I'm happy you're thinkin' about what I offered, Larry. But honestly, maybe we both need a short break. We've been talkin' a while, and maybe you want some time to think about all of this. Huh?"

There is more silence.

Jeff continues, "So, Larry, I'll call out to you again in about ... uh ... say fifteen minutes. How does that sound, Larry?"

Silence.

The principle behind Jeff's actions is often referred to as *the prisoner's dilemma*, that essentially consists of two people who have been involved in a crime, and after arrested are separated from each other so that they cannot communicate in any form with one another. That way, each doesn't know what the other one says to law enforcement questioning. This principle is one of earliest covered during crisis management and interviewing situations training. Here's how it works. Each accused prisoner has the option of telling law enforcement authorities that the other person is guilty or remain silent when questioned. That's the two options. If both prisoners are silent, it is most likely that each will receive a moderate sentence. If both talk, it is most likely that each will receive a long sentence. If one prisoner talks while one is silent the one who talks usually is set free while the prisoner who remains silent receives a long sentence. Since both prisoners are separated neither knows what the other one will do.

Fifteen minutes later, Jeff calls out. "Larry, it's me, Jeff. How's everything?"

While Larry wants to believe Jeff, he's suspicious. He's never really trusted anyone, except for Frankie ... but look at where that's got him. He decides to bunker down … at least for now. "Jeff, leave us alone, I don't believe you!"

"Hey, Larry, I get it. You probably don't trust anybody right now. Yeah, I get it."

"You're full of crap. You don't care about me."

"What about Frankie … do you care about Frankie?"

Larry fearfully answers. His eyes are wild full of fear. "It wasn't my idea … it was Frankie … her stupid idea. I should never have gone along with her." Then he pauses so he can think of something else to say that would make him sound like a tough guy. "Don't try to rush in … we've got guns and we'll shoot if we have to. Understand?"

Fear can be good … it can make you strong, alert, and perceptive but when it's bad it makes you do stupid things.

"OK, Larry, maybe we both need another break, say ten minutes. OK?" He hears no answer but assumes he's been heard by Larry. At least he now knows the target is a male and a female.

Outside but not very close to the scene a local television crew with one female reporter and one cameraman show up. The scene is now shown live on *WRGB*, a local television channel, although it's about midnight.

Mickey, awake, switches television channels as a way to exhaust himself so he can fall asleep. He takes a long sip of *Sambuca* to swallow down the bit of biscotti. Then he sees the live news report on the television screen.

The cameraman first focuses on the street number, 3608, of the house as the reporter narrates the limited information she knows about the situation … not much. However, she mentions the street name, Hummingbird Avenue.

Mickey immediately realizes this is the place where he has temporarily stashed stolen property, drugs to be sold to the addicts, and a load of cash in ten, twenty, fifty, and hundred dollar bills. He can't afford to have law enforcement enter the place. All he needs is an opportunity. He might have to make one himself.

The camera then turns towards Jeff, who is being interviewed by the reporter. This is the opportunity Mickey needs! He yells out to Stone who's sleeping in a nearby bedroom in the same exclusive private suits on the top floor of *Ambasciata*, "Stone!"

Stone reaches Mickey's room within seconds wearing only his undershorts but holding a .38 Caliber Smith and Wesson Model 10, 2-inch barrel gun. Granted, his pistol isn't a Colt .45 Model 1911 that can knock down a large man, even bigger and stronger than him, off his feet flat onto his back because of its heavy bullets, but his .38 can kill just the same, and it's much easier to conceal.

"You OK, boss?" His facial appearance reflects his name.

Mickey doesn't answer that question, but rather he says, "We got a problem, and you're the one who can handle it."

Stone nods his head, proud that his boss thinks that highly of him. This is what he was meant to do. He listens carefully as Mickey explains.

"The dirty cop, Abrams, needs to do something, so I want you to take the lead on this. Understand. Look at the TV."

Stone, still standing, glances towards the television screen. The attractive female reporter is interviewing Abrams. On the bottom of the screen are the words …
DANGEROUS STANDOFF … 3608 HUMMINGBIRD AVENUE … DET. JEFF ABRAMS.

Neither Mickey nor Stone say a thing. Their attention is at the screen. The reporter and Jeff are face to face. She asks, "What's going on here Detective Abrams?"

Jeff takes in a deep breath of air and then puffs it out. He's not really interested in broadcasting the situation to the general public at this time, but it's better to hear it from a reliable source like him than let it become fake news. "We know there are two people inside the house. A 911 call was made by a neighbor who witnessed one of them enter through a back window. The house is for rent. No idea at the present why the two of them are inside or if there are others … don't know why they chose this house. I'm just trying to convince them to come out peacefully. That's it." His eyes dance around to each side of the reporter's head. He's not nervous … he feels in control … but that will change.

Still looking at Jeff, the reporter says, "Thank you Detective Abrams for the update." Then she directly faces the camera as it zooms onto her face. "This is Kelly Sue Marsh, WRGB news … back to you in the studio."

Mickey says to Stone, "We got cash, drugs, and stolen property inside this place. I want to make sure that dirty Abrams does the right thing. Here's the plan. First, find the babe Lilli whatever her last name is. She's got a kid … girl … three or four, something like that … so you're gonna have to deal with that. No big deal. Hold her and the kid if they're together, if only her, so it is. Call me. I'll get one of the other guys, maybe Wolf, to pass for FBI who'll go to the scene, flash his badge, fake of course, and go directly to the dirt-bag and then hand him his cell. I'll arrange all cells are linked up together. You tell the babe she's gonna talk with the dirt-bag that her life and her kid's life are at risk unless he does exactly what I want. Then Wolf calls me on his cell and I tell the dirt-bag that my man will enter the house to remove some personal items … and for him not to interfere. I know exactly what room the stuff's at. I'll remind the dirt-bag to keep quiet, or else the babe and the kid will disappear forever. So, that's the plan. Any questions, Stone?"

Stone shakes his head sideways, "No. Sounds like it's gonna work."

Mickey says, "It's gotta work. Leave now … should take an hour for visual contact with her."

Since Mickey had made sure that a tracking device had been placed under Lilli's car while she and Natalie were eating at the diner, it is easy to alert the two who were following her that Stone would be taking over. He makes the phone calls to relay the information to everyone on the team.

Lilli is showing the stress of juggling so many balls in the air: the loss of Camille, Eric, Vincent, Henry, and Barbara. However, most importantly, she is stressing out trying to be as nurturing of a mother she can be with Natalie. She isn't forgetting how important John and Jeff are as well. Sometimes she just wants to scream, and sometimes she does. It's the freaking position she's placed herself in … the choices that she's made. And now, just thinking about it, she feels a flash of anger take over.

It's dark now, so the car's headlights are on. Natalie, her precious daughter in the backseat, remains sleeping, oblivious to all of what's going on in her mother's life. If it wasn't for Natalie, Lilli's not sure if her life would be worth continuing.

She lowers the driver's side window to let in the cool outdoor air to enter in and in a way for her most recent sad thoughts of those whom she has touched leave the car.

Her heart begins to pound and her lips start to quiver. She spots a rest stop up ahead, so she figures she should pull off the highway to take a short breather … to pull herself back together. She parks the car just a few yards from a rest room designated for females only. Another few yards away there is one for males only. She sits motionless in the car. She feels tension drain away from her body. Her breathing returns to normal. She closes her eyes. She doesn't bother to lock the car's doors and keeps the window slightly cracked open. She should be more careful.

Unaware to her, an hour ago Stone had taken over the detail of following her. He's slowed down to a slow crawl until he stops his car tight behind hers. His car's headlights are off. He silently steps out of his car to walk towards Lilli. There is a knock on the driver's side window that startles Lilli. Her eyes pop open, and then she turns left to spot him.

"You OK, miss?" His voice is soft and comforting as it enters through the partially open window.

"Who are you?" Her voice quivers enough for Stone to pick up. The inside of the window fogs up a bit.

"You just seem a little frightened."

She repeats, "Who are you?" Her heart beat returns to a rapid rate.

"Give me the keys." Now he sounds less comforting and more forceful.

Lilli doesn't answer.

Stone opens the driver side door and reaches in to remove the ignition key. "You two are coming with me." He sounds as if he is giving her a direct order … duh, he is.

"What do you want?"

"Don't panic." He reaches to grab hold of her.

"My daughter!"

He looks towards the back seat to spot the child, still soundly sleeping. "I'm not gonna take you from her." He pauses, gives a rare smile, and says, "Com`e bella."

"Hugh?"

"How beautiful she is."

He pulls out his cell phone, punches in a number, waits for the signal and then says to Lilli as he puts the cell to her face. "Say hello." His smile has disappeared.

She resists, not out of defiance but out of confusion. Then she hears another man's voice.

Mickey says, "Miss Lilli Jackson. How are you?"

"Who are you?" She doesn't recognize the voice.

"That's not important. But what is important all depends on what you do next. Do you understand that?"

"No, no. I don't know what you're talking about!" She sounds frantic and her eyes widen.

"You'll be talking with Detective Abrams in a short time. Don't go anyplace." Mickey's laugh sounds evil.

At the scene of the house break-in with Jeff off to the side far enough away from the reporter Kelly Sue Marsh and the camera, a well-dressed man in an expensive pin-striped business suit, white shirt, solid black tie, and shined black shoes slowly walks towards him. Wolf isn't a large man, about five-eleven, one-eighty-five, trim. There's an expensive looking watch on his left wrist that seems to be out of place for the role he's in. His brown eyes are piercing. His complexion is the color of rich tan. He looks like his nickname. As Wolf gets closer to Jeff he pulls out a fake FBI badge in one hand. "Detective Abrams, may I have a word with you." His voice is military sounding, in total control.

Jeff's look of surprise is quite noticeable. He thinks he might recognize the man, but not totally sure.

Wolf keeps the fake badge visible. "I need to talk with you in private about this matter." He nods towards the house where Larry and Frankie are.

"Sure." Jeff is a bit confused, but in a way thankful that the Feds are here to support him, maybe even take control of the situation if he had his way.

Wolf and Jeff step far enough away to be private.

Wolf takes out his cell and then punches in a number.

Jeff doesn't know what to say or do, so he doesn't say or do anything except wait and frown.

Wolf hands his cell to Jeff. "Somebody you know wants to talk."

Jeff keeps the frown. When he hears Mickey's voice he almost chokes.

"Hello, Jeff. Recognize me?"

"Holy crap!"

"Well, that's not what I was thinkin' of, but yeah, it's Mickey. How you doin'?"

Jeff grips the phone with both hands. "What do you want from me? I've got a critical situation I'm dealing with now!"

"I'm glad you said that. There's also someone I want you to say hi to."

Jeff continues to frown as he hears a clicking sound of some sort. Then suddenly he hears her voice.

"Jeff, it's me, Lilli." Her voice is in a frantic mode.

"Lilli?" His eyes widen in surprise.

"Yeah, please listen to me. Just do what they want. They've got me and Natalie."

"Lilli!" His facial appearance is unchanged.

The clicking sound returns. Suddenly he hears Mickey's voice again. "Listen carefully. There are some personal items inside the house. When it comes time to go into the house, my people will be first. The FBI guy with you will lead the way and I don't want you to enter the house. Nothing will be removed from that house except by my people. Do you get that?"

Jeff struggles to clear his throat. "I can't control that. There could be other law enforcement involved."

"I don't like repeating myself, Jeff. My people will be the first. They'll look FBI. Nobody messes with the Feds. Get it!"

"Uh." His mind goes blank for a split second.

"Hey, Jeff, don't panic. If this goes like I want it to go, nobody'll get hurt. You know, Lilli and her kid. Know what I'm sayin'?"

"OK, alright." He snaps back to reality.

"That's my boy. I got more of my people coming soon. They'll all report to the guy with you now, the FBI guy. If you do anything other than what I'm tellin' you, you'll never see Lilli and the kid again … never … unless, of course you want me to mail them to you in a UPS box."

"Yes, I understand."

The phone disconnects.

Now standing alone face to face with one of Mickey's guy, Jeff momentarily thinks to take-on the guy … or maybe just nod his head to agree. He's really not sure. He tells himself to be careful. Panic can kill. He's got to think straight. There's too much at risk if he does something … anything … stupid.

Wolf says to Jeff, "Look at my badge, memorize the name. That's who I am if anyone asks. I've got three more like me coming here in the next hour."

Jeff stares at the fake badge that looks official to him. His body is so tight that he feels like he's being squeezed by a boa constrictor, dark brown, ten feet long, and can't escape.

"What's the name on the badge?" Wolf demands. He appears to be getting a wee bit agitated.

"Special Agent Green."

"I want you to remember that name … that's who you refer to me. Is that clear?" His voice rises to a louder and more intense sound.

Jeff feels angrier than before, but fights to control showing it. It's not the time or the place to be machismo with the man standing before him. He'll wait for a better opportune time.

"Here's the story. I got a call from D.C. saying you requested help in a sensitive situation, a matter of national security. I dropped everything, and here I am. Got it?"

"Yeah, I've got it. But what if somebody tries to check it out? What then?"

"Let them. It'll check out." He pauses, "What's my name?"

Jeff hesitates, quickly getting tired with the ordeal.

"Answer it!" His voice is louder but his face remains like his nickname.

He takes in a deep breath of air and for a split second considers spitting directly into the guy's face. He doesn't, but softly in almost a whisper replies, "Special Agent Green."

Wolf ignores Jeff's feeble attempt of gamesmanship, but would enjoy pounding his face in. "And why am I here?"

Jeff knows the drill and has temporarily given up trying to be a smartass, "To help out in a matter of national security."

"Alright, just don't screw up. Think of Lilli and her daughter … how you want to protect them … to see them again, alive and well."

"I wish I knew your real time."

"Why's that … so you can send me a birthday card?" He chuckles a bit and then gets back to being serious. "Keep it tight."

"You know, I can't promise you'll screw up yourself or that somebody's gonna find out who you really are," says Jeff.

"Listen man, I don't want to hurt anyone that includes killing. I just want what's in the house and leave with it. That's all, nothing more."

Jeff's phone buzzes.

Wolf says, "You better answer it … could be important."

Jeff connects, "Yeah, Detective Abrams."

"Is Special Agent Green with you?"

Jeff recognizes Mickey's voice, "Yeah, he is."

"Put him on and stay right where you are."

Jeff passes the phone to Green without a word, and then watches him listen, looking for any body language that might be helpful.

The call ends quickly and the cell phone is returned to Jeff without anything that Jeff can use to help himself out.

Wolf says, "It starts in an hour from now."

Inside the house Frankie has come to, yet she's still groggy and staying motionless on the floor.

Larry watches her body twitch just enough to see her slowly move. He keeps quiet for the time being, but thinking about getting out of the place alive. He's already confessed to Jeff that it was all her fault. But why hasn't he just walked outside with his hands raised above his head? What is he afraid of?

Jeff not only feels traitorous, being unfaithful to his law enforcement duties and obligations, but also betraying himself as a human being. He was once one of the good guys. He wonders if he should … make that must … re-evaluate the choice he has made. Everything he's recently been through seems to get heavier and heavier to bear, pressing down on him with intensity. Enough pressure eventually breaks things open and spreads it all over the place, often times unrecoverable. He doesn't want to fail Lilli and Natalie, as well as himself. It's a long shot and a risky one, but he doesn't believe he has an alternative.

Green has stepped away leaving him alone. Jeff calls John Walker, betting the call is private.

"Hey Jeff … longtime." John is cautious but doesn't sound that way. He's experienced, but the information given to him from Hoskins about Jeff is very worrisome, yet still hard to believe any of it.

"Glad I got you. I, uh, have a few things to say, but you gotta promise me it stays between us … only us."

John remembers hearing the same from Hoskins. "Sure, Jeff, you got my word on it. I'm listening."

Jeff slowly begins to explain a lot about his life … the good with the bad … much like a sinner would confess to a priest during a confessional. It takes Jeff a solid uninterrupted twenty-five minutes, although he could have gone on for a full hour or so. He feels drained and yet happy to have done the data dump, but there's going to be some form of penance for his sins.

"Incredible." It's the first thought that comes to John's mind to say. He continues. "You know you're confessing punishable crimes … you could spend time in prison and never be allowed to work in law enforcement again."

Jeff sounds sheepishly but in a way cleansed inside. "I understand. But it's time to do the right thing."

"Anything that involves Lilli?"

"Bingo … right on … and there's more."

John continues to listen without prompting Jeff to say anymore. He feels his body tense.

"I need your help," says Jeff, almost in a plea.

John was wondering when the bomb would drop. "Tell me." He grins that is not even evident to him.

"I want three visible FBI Special Agents who know how to mentally and physically handle this, to replace the ones … whether they're the real thing or fake like I'm sure Green is. We'll rush the house, even if it means harming Larry and Frankie. Then the three FBI Special Agents will search the house for the stuff that Mickey wants removed. All of this has to be done quickly, and it has to start now. There's no time left to make this happen, so we'll manufacture some. Oh, one more thing. The television crew needs to be diverted to another situation. Whaddaya say? Can you do it?"

"What about Mickey Zitano and the rest of his crew?"

"He's usually at his private suite at *Ambasciata*, well-guarded. All communication from and to him has to be cut off. His claws are too long." He pauses, and then says, "I hope he's not listening in to this talk."

"Let's hope not, but if he is, it's too late to change. I gotta make a few calls. What's your drop deadline?"

"I hope it hasn't already passed, but I'd say less than zero hours from now when it all begins."

"So, immediately, is that it?"

"Yeah." His voice remains anxious and serious.

"OK, Jeff, I'll get back to you … faster than a speeding bullet. Keep your cell handy."

The phones disconnect.

Less than one-half hour of time passes when Jeff's cell buzzes. He picks it up quickly recognizing from caller-ID that it's John.

"Faster than a speeding bullet. Hell!" Jeff is excited.

"Jeff, I've got FBI Director Price on the line. Director Price, here's Detective Abrams. I'll let the two of you talk while I listen."

Jeff's eyes bulge with surprise.

The Director sounds very certain of himself, choosing not only the right words to use but how he uses them including the inflection in his voice. He's been the Director of the FBI for three different U. S. Presidents from both political parties, so he's well respected. His reputation is tough, fair, honest, and composed, rarely losing his temper. His face is long and narrow with wide cheek bones, a long square chin, and a low hairline that reduces the shape of his forehead. His eyes are closely set to one another as is his nose to his mouth. When he smiles, which is rare, it is uneven and without a twinkle from his eyes. He has square shoulders and a thick neck. He speaks in a monotone to Jeff.

"Zitano has to be stopped … that'll end your situation for certain and many more you don't even want to know about. Stopping him will also present future ones from arising. I've been informed that you've been at his place, *Ambasciata*, so you know it's like a fortified bunker. But once inside, there's the probability things will be found that he doesn't want anyone to know about. What I'm saying is that if we want Zitano badly enough, and I certainly do, he has to be approached directly … straight to him."

"Sir, can I ask a question?"

"Go ahead but cut the sir."

"OK." Jeff clears his throat. He hears John chuckle in the background, but he needs to put that insignificant thought aside. "So, you're saying we literally need to rush the place and in a way take no prisoners?"

"Can't literally do that, but there are other ways."

"Like what, if I may ask? I want to help."

"OK, I'll let you help. So listen carefully."

Zitano has been listening in the entire time, but it might be too late for him to do anything about that or maybe not.

A short time later, Jeff is able to distract Wolf/Green just long enough to disarm him and put cuffs on his wrists. Then Jeff pulls out his gun to point at the head of the fake FBI Agent. "You're gonna call whoever it is who is holding Lilli and her daughter and tell him he has orders from Zitano to release them, immediately. I hope I'm making that clear enough ... or else this will be your last day." He cocks the gun and touches it firmly against the forehead of Wolf/Green.

The click sound from cocking the gun is not unusual to Wolf/Green. He's been in similar situations before. "I can't do that. My orders have to be followed ... no improvising." Wolf/Green is composed for the moment.

"I don't think you heard me, so I'll repeat it one more time. "Release Lilli and her daughter, or else you die right here and now." Jeff smirks but his eyes don't. His hand remains firmly clasped on the gun, steady and ready to pull the trigger. Then he quickly lifts his right leg so that his knee squarely hits the fake FBI Agent in the groin.

Wolf/Green doubles over and lets out a moan.

"I think I've been clear enough. Call now."

"I – I don't have his number."

"Oh, you do. We both know you do. So, I'll count to five before you're dead. One, two, three, four, …."

"OK, I'll do it." He extends his life, but isn't sure for how long that will be.

Stone releases Lilli and Natalie.

At the same time that a search warrant is issued to allow the FBI to rush and then search the house where Frankie and Larry are, search warrants are also issued to search Zitano's private suite at *Ambasciata* along with the bar, restaurant, and full stage area where the entertainment takes place in addition to eleven specific rooms on other floors of the enterprise.

Frankie and Larry are arrested and plead guilty to a misdemeanor, serve five days in County Jail, and then are released.

Inside the house, where Frankie and Larry were held up, FBI Agents find cash, drugs, and stolen property that

Zitano's people were temporarily storing until the drugs and stolen property could be peddled.

Inside *Ambasciata* another team of FBI Agents finds one hundred seventy-three thousand dollars' worth of crack cocaine, two cases of stolen rifles, and approximately seventy-nine thousand dollars of stolen jewelry and pieces of artwork. Additionally, over two hundred videos displaying some of *Ambasciata's* wealthiest and well-known male customers engaging in sexual acts with mostly underage prostitutes along with nearly fifty CD's displaying financial spreadsheets of illegal financial transactions between Zitano and his clientele.

All the evidence is found admissible and it results in charges against Zitano and many others.

Nine weeks later after the evidence is analyzed trial dates against Zitano and others are determined.

Jeff Abrams pleads guilty on all charges. He is fired from his law enforcement position, loses all benefits that he has accrued with every law enforcement position he ever held. In return for the guilty plea and assisting in taking down Zitano and others, he is sentenced to one year in a Federal prison.

Zitano and his entire crew are all sentenced to life in a Federal prison with no chance of an early release.

Lilli Jackson and Natalie are doing fine. Lilli kept in constant contact with Jeff during the first few months in prison, developing a strong personal tie to one another, including several conversations about getting together after he's released, but their intentions with each changed quickly … prison time will do that. She and her daughter took in Jeff's dog, Lady. Lilli accepts an admin role with *Verity Security*, reporting directly to John Walker with a career path to take over the Company in a few years when John retires. She finally gets to wear a skirt and blouse with nice shoes to work.

CHAPTER 33

Jeff's one year sentence to a Federal prison doesn't last long ... not that it is shortened for good behavior or anything close to that. The truth of the matter is the prison term is extended to 5 years total because of bad behavior.

If you think about it, people serving prison time are there because they violated a law ... in other words did something illegal ... wrong, for the most part. Yes, there are some unfortunate situations when someone is jailed and remains there for a while who actually is innocent of the charge. Unfortunate things happen all the time ... that's life. But that's not the typical situation in the U. S. legal system.

And those in prison are usually anti-law enforcement types because it's law enforcement personnel who are the ones who apprehended the bad guys/gals that led to their trial and sentencing. And when someone from law enforcement is imprisoned they become live meat, so to speak, with a variety of adverse actions from others. In fact, the gangs that are created and perpetuated within the prisoner ranks take pleasure and even pride in making the law enforcement types suffer. That's just how it is.

When Jeff is imprisoned word spreads quickly in prison that a former Detective has been incarcerated and several gangs put together a variety of plans to teach him and his types a lesson or two. He isn't one of them and never will be accepted. There's no room for pretending anything otherwise.

Jeff is beaten up several times and close calls to his death occur during the five years that led to him being placed in solitary confinement in order to protect him. But it is because of those instances that he develops a stronger commitment to eventually get even with the gang members ... and on several occasions some of the prisoners are killed, but nobody is talking.

Jeff begins to realize something about him during the five years. He isn't either a good person or a bad person with an internal conflict fighting his good side against his bad side, and the theme of original sin. Jeff takes on a fundamentally different view of good and evil or the idea of heaven and hell. More precisely, human nature is inherently both good and evil, and these two options manifest themselves through the choices individuals make in their lives. Jeff is transformed and is comfortable with that.

And without having to point this out, it puts a damper on his relationship with Lilli. Their frequent conversations and some face-to-face meetings end.

Eventually, Jeff is released after serving the full five years in Federal prison, but has no job waiting for him, or so he thinks. However, in a strange way, he finds a family of sorts during his imprisonment who are hired for service merely for pay … in other words, a mercenary. Yet, he still considers himself a patriot who has the capacity to switch between good and evil through the choices he makes.

There's a full moon and Jeff is hidden outside a three story no-expense-spared mansion on a private island in the South Pacific Ocean. The walls of the place are as tall as the tallest part of the Great Wall of China with one side facing a dense jungle and the opposite side facing the Ocean. The flowers from the jungle smell as if they are very close and touching his nose.

He spots several cameras attached to the mansion that can easily pick up sound, motion, and foreign odor. Security is tight as to protect the owner of the building as well as whoever and whatever is inside.

Jeff thinks how cool it would be to live in a place like this.

He has gloves on his hands as he holds a high powered Smith and Wesson rifle with a telescope. He points the tip of the Smith and Wesson towards the mansion while looking through the telescope hoping to spot an open window or even a closed one without any covering so that he could check out where the target is. The guy he's hunting is a known terrorist, a pedophile, a drug and human trafficker and a low-life sonofabitch who has no right to be alive.

With no luck in spotting anyone inside the place, he uses his Dick Tracy-type wristwatch that counts time among other things to make contact with his partner, Desert Hawk … birth name Angel Hawk but nicknamed

Desert when he was young due to his physical appearance and sound of his coarse voice.

Desert Hawk is six feet three inches, lean and tough looking. His brown skin and set-in eyes accentuate his distinct jaw bone and jet black hair that is combed straight back underneath the ski-like black hat he wears. Just above his left eyebrow is a scar, the remnant of his final amateur boxing match in Chicago a while back when he suffered a severe concussion that almost cost him his life. Without much formal education past the eighth grade, he took up odd jobs to make it through life after he ran away from home ... a drunken and abusive father who couldn't keep a steady job and a mother who paid most of the home expenses from being a prostitute to whomever had the money. She preferred to refer to herself as a female escort with benefits.

Boxing was to be Desert's pathway to success, financial security, and eternal happiness ... what a pipe dream! At twenty-two years old, unable to box anymore for fear that just one more punch to his head would end his life ... so the doctors said ... he decided to put to use his innate interests and skills ... understanding people so well that he could read their body language, analyzing issues to focus on what really matters while ignoring the rest, and physical endurance coupled with strength. He's always believed that hard work would beat talent when talented people didn't work hard enough.

Now, at thirty-eight years old he has a reputation within a small and guarded community of warriors. He is paid very well and very much enjoys being a mercenary.

Jeff Abrams is one of his best friends, maybe his best, but Desert doesn't admit that to Jeff ... too mushy sounding.

On prior assignments, they've saved each other's life so many times they've stopped counting. They think of each other as warrior brothers, willing to protect each other at any cost, at any time.

Desert is equally equipped with identical weaponry as Jeff.

His identical Dick Tracy-type wristwatch that is electronically linked to Jeff's sends him a pulsating signal. He listens.

"See anything?" Jeff's voice is calm and focused without any sort of emotion.

"Nothing, no movement," replies Desert with an almost identical vocal sound. "But some of the windows on this side are covered with what looks like curtains. Maybe that's where the target is."

"Could be more than one … is that what you're sayin'?"

"Yeah … it's a freakin' large place … could be armed or could contain a crew just waiting to see what happens. But I doubt that since there's no freakin' way they could've known we were comin' … won't know for sure unless we get closer."

"We could chuck grenades though the windows. The chemicals would cause a lot of damage. And with fire and smoke they'd have to leave the building, and then we'd be in control."

"Sure, but how much fun would that be, bro? I say we wait it out a little longer. Somebody's gonna take a peek out of one of the windows and that will be the end of that."

"You sure, bro?"

"Hell no!" He chuckles.

"The guy's a piece of crap! I don't care how he dies … as long as he does."

"See the Porsche Turbo outside? Hate to see it go to waste if we blow up the building." Desert chuckles.

"We could move it far enough away from the place to secure it." It's Jeff's turn to chuckle.

"Could be cash inside too that'll burn away if we blow up the building," Desert adds, along with another chuckle.

Then there is silence between them for a short time as each of them thinks the same thoughts: wouldn't be right in taking the Porsche, the money, or anything else from the scumbag. Each of them will earn considerable U. S. dollars off their contracts once the dooshbag is dead.

"I say we move in ... take out who we find ... finish this deal." Jeff waits for Desert's response. When there is only silence he's about to repeat his idea, but he doesn't have time to say anything before it happens. He hears a sound similar to a baseball bat smacking a baseball that's thrown at ninety-five miles per hour straight over home plate in the strike zone. He knows what just happened, so he smiles.

Desert's voice is once again calm and without emotion. "He should've never looked through the window. I'd say it's safe for us to enter."

"I'll take the front two doors, you enter the rear." Jeff too keeps emotion out of the conversation.

"Roger that. The target was on the third floor where the den is. That's where we'll find the body."

Entering the mansion is easier than what Jeff or Desert thought it would be. The two front doors are unlocked which makes it super easy for Jeff to enter.

In the rear of the place, a kitchen window is slightly ajar so Desert only climbs through.

Separately, each of them silently and swiftly creeps through their respective areas to make sure no one else is inside, and if they find someone, they'll immediately secure the area. They find no one else as they move from room to room regularly checking with each other saying the same, "area secure."

They both reach the den on the third floor at the same time to find the target's dead body, face up on the wooden floor near the curtain-less window. There is a single bullet hole in the man's forehead and blood is slowly creeping out onto the wooden floor.

"Piece of waste," is all that Jeff says.

"I'll take a photo of him as evidence. Sorry you didn't have the pleasure of putting him down." Desert takes a photo using his Dick Tracy-type wristwatch.

Jeff lowers his rifle, but then seems to change his mind. He raises it towards the dead man. "Yeah, you should have let me take him down."

"Jeff, no … don't do it."

Jeff ignores Desert's remark as he shoots the dead body in the forehead. He smiles but his eyes don't. Then he blinks at the dead body as if he's someone interested in doing something more. His hands remain firmly clasped on his rifle longer than normal, reinforcing some internal dilemma he's struggling with. He's blocked out all external information and sound.

He visualizes a grayish shaped bald eagle moving through the cloudless sky, beautifully navigating itself, graceful and yet strong and determined. The bald eagle slowly drops to the water's edge, letting its six foot wingspan take over its flight. Then, suddenly, swiftly, accurately, forcefully, it snatches its prey with its powerful talons and then ascends upward.

Then Jeff's head slightly snaps back, still looking at the dead body. He grin is an evil looking smirk. "OK, we're done here."

Jeff and Desert leave the mansion with their target dead in his den, proud of the completed mission.

CHAPTER 34

Lilli stands in the doorway of her kitchen. It's seven in the morning, Tuesday, another work day at *Verity Security*. She feels energized in spite of what she believed to be a restless sleep.

Natalie, now eight years old growing fast to become a teenager regardless of how much her mother wants her to remain her baby, is mixing Lady's breakfast. Amazing how the two of them … young girl and old dog … get along so well. Wouldn't the world be better if we all could just get along with one another like they do?

Lilli continues to smile at them realizing that Natalie will be a teen before too long with the probability, as many teens do, of seemingly behaving like frustrated attorneys during a trial … asking seemingly stupid questions, challenging the smallest most unimportant piece of information, and acting as if they are a know-it-all with strange looking facial expressions and hand movements included. She reminds herself to enjoy the present.

They'll be a time when Lilli and her daughter will not see each other as much as they do these days. Natalie will be growing up, and Lilli will have to let her grow up and let her go, leaving herself alone for the most part, unless of course, she finds a man to be by her side. But now is not the time to think of that.

Natalie finishes with Lady's food preparation, pets the dog, and stands. Then she turns to her mother with a big beautiful honest smile ... eyes twinkling like bright stars in the sky. "How did I do?" She points to Lady eating her breakfast.

Lilli thinks her little girl is all grown up, but still her baby. "Fantastic. Thank you."

Natalie runs to her mother's open arms for a long hug.

"After breakfast, we'll each get ready ... you for school and me for work." Lilli feels confident that within a year John will hand over the full operation of *Verity Security* to her, and then she and Natalie will look for a bigger and nicer place to call home. Natalie needs a bedroom of her own. And with a probable salary bump, she'll be able to start putting a few dollars away on a regular basis to save for her daughter's college tuition. She doesn't want Natalie to have money problems, especially starting at a young age.

The day's work starts out routinely for Lilli. John is reviewing some contracts that are about to renew along with a few new ones. His attorney, Lester Brey, has taken a thorough review of a few of them so far and written comments in the margins so John could see. There's not much noise inside the office that he now shares with Lilli.

She, on the other hand, is given the contracts that both John and Lester have reviewed in order to offer her point of view that would include suggestions. The three of them have found this method to be valuable for everyone, especially Lilli so that she can better understand the business.

Lilli's desk is jammed face to face against John's desk. This office arrangement doesn't leave much room for much of anything else besides file cabinets, a coat rack, and one chair besides the ones that John and Lilli sit in.

John takes off his reading glasses, rubs his tired looking eyes that have noticeable bags below them, and then stretches his arms over his head. He yawns loud enough to interrupt Lilli's concentration.

She pops her head away from the contact she's reviewing towards John. "Break time?"

"Yeah," he says and then lets out a deep breath of air. He stands, now facing her. Their desks are the only items separating them. Then he grins. "I've been thinking about a transition plan."

She, at first, isn't sure what he means, but then quickly picks up on the message. She grins, "You mean …." She feels her heart beat pick up before completing her thought.

"Bingo." He interrupts her. Then he clears his throat as his fingertips touch the top of his desk. "Lester advises me to develop a timeline and put it in writing. His experiences in leadership transitions say that when it's written and agreed upon, it's more likely to happen smoothly … you know … especially if something unexpected happens to me."

She's momentarily speechless, yet thinking to herself that it's really going to happen. Then she focuses on something else. "Nothing's going to happen to you, John. Don't even think like that." She thinks she might be sounding more like a mother to a child than someone getting prepped to take over an entire business.

He smiles, "Now you're sounding like a wife." He laughs.

She joins in with a chuckle of her own while keeping her thoughts of mother and wife to herself.

"Anyway, I've got a rough draft here in my desk." He opens the middle drawer to pull out a heavyweight clasp envelope that contains the draft document. He extends his right arm holding onto the envelope to her. "Take a look at it. Let me know what you think. OK?"

Her eyes widen with pleasure and surprise at the same time. "Sure." She feels giggly in a way.

"It might seem aggressive but you've learned so much about this business already that I'm not worried at all. I'll stay on as your consultant for as long as you want and I'm productive. I trust you."

She feels her eyes moisten and her nose watery, almost starting to dribble out droplets of liquid. She sniffles. Then she walks around her desk and his to stand in front of him, extends her arms around him, and presses her head against his chest. "I'm so thankful for everything that you're doing and have already done."

They remain in that pose for only a few brief seconds, but it feels much longer to both of them.

John clears his throat. "OK, back to the contacts."

She returns to her desk with the envelope still firmly clutched in her hand as John sits down.

He says, "Oh, one more thing."

Lilli thinks to herself … "This is the bad news."

He continues, "I want to have a celebration, nothing real formal, just a party of some sort once we agree on the terms and conditions. I want you to officially meet some people who you'll be closely working with … sort of who you'll be depending on. No speeches or anything like that … nothing fancy, just, you know … a celebration. OK?"

"Whatever you say, John, I'm in."

CHAPTER 35

The Phoenix isn't a cheesy club nor is it a five star establishment, yet it's the right place to celebrate the leadership transition from John to Lilli. And, it's not as if *Verity Security* is being brought back to life as the name of the place might suggest. It's one of *Verity Security's* clients and the food and service are top rate. There is a private room in the back to the right where a bar is set up and a wide variety of hors-d'oeuvres are served before a sit-down dinner takes place.

Lilli doesn't recognize most of the people present, just a few like Detective Parsons, Detective Hoskins, and Lester Brey. That's when it hits her that many people she has been close to aren't around anymore. It would be nice if Natalie was by her side, but the evening is really geared towards adults, and her daughter would most likely be bored to death. Her daughter is in good hands … the parents of one of Natalie's school friends offered to help out … although she'd rather be with Natalie and Lady.

There's a photographer roaming around taking mostly candid pictures, a few posed. She doesn't like photos taken of her alone, but with Natalie and Lady by her side is something else. Everyone is dressed in casual-style clothes. Country music plays in the background … Willie Nelson,

Garth Brooks, Charlie Pride, Dolly Parton, Shania Twain, and Johnny Cash. She doesn't recognize any of the music or performers … not her preferred music. While the music might be full of life, she can't hear the lyrics.

Lilli isn't a drinker like with shots. A glass or two of wine suits her fine, but it seems she's out of place with those present. She wonders how often she'll be expected to socialize with them once she's in charge of *Verity Security*. She might not want to, but she'll probably consent.

She smiles and nods her head, even a laugh or two, as if on cue. She takes the lead from others who she's immediately with. This is all new to her and not as comfortable as she'd like, but it is what it is.

"Well, well," John says as he looks over her shoulders towards the door entrance to the room. "Look who's here." He has a big grin on his face, happy to see the man.

Lilli turns around to see a man standing in the doorway. He's dressed in dark pants with a cowboy style dark blue belt and matching silver buckle, open collar western style dress shirt, and dark blue cowboy boots. She figures he's an inch or two over six feet, light bronze skin tone, perfect looking teeth, and wavy black hair parted to the left side. She almost drops the wineglass she's holding onto. She doesn't recognize him, but intends to get acquainted if at all possible at the first possible opportunity.

The man walks her way … or is it towards John? It doesn't matter, she's staying right where she is.

John extends a welcoming handshake. "Eddie, so glad you could make it. You know most of the people here, but I don't think you know Lilli Jackson." He nods towards her.

Eddie smells good to Lilli. She thinks the fragrance might be a pine and cedar combination. It must be his aftershave. She has no choice but to look at him, and then she smiles as she extends her hand, "I'm Lilli." She feels her heart beat pickup as if she is a young girl again. She's got to stay composed and not be teenager-like … friendly, but not flirtatious. She doesn't want to embarrass herself or John.

He grabs her hand with his. She's too taken with him to notice a slim elegant dress watch by Rolex on his wrist. They momentarily stare at each other before he says, "I'm Eddie Wing. I have contracts with employment agencies that represent highly qualified candidates who've already been vetted in the security field. We can't let the wrong people work in security."

John interrupts, "And he knows people. He can be trusted."

"Thanks, John, I appreciate the recommendation." Then he turns to Lilli, "When you're ready I'd like you to get to know me and my business well enough to consider continuing using my services. I promise I won't let you down … ever." He smiles with a noticeable grin of pleasure.

She feels her legs shake a bit so she takes in a deep breath to focus her attention. "Thanks. Do you have a card?" She smiles.

"Sorry, not with me, but John knows how to find me. I really wasn't thinking of my business at the time … you know, sometimes you just got to take a break." Her smile is magical to him.

They are suddenly interrupted with a shout. "Hey, Eddie!" a voice springs from across the room.

Eddie turns towards the voice, sees a hand holding a glass of whiskey that seems to wave him to join. He recognizes the man and the *Knob Creek Rye Old Fashion* he is holding. He turns to John and Lilli, "Excuse me. I've got to catch up with Tip. He and I go way back and well, it's long overdue."

"Sure, go catch up," says John. "I'll get you and Lilli hooked up soon."

"Nice meeting you, Lilli," says Eddie.

"Yes, likewise," answers Lilli.

Eddie moves away, towards the man he calls Tip, along with his manly scent. She stares at him but is interrupted by John.

"He likes you and you like him … quite obvious."

"Huh?" She's out of her trance.

"I can tell when a guy is interested in a woman and vice versa. The body language and the sound of the voice are the obvious "*tells*." In fact, there's not much difference between the two sexes."

Lilli frowns, "Huh?" She's still thinking about Eddie.

John explains, probably more than he should, but that's John. "It seems to be the popular thing to say that women are the weaker sex, more emotional, and often times irrational in what they do and what they say." He shrugs his shoulders as he continues, "You wonder what fools believe that." He continues, "Many men don't know how to relate to strong willed women, those determined to do and say something, confident and secure in who they are. And a man in love or infatuated with someone, something, even himself is a personified weakling. He can really be manipulated when he's in that emotional and mental state. Or, maybe there're very little emotional and mental differences between women and men?" He takes a break and then picks up again. "Sure, there are examples of some men being stronger than women in some instances under certain conditions, but there are also plenty of examples where women are stronger than men. In fact, no two people, men and women, are exactly the same. They may be similar perhaps but not exactly the same. Even so called identical twins have their differences. This, therefore, makes each and every one of us unique, different, and special from everyone else."

She can't hold back a grin to herself, not really listening to what John has said. She's thinking of Eddie.

But John continues as he grins to her. "He's gonna ask me for your e-mail and phone number. Do I give it to him?"

She thinks to herself … "I'm never too young to start dreaming, and I'm never too old to believe my dreams won't come true because dreams have no expiration date."

"Well, Lilli, do I?"

She looks at John in the eyes. "Maybe I should call him … maybe he should call me? Only give him my contact information if you give me his too."

CHAPTER 36

It's been ten days since the celebration party, and Lilli's stomach is tight as a drum, almost to the point of cramps. She feels anxious and hopes that she'll be able to eat dinner tonight with Eddie. The new clothes she bought feel just right for the occasion … a first date … not too revealing nor too conservative, at least that's what the saleslady told her … a plain black dress that falls just below her knees, a white silk blouse along with black heels not too high. She wears little makeup. Her hair is short to accentuate her eyes and cheeks. She wonders about the flirting part of a first date … teasing with each other … she has no idea. She'll figure it out, even if it's spontaneous.

When Eddie called her, which was her preference, she said she'd meet him at the restaurant because she wanted to cover all bases. She didn't want to be dependent on him picking her up at her place and then if things didn't turn out positive, the drive back to her place would be uncomfortable. There's nothing like planning for a worse-case scenario so that's why she preordered an Uber to and from the restaurant.

As she steps towards the restaurant's door, an older man dressed in a business suit, dress shirt with tie, and black shoes opens the door. "Good evening, Miss. Enjoy." He nods just enough to be noticed and isn't able to conceal a smile of pleasure in admiring her looks.

Once inside the restaurant, she spots Eddie at the stylish bar. She begins to feel nervous all over again. It's been a while since she's been out on a first date. She hopes he doesn't notice.

He steps towards her and close enough to touch her hand. He says, "I was actually wondering if you would cancel." He learns towards her just enough to kiss her on the cheek.

She smells the same pine and cedar fragrance, and notices he is dressed differently than when they first met. His clothes are more traditional yet stylish … fitted shirt without a tie, unbuttoned at the top, and a suit with dark polished shoes. Her voice is unusually low, yet clear. "I wouldn't do that."

"You look lovely … actually breathtaking." They stare at each other for a few seconds.

A head waiter appears. "Mr. Wing, your table is ready."

Once seated the head waiter hands them a large-sized menu as he asks, "Something to drink before dinner?"

Eddie asks Lilli, "Do you prefer wine or something else?"

"Chardonnay is fine, but only a glass."

Eddie looks at the head waiter, "Make that two *Coppola's*, and give us a little time to review the menu."

The head waiter disappears.

"You've been here before, I assume," she states while she smiles.

"Yes, this restaurant has been here for a while, family owned and operated. I'm loyal."

"That's nice to hear." She's referring to his loyalty, not that the place is family owned and operated.

"If there's something that's not on the menu that you prefer, we can tell them, and if they have the ingredients they can make it."

"What do you suggest?"

"Beef, fowl, fish, veggie … what's your preference?"

"Fish."

"Their fresh salmon with spicy red sauce is fantastic."

She puts the menu on the table top, smiles and says, "I guess that settles it. Don't make easy decisions more difficult to make." She feels settled down.

"Any hobbies?"

She figures he's diving right into getting to know her. Bravo! She doesn't want to sound foolish. She smiles, "I have an eight year old daughter who's growing up faster than I'd like. She takes up time and I love her so much. Husband left a long time ago and recently died. She never met him and I never talk about him."

Eddie thinks to himself … "So much for small talk." Then he says out loud, "Oh."

"Which part?" She smiles but needs a bit more clarification.

"I'm sorry about your ex, but you're lucky to have a daughter you love."

"And you?"

"Never been married … no children … spend all my time working." He lies, something he's good at.

"Nothing else?" She's surprised, but doesn't press the issue, at least not now, maybe later.

"Nothing else. Never been arrested or anything like that, or even robbed a bank and gotten away with it." He holds back a grin.

"You're funny, in a way." She doesn't want to sound too flirty.

"Lilli, I like you. I know we've only known each other a little, but I like you and would like to know more about you."

She takes in a deep breath of air. "There's really not much more to know than what I've already said." She wonders if that sounds too defensive. It seems he's coming on to her quickly and strongly.

"Honestly, I don't believe that." He smiles, thinking he'd like to jump in bed with her right now.

Somehow his pine and cedar fragrance settles on her.

Another waiter appears to place a glass of Chardonnay in front of each of them. "Two *Coppola's.*" He looks at him and then at her. "Are you ready to order?"

Eddie says, "Thank you, but give us a little more time."

"Of course." The waiter leaves their table.

Each of them raises their glass of wine to each other. Both of them hesitate while their eyes look deeply into each other wondering who's going to say something first and what it will be.

He's the first to speak. "To your continued health, happiness, and success."

Although Lilli is somewhat relieved he had spoken first ... the pressure is off her ... she'd like to have him say something else, something more personal than job related, although she's not sure what that would be. "And to you as well." Better to be safe than sorry.

Each of them takes a sip of wine.

She wonders if he's disappointed in what she said. She hopes so, but she can't tell. He has a way of couching his feelings and even some of his thoughts until he's prepared to share.

They each order the fresh salmon and continue to talk about this and that, nothing very personal or interesting to each other, but it's probably the safest thing to do … just enough to keep each other's attention with the hope there will be a second date sometime soon. Life is a succession of events, some obviously linked to each other, others not so obvious, yet still linked.

He thinks to himself how beautiful she is, externally and internally. He knows more about her than he's willing to share right now … the results of a little investigation. He could be so fortunate if things fall into place between them. He wonders what she's thinking, but decides not to push it right now. And there are a few things about himself that he intends to keep hidden. He thinks about having sex with her.

The ten o'clock hour arrives. They've finished their meals along with a second glass of *Coppola* each. No desert. They both are more relaxed with each other and themselves than when they first met earlier in the evening.

Eddie offers Lilli a ride home. "Can I take you home? It's no bother."

"Ah, I've already reserved with Uber. Just need to call in." She wishes she hadn't, but she could cancel.

He wants to suggest she cancel the Uber but doesn't ... that might come across too aggressive.

"At least let me wait with you outside until the driver arrives."

"Thanks, that's nice of you."

She makes the call before they leave the restaurant and after Eddie pays the bill. "Ten minutes top."

"Darn, I was hoping they lost your reservation." He smiles. "Can we do this again?"

She hesitates as if she's not sure or just surprised. "Yes, I'd like that."

Once outside of the restaurant, the Uber is already waiting. "Fastest ten minutes I've experienced." His tone isn't clear enough to interpret.

She asks herself ... "Does he mean sorry it wasn't longer or happy we don't have to talk anymore?"

He opens the back seat door as she gets in, but not before he gives her a kiss on the cheek. "Soon."

The vehicle drives off leaving Eddie watching.

Eddie Wing isn't her boyfriend just yet, but there is that possibility, so she thinks. There are enough ... make that too many ... jerks out there who'd love to have just a single one-night stand, or even just an hour of sex with her. But she has no interest with those types of guys, especially the ones who are too consumed with themselves.

She wonders what he thinks about her, other than ... "I'd like to get to know you, or whatever it was he said." And then there was ... "Can we do this again? What the hell does that mean?" But still lingering in the back of her mind is something about him that she can't put her finger on ... aloofness or maybe shyness or maybe intentionally hiding something ugly from her or maybe her own apprehension about getting too close to a man again. Look what happened with Eric and Jeff.

She tries to turn her attention away from him, but that's harder to do than what she'd like, considering her rocky history with men. And now it's Eddie, first friends and then lovers? How much she would love to be touched by him in all the right places ... and of course ... he with her, as if they had memorized each other's body map so well in such a short time. She feels her body is ready for that again, now, in fact more than ready, but it's her damn logical mind that's distracting her. Damn it! She has to find a way to get a handle on what she's going through, yet she knows it will be much harder now. As quickly as she thinks she feels him emotionally disappear, she is surrounded by his scent, the sound of his voice, and the warmth of his body. Then, as quickly as possible, she snaps out of the daydream.

She looks out the back seat window seeing her reflection. At first she's not sure who she's seeing. The face in the window seems to be worried, and then she flashes forward ... way forward ... if or when they're married. At that point in time they each ask the other a question about something that really doesn't matter because it's just a simple question for each of them to have an opinion on ... no right or wrong answer, just an answer. They look at each other as if each of them has no ready opinion or maybe each of them is waiting for the other one to go first. Oh crap, is marriage worth it ... ever ... any time? But why can't she be who she is, a woman with her own opinion regardless of whatever anyone else thinks? She's an individual with an opinion who wants to tell. What's wrong with that?

And then quickly she tells herself that she's not going to get off the imaginary therapist couch before her time is up.

She thinks how nice it would be if she had someone special she could talk with about any or all of this, even if she hasn't regularly talked with her, him, or them in a while. John comes the closest, but she's not sure about sharing some of her most inner personal thoughts with the man who's turning over his Company to. He might change his mind about the transition. She feels lonely and alone, except of course for Natalie and Lady, but they're in a totally different category.

While Eddie stares at the Uber driving away Lilli, he too has a few things on his mind, and the perfect one to talk with. He speed dials.

"Yeah" The voice is coarse sounding.

There is noise in the background that is all too familiar to him. "Knew you'd be at *McGuire's.*"

Tip answers, "And?"

"I'm on my way. You can help me think through a few things."

"Ah, so she wouldn't go to bed with you." Tip chuckles.

"Something like that. You sober enough to carry on a conversation?"

"I'm sure I've got a few tips of the glass left," Tip replies.

"Funny. Don't go anyplace."

"No intentions."

Eddie shuts down the cell phone and then walks to his valet parked 2020 milky white Carrera 4-S. He waves to the guy who recognizes him immediately. Within a few minutes Eddie is driving to *McGuire's*.

There's no valet parking or any other organized parking at *McGuire's*, so Eddie cruises the streets to find a suitable spot on the street underneath a lamp light and in full view to park where it is safe.

He enters the bar that is still packed with mostly regulars, but not entirely … singles and couples of various races, religions, and nationalities … all of whom are well above the legal drinking age. There's music blaring that is mostly unrecognizable by most and that's just fine since that's what it is intended for … unrecognizable blaringly loud music. There's no one at the front door to welcome you in or thank you when you leave, but there are three large-sized men with mainly muscle who are crammed into tight fitting short sleeve green tee-shirts wearing dark pants, and Adidas shoes. The name of the place, *McGuire's*, is clearly visible on both the back and front of the green tee-shirts of each man who will settle any and all disputes that may arise within the boundaries of the establishment.

The thirty foot long bar is immediately to the right as you walk in. Three male and two female bartenders are serving drinks … beer, wine, rye, scotch, whiskey, gin, vodka, and tequila, as well as specialty concoctions such as *Organism*, *Climax*, and *Screw*. There are five female and three male servers who roam around taking orders from those not seated at the bar.

Except for the name, *McGuire's*, on their tee-shirts, the rest of their clothing for the bartenders and servers is of their choosing. No two people are dressed alike.

The bar room also contains fifteen chest-high cocktail tables with adjoining chairs.

To the left of the bar is another room of the same dimensions with another fifteen chest-high tables and adjoining chairs.

All seating is filled which means many others are simply standing, talking, and drinking.

Food is only served on Sundays between 9 am and 3 pm in the form of a brunch.

Eddie knows exactly where Tip is … a seat at the far end of the bar just a few feet from the separate male and female restrooms. Tip has been a regular for so long that there's a sign on the back of one chair identified as *Reserved*. He's tipping a *Knob Creek Rye* when he hears his name called out over the blaring music.

"Tip!"

He doesn't need to turn around because he recognizes Eddie's voice, even over the blaring music, but he's not real happy that he might have to end the conversation he's having with Phyllis, someone he just met and who is new to the area. But that's what buddies are for!

Eddie immediately notices Phyllis, a strikingly beautiful woman about the same age as Tip, probably a little over six feet, slender, with clear complexioned skin. Her crossed legs display slender yet apt muscles as if she is or was an athlete of some sort. Her blue eyes contrast nicely with her skin tone as does her short straight black hair.

Eddie nods to Phyllis who doesn't respond, and then he says to Tip, "I appreciate your time." There's no vacant chair to sit in so he stands next to Tip.

Tips smiles to himself because he's just figured out a way to be with both Phyllis and Eddie at the same time. He says to Eddie, "This is Phyllis. She's new in town. Works in *Human Resources* at *American Staffing*." Then he turns to Phyllis, smiles, and says, "This here is my best friend, Eddie. He's ancient, been around the block a few times."

"Glad to meet any friend of my new friend, Tip." She smiles showing off her perfect white teeth.

"You know, Eddie, Phyllis here might be helpful to your situation." Tip turns towards Phyllis as he opens his eyes a bit wider.

"I'm game." She pauses, "Whatta you drinkin'?"

"Same as Tip."

Phyllis turns to the nearest bartender to order Eddie a *Knob Creek Rye*.

"Busy tonight," Eddies says, not sure how to start the conversation now that Phyllis has joined.

"Yeah, but not surprising." Tip knows exactly what Eddie's doing, waiting for the right opening.

Eddie's *Knob Creek Rye* is placed on top of the bar in front of him. He reaches for it, pauses, and then says, "To friends."

All three take a sip of their drink.

Phyllis figures she's got nothing to lose by starting the conversation. "H. R. issues at work?"

Eddie nods, "No, it's a little more complicated."

Phyllis grins, "That can only mean one thing." She takes a sip of her specialty drink, *Climax*.

"And what's that?" Eddie asks.

"Woman."

Eddie and Tip laugh in unison.

Then Tip adds, "Was I right about Phyllis or what!"

Phyllis takes up, "So, you're having a problem with your wife, ex-wife, girlfriend, ex-girlfriend, or someone you're not too sure about, meaning if she is the right one or not. How close am I?"

"You covered all the possibilities, but it's the last one. I'm not a kid. I mean, I've been around a little so I'm not naïve, but, well, I'm confused about Lilli. I just met her ... had dinner with her tonight."

Phyllis looks at Tip, grins, and then says, "Confusion, all too common." She turns to look at Eddie. "Tell me what you know about her, what you don't, what you wanna know, and what confuses you."

Eddie answers, "Feels like I'm lying on a couch while a psychologist is examining my every thought."

"Well, Eddie, that's what I do for *American Staffing*. I interview job candidate finalists in order to determine if they are a good match with the client's values and culture. That's probably the single biggest criteria for success with any company ... do you match the values and culture of the company you think you want to work for. The company's values and culture aren't going to change, and if there's an incompatibility, either the person changes or else gets fired because the company isn't about to change its values and culture to fit the individual person. And, further, in my opinion, the number one criteria for a happy, long lasting relationship between two people is this fit. Some say it's simpatico. So, what I think I hear you saying is you want to know more about her to figure out if there is a simpatico between the two of you. Therefore, tell me a little about what you know about her."

"She's a single mother of an eight year old daughter who she loves very much. She and her husband split that gave her full custody of the child. He died ... I don't know the cause. She's a hard worker, thoughtful, and conscientious. She's protective of her personal life, at least that's what I suspect. I think she'd like to get to know me better, but maybe that's just my personal wish. I could be all wrong about that. She's gonna be the head boss of *Verity Security*, personally selected by the founder and current head guy who wants to step aside. I'm a bit surprised of his decision because she's really not deeply skilled in that arena, and has never managed other people, not to mention an entire company."

He's decides not to tell Phyllis what else he knows about Lilli through other contacts, for example, the Conroy's deaths, Abrams situation, the old guy who proposed to her, Detective Parsons, and Lester Brey. There's no sense to that since he'd have to explain how he knows.

Phyllis leans towards Eddie, "Listen to me. This was your first date. What did you think was going to happen ... get her in the sack and then each of you explains in full detail everything about yourselves? Hell, that's not likely ... maybe the sack part is, but definitely not the rest."

She then turns to Tip who's been mostly quiet. "Or am I missing something?"

"You've said it more clearly than I could have, but no." Then Tip turns to Eddie, "Getting to know someone and to open up to someone as we get older isn't easy. Hell, I'm more protective of who I am today than when I was eighteen. I don't think I've made close friends for a bunch of years."

Phyllis interrupts, "Does that mean I've got to break you free?" She broadly smiles at Tip.

"I'd be worth it." He tries to match her smile but falls short. Then he touches her hand that doesn't pull away. Their eyes stay glued on each other for a short time.

Then, Phyllis looks at Eddie. "So, my advice is to ask yourself how far you'll go to open up to Lilli as to how you feel about her and about yourself. In a way, it's a good definition of freedom … to be who you are regardless of who cares. Although I suspect you want Lilli to care, but that's the risk, isn't it. And, you're hoping that she'll do the same with you. Do you want a relationship with her that is 50 - 50, meaning each only gets half of what they want? Not for me! Or, is it something else that gets both of you the maximum freedom and love from each other possible? Yeah, that's what I want!"

Eddie wasn't expecting the conversation to be like this. He has to figure out what he wants and what he's willing to do to get it. He blinks his eyes a few times, takes in a deep breath that he slowly releases, and then looks at the mostly empty three drink glasses on the bar in front of them. He says to the bartender, "Another round."

That evening, alone in bed, while Natalie and Lady are staying with the family of her daughter's best friend, Lilli tosses and turns, unable to sleep, consumed with mixed thoughts.

The more she thinks about the leadership transition from John to herself, the more unsettled she becomes. It's not that she doesn't think she's smart enough to run a company. It's just that this particular industry, security, can be emotionally challenging. She's already faced some awful situations that have challenged every ounce of emotional strength. Will she have to become emotionally numb to crime, criminals, victims, and all the consequences associated with it … in other words, to not feel the pain so as to not be influenced at all? Or, will she be able to place herself in a situation to feel the agony of others, to be passionate, but not to let it adversely affect her? Might she have to become non-human and more robotic?

Not everyone is emotionally equipped the same way. She wonders if she's headed down a one-way path that she'll regret and then have no way to change course.

And how might her decision to continue with the transition influence her personal life … especially with her daughter, Natalie, not to mention any chance of a real adult relationship with someone, whoever that might be?

She might never hear the sounds of her man in the bathroom as she lies in bed while he brushes his teeth and gargles with mouthwash before he joins her in bed to cuddle next to her and touch her in all the right places that make her feel perfect, and then wake up next to him the next morning. And she might never hear water on his naked body while he showers, nor visualizing him naked as he shaves, nor smell the fragrance from his aftershave lotion.

She might be preventing Natalie from having a father who loves her, no one to quiz her daughter about the boy she's seeing and what they do when they're together alone.

There might not be any Thanksgiving dinners with turkey, gravy, bread stuffing, mixed vegetables, cranberries, and pumpkin pie with even a little glass of wine or two.

Her whole live might be very different.

None, all, or some of this may happen. She doesn't know for sure. Who does? Lilli asks herself if that's what she's willing to give up to be the leader of *Verity Security*.

CHAPTER 37

Earlier the next morning, much earlier than she prefers due to the restless sleep, Natalie and Lady are with her in the kitchen and they're eating breakfast. All seem to be very happy to be back together even though they weren't really apart very long. But, just the same, they're a happy family.

Lilli isn't very hungry, but she enjoys the presence of her family. She sips on her third cup of coffee.

Lilli arrives at work at her usual time. The front desk where Fred used to sit has been eliminated. It's now open space. John is reviewing some paperwork as he drinks some of the worse tasting coffee ever made. She's not sure how she'll respond to any questions she might get from John about last night's first date with Eddie. She's not sure herself how she feels … it's all still confusing to her. But, why would John care one way or another about her personal life? And even further, how would he know that she and Eddie had dinner together? She's not mentioned it, but did Eddie?

"Good morning, John."

"Uh," he doesn't even look up to make eye contact.

Antonio F. Vianna

She senses through his response and posture that he's preoccupied with something more important than a simple ritualistic morning greeting. Maybe he's waiting for her to offer something else. She heads toward the coffee pot to pour the worse tasting coffee ever made. It's a simple ritual. Then she takes a seat in her chair behind her desk that faces him.

His head is still tilted downward as he speaks, "Something's come up."

"What?" she asks.

"My cousin Denny."

She's relieved he's not asking about last night's dinner with Eddie. "You know something?" She doesn't wait for a reply. "I didn't know you had a cousin Denny."

"Really, never mentioned him?"

"No, not to me." She shrugs her shoulders. "It's none of my business, anyway."

"Maybe I work too hard ... you too. Rarely anytime to chit chat." He forces a smile that doesn't fool her.

She doesn't smile.

His first reaction is to end the topic right now, not to go any further. It doesn't concern her. Still, he thinks that she needs to know what's happened because it will affect the transition plan. He decides to tell her. "Denny is the oldest son of two boys of my father's younger brother. Denny is about 10 years younger than me. His dad died unexpectedly from something that nobody in the family talks about, even to this day. Too fishy for me ... but I've never nosed in ... it's none of my business. Anyway, Denny went ballistic when his father died. They were really close. And then, his mother remarried soon after and guess what? THAT guy died! Can you believe that!" He pauses to catch his breath.

Lilli knows the comment is rhetorical, not really a question that is searching for a response, so she keeps quiet.

John picks up where he left off. "She married again, but then HE died a few years later ... her THIRD husband! Mindboggling, I thought maybe my Aunt was killing off her husbands. I was in law enforcement and security at the time but I didn't ask anybody also who was ... to help check it out. Maybe I should have, but I didn't. And, nobody else in the family did anything!" He pauses then restarts. "So what has this to do with Denny? Well, he emotionally didn't take well to all of this, especially his dad's death, but on top of that the remarriages and their deaths. He mentally became impaired, as the doctors like to say ... went through counseling and even, get this, electrical shock treatments! Can you believe that! He was put in a State Hospital for the mentally impaired ... was restricted from even marrying, having kids, having a driver's license or use of all non-prescriptive drugs including alcohol. A few years ago he was released to the local branch of the Y. M. C. A. where he was given a room and meals. He wasn't allowed to travel anyplace, anywhere. Nobody in the family, as best as I know, ever made an effort to connect with him, except me. They all treated him as if he didn't exist, even his mother who's now living in a fancy retirement home. She didn't marry the fourth time." He blinks his eyes a few times to dry up the moisture that has accumulated.

Lilli isn't sure if she should say something or just keep quiet and listen. Maybe this is John's way of dealing with his lack of relationship with his cousin Denny ... maybe cathartic ... maybe something else.

John continues. "Thanks for listening."

Lilli smiles and nods her head. She can't think of what to say, so she doesn't say anything. She thinks the one-way conversation has ended, but it hasn't. There's more John wants to say, so she continues to listen.

John restarts. "We've exchanged letters a few times over the past few years … not much to talk about … but he reached out to me first. I've never asked him how he got my mailing address and why he contacted me. Really doesn't matter, does it. He says he's doing good, but he never mentions anyone from the family, not even his mother or younger brother. What a freakin' horrible way to live. I don't know if he has any friends at the Y. He must, though, don't you think? He has to, even if it's only one. I have to believe he's got at least one friend. Anyway, his letters are coherent, neatly handwritten, and short. He'd probably go bananas if he knew that I am partially subsidizing his upgraded room, all meals, access to an exercise/weight room, and healthcare. He'll never hear about that from me. He'd be too embarrassed."

He pauses, and then continues. "The Y contacted me … why me I don't know … to say he abruptly left the place, which I assumed he wasn't allowed to do, to leave the place. I thought he was under strict supervision, I guess not. They didn't seem worried. When I heard that I made a few calls to a few people I know to find out where he went … some vacant building in the mountains … could even be a shed, but minding his own business. But I know him better than that … he's gonna get into some kind of trouble that won't be happy to anyone. Somebody could even get hurt, even him. I really don't think he can take care of himself."

John looks away for a second and then back to Lilli. "So why am I telling you this?"

He takes in a deep breath of air and then slowly lets the air back out. "I've got to see him. I know where he is. Maybe this is my way of dealing with him in the pathetic way I have in the past as well as other family members. So, this means I can't wait for an extended transition of leadership. I've got to turn over the reign to you now. Lester has updated the paperwork. I've almost finished looking it over before signing it and then you. And then I'm off. Don't know how long I'll be gone, but not like a month, more like a week I suspect. I'll always have my cell in case you need to talk. You know enough about the business, you're smart and honest, and there are people who you've already met who you can turn to for advice. If you get stuck, Lester knows who to contact."

He stares into her eyes to figure out if she's really up to the change in plans. He's sure about it but is she. "Listen, Lilli, I wouldn't turn over *Verity Security* to you if I didn't have full faith in you. I know you can do this. It's like when you first drink coffee, it tastes bitter. And then, after a few more cups the taste changes to something you really like and can't live without. And then you figure out which blend and brand fits your taste."

Lilli isn't too sure the coffee analogy works, but she's not going to let John, herself, and Natalie down. "Count me all in." Her smile is full of confidence. Talking about Eddie is off the table.

Later on the same day, Eddie gets an unexpected phone call. It's from his wife, Kathy.

"Kathy?"

"Yeah." She doesn't sound pleased in talking with him, more like a crazy combination of panic and depression. "Bobby is seriously ill."

"What?"

Eddie and Kathy aren't officially divorced, just living apart from each other, she with their son and daughter, he paying non-binding support. They agreed to this arrangement thinking that they just needed to get away from each other for a while ... to simmer down about their respective anger towards each other while not injuring the children. But now, eleven months later, they still haven't resolved their problems. Have they grown so far apart faster during these past eleven months than they expected? Have the children been hurt more than when they were living together? Eddie continues to work unreasonable hours and regularly interacts with some of the most obnoxious and worthless people as part of his job, while Kathy hasn't given up her urge for short-term male sexual partnerships and booze.

"The doctors don't know for sure why he's so ill. But he's unconscious in the hospital. He passed out during a gym class and hasn't woken up." Kathy starts to cry.

"Hell!" Eddie's pain is obvious from the sound of the torture in his voice, ignoring how Kathy might be feeling.

She shouts. "I don't want you to come here!" It's unclear if the words are slurred because of her emotional distress or if she's been drinking. It could easily be both.

"No, I've got to see him!" He yells in a high pitch that is even foreign to him.

"Eddie, listen to me! He's unconscious! Do you not understand that?"

"How's Cindy?" Now he sounds almost broken and sore from his agony.

"She really doesn't understand. Just thinks her brother has a cold. That's what I told her."

"Hell, I'm their father!" He now sounds as if he is pleading with her.

"But we agreed! Stay away!" She disconnects her phone before he has a chance to continue the argument.

Eddie's cell still remains firmly clenched in his hand. He is fuming with anger. He wants to shout out to Kathy, to scream that she can't do this to him, but he knows that's useless. He feels empty … no family … no soul … nothing. He cries long enough to wash away some of his feelings. His mind goes blank, and for a quick second he's not sure where he is. Then, suddenly, he thinks of one person who might be willing to listen. But if he calls Lilli he's going to have some explaining along the way. "What the hell!" He dials Lilli's cell number. What does he have to lose? He'll soon find out and won't like it one bit.

Lilli has just finished signing all the paperwork giving her full reign of *Verity Security* with John still owning

100% of the organization and categorized as *Paid Project Consultant*.

"How does it feel?" asks John.

"Honestly, still somewhat unreal, yet ready, willing and able. Thanks for your confidence in me." She glances next to Lester Brey. "And you as well … I won't let you down … I promise."

Lester replies, "John's very good at sizing up people. He'd never support someone he wouldn't trust with his life. And that is good enough for me."

"OK, enough of this." John clears his throat. "I gotta get out of here. Maybe I'll be gone a week, tops, but I'll keep you both posted." He stands, faces Lilli, and instead of a handshake, he extends his arms to hug her, that she willingly accepts with her arms wrapped around him.

Once John has left the room, Lester says to Lilli, "No need for me to stay here. You've got work to do and so do I. You know how to get hold of me … 24 – 7." He extends his hand to shake and says, "Congratulations."

Lilli decides a hug is in order, so she wraps her arms around him and says, "Thank you for your support."

Lester exits the room leaving Lilli by herself.

Lilli's cell buzzes almost on cue with Lester's exit. She recognizes the caller-ID and feels the beating of her heart. She connects, "Eddie?"

"Hi. Can we talk about something really important … like now?" No small talk, right to the point.

She frowns a bit. He sounds anxious, something she thinks is unusual. "Sure."

"I'd rather it be face to face, not on the phone."

She can't imagine anything so important between them that a face to face demands. She's confused. "Uh, sure. I'm at the office. Come on by."

"Be there in thirty minutes. Appreciate it." He disconnects.

Lilli remains motionless for a short time, then shuts down her cell, places it on top of her desk. For the time being she's decided to keep her own desk and let John keep his. They'll figure out together what's the best plan when he returns.

There are many renewal contacts she's got to review, to decide on whether to renew them, offer an alternative deal, or not renew at all. This is a relatively easy set of decisions because both John and Lester have already given their thumbs-up. Just the same, she begins reading the first renewal contact, doing her best to put aside Eddie's call and soon-to-be face to face. Easier said than done.

Forty minutes later, ten more than what Eddie predicated, her cell buzzes. She looks at caller-ID and then picks up. "Yeah, Eddie."

"Hi, I'm outside. Just need you to buzz me in."

Lilli looks at the monitor to her side that through the camera at the building's entrance shows Eddie. She presses a button to let him enter. Thirty seconds later, Eddie walks into the office.

He stands motionless for a few seconds, appearing nervous for some reason, like a kid who just got called to the Principal's office. He actually feels much worse than that. "Thanks for seeing me so unexpectedly." He takes a seat alongside her desk without a hug, handshake, or bright smile.

Lilli knows something is up … big time … but has no idea what-so-ever.

Eddie swallows and then clears his throat. His head is tilted away from her eyes. "I'm embarrassed at what I'm going to tell you. I hope you'll understand … and … even forgive me."

Lilli feels her own heartbeat pick up. It's show time! "I'm listening." She looks at him … a light yellow shirt unbuttoned at the collar, jeans, black suede shoes, and a blue sport coat. His boyish face that she remembers during their dinner date is replaced by a man looking as tense as a drum. He doesn't seem happy about the situation.

"I haven't been honest with you." He doesn't blink but his narrow lips begin to quiver slightly. "I didn't want to fall in love with you. I thought we would only be friends."

Lilli wonders where this is headed. She thinks to herself … "Is he trying to tell me he's gay or maybe he's married?"

"My relationship with Kathy … my wife … is strained. She has custody of our two children, Cindy and Bobby. We haven't slept together for a while. They live out of state, and I haven't seen any of them for a while … that was my promise to Kathy. But now, Bobby is sick … really sick … and I've got to see him regardless of what Kathy will do to me." He pauses as if he's rearranging his thoughts.

Lilli doesn't move an inch, but her head is throbbing and her forehead has a large number of wrinkles.

Eddie continues, "You turned out to be someone wonderful to me, so different from any other woman I've ever met ... and we've only known each other for only a very short time. You're beautiful and magical." His breathing rate picks up.

Lilli, now, isn't pleased in spite of his compliments. He's betrayed her but now he wants her to forgive him! The bastard ... no way!

"I don't want to leave you or for you to leave me. I can't let you leave my life." He sounds desperate as his eyes start to water. Then he sniffles and rubs his nose with the back of his left hand.

Lilli really wants to punch him in the nose. She feels her body tremble a little. His fragrance is gone.

"I was going to tell you before our dinner. I swear I was. I was working up to it. Really I was."

Lilli now wants to kick him in the groin, but settles to watch him twist-turn-burn in front of her.

"But then Kathy told me about Bobby. I've got to see him. But when I return I want us to be together." He lowers his head. "The truth is I don't want to live without you. All I ask is that you be patient while I make it work out. Then we can be together."

Lilli's prior thought of not being able to get him out of her mind has vanished.

He continues, "I promise I'll never hide anything from you again. I just need a little time."

Lilli thinks to herself ... "Sure and everything will be just hunky-dory. What do you take me for ... an idiot?" Now she'd really like to punch him full in the face. She leans back in her chair, grins … not the friendly type and says, "No." She firmly crosses her arms.

"What?"

"If you ever get divorced, which I doubt, don't even look me up. But here's some advice. Go back to your wife and kids. Make up for whatever you've done in the past, ask them all for forgiveness. I don't ever want to see your pathetic face again. Is that clear?"

"But Lilli, you've become everything to me."

"But Eddie, you haven't become that to me." Her arms are no longer crossed, but she leans forward towards him glaring with angry eyes.

"What are you saying?"

"Eddie, let me say it another way. I've got a daughter whom I love with all my heart and all my soul. I'd do anything for her. She should have a father and I should have a husband … I get that. You're already married with two children. If you get divorced then your kids won't have a father and your wife won't have a husband. If you get divorced don't look me up. I won't be available. Do you understand that? A simple head shake will suffice."

"I see."

"I don't think you really do, but if that's all you've got then it is what it is. Have a nice life, and goodbye."

He can't hold back his tears. He places a note on her desk that she doesn't acknowledge.

Lilli stands and then points to the doorway. "That's the way out."

Eddie stands, turns towards the door, leaves the room, and then exits the building.

His compliments to women … not all women were the recipients of his compliments … were never totally honest because he held back what he really felt, embarrassed if he shared too much. However, not this time with Lilli, and look where it got him. Even as a young kid he fell for unattainable girls whom he saw in real time as well as what was in his imaginative mind. Not just a crush, no that's not the word, but more fanciful, vivid, passionate, gorgeous, and of course always unattainable, yet it still caused an erection. He lied to Kathy, his wife, and look what happened with that. Lilli, however, is very different and now he knows his form of love will continue to be a dream that will never come true.

She sits back into her chair, watches him on the monitor, and says to herself … "What a way to end it." She feels very good about her decision. She takes a look at the note Eddie left on her desk. It reads … *I will always love you regardless of what happens, Eddie.* She crumbles the note in her hand as if to suffocate the words … to forget … forever.

It dawns on Lilli that she might never marry and in turn never give her daughter a father. She thinks she might not even consider dating again, in a way trying on men as if they are dresses, hoping that one day she'll find the right fit. She feels sick … of herself. She wonders if it's really possible to find the right match … sharing the same interests and the same values, not to forget about a sexual buzz … bottom line, wired the same way. Sure, someone who's rich, famous, good looking, and influential are important, but not nearly as much as other qualities of honesty, kindness, helpfulness, and supportiveness, for example. Years from now she'll probably look back on her decisions to conclude that she did what mattered, and did her best to ignore the rest. At least, that's her wish. She doesn't know for certain until that time.

Lilli figures life will go on regardless of her decisions, her marital status. People will be born and others will die. People will go to school, to work, to church. Teenagers will have crushes on each other. There will be broken hearts at an early age for some, but the probability is that they'll all recover. Some husbands and some wives will share their non-marital lover's bed for a night and return home before their spouse does. The universe will continue in spite of global climate change or whatever liberals will call it in the future, plastic trash in the ocean, and wars.

Some people will figure out early in their life what they want to do with the rest of their life, some will take a little longer, and some never. For those who take a little longer and especially for those who never do, they'll ask how the hell are they going to figure it out ... does it really matter. Sometimes much of one's life is determined in a split second.

She feels a swell of emotion take over her body. Maybe that's what life is really all about ... figuring what life is really all about ... figuring out what life is, what she wants her life to be, and how to achieve it. And, sadly as it is, to realize that some things that are important to her might never be achieved even when those opportunities are present.

She feels anxious about the time when her sweet eight year old daughter turns to a teenager. Will she wear skimpy clothes and use make-up? And will she talk in grammatically incorrect sentences with an exaggerated attitude and an animated behavior that is in a borderline abrasive, opinionated, and sarcastic tone? Will she think all adults are as relevant as the Middle Ages? Definitely not on Lilli's watch … none what-so-ever. At least that's her current plan, but she knows she can do only so much.

She turns her thoughts to herself, as if she is both a trial lawyer and the witness she is questioning during a trial. She can only be who she is, nothing more, nothing less, and nobody else. Her realization through this internal question and answer session leads her to only one reasonable conclusion … live her life based upon who she really is, not what's in her mind. Fortunately, she has no addictions to worry about and she's worthy of something wonderful to shine on her.

Lilli speaks aloud that which she has spoken to herself in silence, "I want IT so badly!" It almost sounds like a desperate plea for help, maybe even a prayer. Yet, while IT is what she wants so badly, she's unsure what IT really is, and therefore no way of achieving IT.

CHAPTER 38

Two days later, John drives a red Jeep in the Adirondack Mountains headed towards the remote location where his cousin Denny supposedly is. He's not sure if his cousin is being pursued by anyone from the Y. M. C. A. or anyone else. That doesn't matter to him. His mission is to find Denny and talk. Whatever happens as a result of the talk happens.

His destination is between Glenn Falls and Lake George.

The Jeep handles very well, especially on dirt roads off the paved highway U. S. 87, also called *The Northway*. He takes Exit 20 onto Route 9, then to *Bloody Pond Road*, and *East Shore Drive* towards *French Mountain*. A place called *Ryan's Farm Market* isn't far away before he spots the worn down wooden cabin that looks useless for any purpose. He stops, exits the Jeep and slowly walks towards the cabin. The closer he gets to the cabin the worse it looks as if no one has inhabited the place for at least a dozen years … probably more. But that's the idea of finding a place to go into hiding where no one will find you. John wonders how Denny even knew of this place, how he got here, and how he expects to live his life. He'll forget asking those questions once he's face-to-face with his cousin.

He stands about 20 yards from the damaged wooden stairs that lead to the front door when he hears dry leaves and pine needles crunch behind him. He knows what that means, so he raises his hands high over his head as he slowly turns around.

Standing before him is a white male with a brown ungroomed long beard that looks like it hasn't been trimmed or washed in quite some time. The white male, about five feet eleven inches tall and no less than one hundred seventy pounds, is holding a shotgun to his shoulder while his right index finger is on the trigger.

"Private property! Get out!" The voice is coarse sounding just like his appearance. He squints because he needs glasses. His face is wrinkled beyond his age. He wears worn out boots, worn jeans, a dirty black shirt beneath a dirtier brown outdoor jacket, gloves, and a red baseball-styled cap covering his long brown hair.

They stare at each other as if it is a contest to be the last man staring.

"Denny, is that you?" John is in disbelief.

Silence returns between the two men until the one holding the shotgun slowly at a snail's pace lowers his weapon. "John … John Walker, my cousin?"

"What the hell are you doing here? I thought you were at the Y!" John knows his cousin will quickly sense the fabrication.

"What the hell are YOU doing here? It's a long way from where you live!" Denny is content in playing the same game.

Stillness returns until, as if on cue, both of them laugh.

John continues, "I've been told that maybe you're having a hard time, so I decided to give you a visit."

Denny replies. "Don't trust anyone, John. You can't trust anyone. Trust me on that." He wonders to himself how John knew where to find him, but doesn't ask.

"Is that gun loaded? It's making me nervous."

"Hell no, I don't even know how to shoot. I don't know if it even works … just found it inside the place. But it put a hell of a scare in you. Huh?" He chuckles. Then he drops the shotgun on the ground in front of him.

"Got anything to drink inside?" John makes a head motion toward the cabin. "I'm thirsty."

"Haven't been here long enough to stock up. Do you have a COSTCO membership? I hear you can buy a lot for less?"

"I can do better than that." John smiles at the idea that somehow just popped into his head.

Denny tosses his head slightly upward. "And what's that, cousin?"

"You come live with me. I'm by myself and could use the company, even though it's you." He laughs.

Denny's response is slow in coming. Then he laughs as well, sounding in an uncanny way very similar to John. "You lookin' for a housekeeper, a bodyguard, a cook, or something else?"

"I want my cousin to live with me. We've got a lot of catching up to do. And our infrequent letters have been too short in length." John pauses and then continues. "You're not wanted for a crime, are you?"

"Crime, what crime would I do?"

"Hell, Denny, I don't know. I'm just asking. Are you?"

"Nope, but I've got a few mind challenges, you know like in the head. Sometimes I'm difficult to be around."

"Then I'll just crack you on the head a few times to drill some common sense into your thick skull."

"But, are you a COSTCO member?"

CHAPTER 39

It's been two days since John took off to be with his cousin Denny. Lilli sits in their joint office, squirming like a child in a school seat impatiently waiting for the school bell to ring to end the day's classes. She decides that while it's relatively early for her to take off from work, it's been slow and she's bored. She checks all the doors and windows to make sure they're secured, turns on *Verity Security's* answering machine and then heads to the front door. Once outside the building she turns on the entire building's security system with a simple push of a button on a remote control device.

She drives to the town's center where she parks her car in a self-parking facility and then heads to *Soft Optics*, a relatively quiet restaurant and bar combination that happens to be one of *Verity Security's* clients. She's recognizable to the owner and most of the employees by sight, as they are to her.

It's just a little after four in the afternoon and the place isn't yet crowded with business-type people from local establishments and those traveling on business from other places, but that will easily change within an hour or two. This is just what she needs now … time to wind-down.

She checks her watch. There is just enough time for her to have a drink and then pick up Natalie at one of her girlfriend's house. She feels she needs the time alone right now to think about things. So many changes have happened to her life within a relatively short time that she needs "her-time" to process it all … to get a clearer perspective of it all.

She sits alone at a small table in the back waiting for her Chardonnay when she suddenly feels someone staring at her. She hasn't got accustomed to stares since she turned to wearing skirts, blouses, nice shoes, and other womanly clothes … it still makes her feel a little uneasy, especially when she's by herself, as she is now.

The waitress places her drink on the table. Lilli says thank-you and hands over enough money to cover the cost of the drink along with a generous tip. It's then that she glances to the side to see an attractive light skin toned woman about her age with a soft distinctive smile looking her way.

It doesn't take her long to recognize the smile, yet the complete recollection of who this person is comes in increments. The woman is dressed in a clingy white silk blouse without a bra that clearly accentuates her breasts, especially when she takes a deep breath in and out. Her short dark green skirt shows off her slender legs, and her black low heeled shoes are shined to a glow. On the woman's left wrist is a bracelet studded with sparkling diamonds. There is a slight tint of lipstick on her full lips. Her ears are without earrings. Finally, Lilli recognizes Sheena Lee. She does her best not to wince.

While Lilli now has a career where she can wear a skirt, blouse, and nice shoes to work if she wants to, it wasn't always like that. With Sheena, when Natalie was approaching her first birthday, nothing really mattered except of course her daughter whom she pledged to protect from knowing anything about her personal affairs, especially with Eric and then Sheena.

During those days … it was less than a three month relationship … a sister she never had … a family to be with. She felt good, not complete, but good in the way that another adult appreciated her as much as she appreciated the other adult. The air smelled fresh and clean, sort of sweet in some respect, and she laughed at Sheena's funny jokes. But now, she wonders how her life would be different if she took Sheena up on her entrepreneurial idea of hustling men … sex in exchange for money, lots of money Sheena proclaimed. These men would become their human ATMs! No more would either of them have to worry about meeting all their basic needs of food, clothing, and shelter so that they could focus on higher order needs like love, respect, and freedom. Natalie could attend private schools and have no worry about tuition, even to college if that's what her daughter desired. No more would they be rag dolls, and in its place they would become unbridled women free to do whatever they wanted.

It seems to Lilli that Sheena just might have arrived at that place now. But now she has to hide her history with this woman, yet she'll never forget it herself.

It seemed so sudden that Sheena walked away from her, but there was a reason, a sort of excuse, and a brief explanation, just a short note handwritten on a torn piece of paper that said … *It's been fun, but we're each looking to be free and respected in different ways. You'll always be someone I respect, to look up to, and you'll always be my sister.*

Fortunately for Lilli, there was Natalie, whom she pledged to honor, love, respect, and protect. She was a fool to think it would work out long term with Sheena, and she now concludes that Sheena had already arrived at that opinion much before her ... maybe even at the very start of their very short relationship. Nothing good was to come of it, so keep it short and then cut if off. At least she felt at that time she had a sisterhood with Sheena, and maybe she still does in some strange way.

Sheena and Lilli continue to stare at each other with a distance about sixty feet ... no body movements, not even an eye wink or nod of the head, yet an obvious recognition of each other. Then Lilli frowns and breaks eye contact first. She turns her body in the chair so that her back faces Sheena. Consequently, she doesn't notice a well-dressed man in an expensive business suit walk up to Sheena to carry on a conversation.

Within a few minutes, and after two sips of her wine, Lilli sees Sheena and the well-dressed man in an expensive business suit leave *Soft Optics* together. His arm is wrapped around her waist. And then Sheena turns her head back toward Lilli to share the same secret that both of them know to be true and the choices they've made.

Fade Away

ABOUT THE BOOK

Sometimes we try so hard but do not succeed. Sometimes we get what we want but not what we need. Sometimes we love so much but never get love in return. Lilli Jackson, a divorced single mother of three year old Natalie, works as a Public Safety Officer for Verity Security, a property security firm, in a job she doesn't like, but her boss is a gem and she's paid enough to meet her and Natalie's basic needs. She'd really like to meet the right guy, and wear a skirt and blouse with nice shoes to work. She feels trapped. The choices she's made that got her to where she is now will not get her to where she wants to be in the future. But figuring out where she wants to be isn't clear, which makes the choices even fuzzier. She meets an array of people, each with their own desires, secrets, wishes, rules, fears, duties, and obligations. And those people meet others, each making their own choices. No two people are identical. She believes there are people who will try to take advantage of somebody else as well as people who are kind, courteous, loving, and helpful. So she has to figure out who is doing what, in other words who to believe. It's sort of like watching two people arguing about something, each of them using different and contradictory information they claim to be factual objective information. You suspect one is lying and one is telling the truth, but figuring out which one is lying and which one is telling the truth can be difficult.

Printed in the United States
By Bookmasters